A DREAM OF ICE

Also by Gillian Anderson and Jeff Rovin

A Vision of Fire

GILLIAN ANDERSON

& JEFF ROVIN

A DREAM OF ICE

BOOK TWO OF *THE EARTHEND SAGA*

SIMON & SCHUSTER

London · New York · Sydney · Toronto · New Delhi

A CBS COMPANY

First published in the USA by Simon 451, an imprint of Simon & Schuster Inc., 2015
First published in Great Britain by Simon & Schuster UK Ltd, 2015
A CBS COMPANY

1 3 5 7 9 10 8 6 4 2

Simon & Schuster UK Ltd
1st Floor
222 Gray's Inn Road
London WC1X 8HB

www.simonandschuster.co.uk

Simon & Schuster Australia, Sydney
Simon & Schuster India, New Delhi

A CIP catalogue record for this book is available from the British Library.

Hardback ISBN: 978-1-4711-3774-7
Trade Paperback ISBN: 978-1-4711-3775-4
eBook ISBN: 978-1-4711-3777-8

Printed and bound by CPI Group (UK) Ltd, Croydon, CR0 4YY

A DREAM OF ICE

PROLOGUE

Exile.

The word stuck in Azha's memory like an angry barb. The only thing that stung more was the name and face of the traitor, that serene lunatic who had assumed rights and powers no Galderkhaani should ever possess.

We trusted each other with everything, she thought angrily, *but now I alone pay for his sins*.

Wisps of wet cloud and red hair whipped across Azha's face as her airship glided east, hundreds of feet above the white, icy surface. Balanced on the rigging with several dogbane-fiber ropes looped over her forearms in case she lost her footing, the former Cirrus Farm commander sidled along while completing her scan of the enormous inflated *hortatur* skin above her. She did not like what she saw.

Cursing it all—but at this moment, mostly the ship—she climbed down to the gondola as carelessly as she dared, her movements as natural and familiar to her as breathing. She dropped the last few feet. The seventy-foot-long, wicker-ribbed basin was empty but for two other people: Dovit, her man with black dreadlocks to his waist and touches of gray at his temples, and Azha's younger sister, Enzo, her short-cropped hair black as coal.

As Azha leaped the last few feet into the gondola, she cursed again in frustration.

"I couldn't see any leaks so there must be one higher up," she groaned. "Naturally, the bastards gave me the oldest ship in the fleet."

"Exile was not designed for comfort," the man remarked.

"And these ships were not designed for this much travel over land," Enzo added cautiously. "It dries the fabric. The ocean's thermal updrafts are what really keep them aloft—"

"Enough!" Azha slammed her hand down hard on the console. "What I need are solutions, not a discourse in cloud farming." She glared at Dovit and then her sister. "I don't even know why you came! You had your own life, your own—people."

"Because I couldn't let you face this alone!" Enzo said.

"Neither of us could," Dovit said, putting a hand on Azha's arm. "And my 'people,' as you call them, supported me in my love for you."

"Love," she said, pushing his fingers off. "Is that all?"

"What more?" Dovit asked.

"Nothing," Azha said, glaring at her sister again, her red hair rising and twisting in the wind like slender serpents. "This is my doing, my choice, but it's a sign of how perverse our society has become. I'm banished for trying to stop someone from committing genocide."

"You were banished for trying to enter the Technologist Inner Quarter with a spear, two knives, and a grapnel," Dovit said, correcting her. "There are far more legal and far less dramatic ways to express dissent."

"Dissent," Azha muttered, glancing up at the swaying balloon. "It wasn't about 'dissent,' Dovit. It was—an impulse. I learned the facts and had to do something."

"A legitimate reaction," Dovit agreed. "But, as I said, there are legitimate forms of redress."

"None that would have worked in time," Azha said.

"So say you," the man replied.

"Dovit, *you* were on the Technologist Council. You heard that someone was going to initiate the Source before the council decided it was ready."

"We all heard those rumors, mostly from Priests."

"You know how I hate to side with those people, with *any* of your mad allies," Azha said, "but they *weren't* rumors."

Dovit shrugged. "That is irrelevant. Most did not accept the rumors as true. They still don't. Action requires belief."

"It was true, it *is* true," Azha said, turning to face him. "And it will kill them all."

"We went through all of this at your hearing," Dovit replied patiently. "You offered no proof."

Azha's gaze fell. "I couldn't."

"*Why?*" Enzo pleaded, bracing herself against the rocking gondola. "There is no harm in telling us now—we're not going back."

Azha looked at her sister and then at the man who meant so much to her, especially now. She didn't wish to reward his sacrifice with hurt.

"Azha?" Dovit asked, reading her mood—as always. "Please tell me. What is it?"

"You really want to know?"

"That *is* why I asked," he said with a wary smile.

Azha sighed, casting her eyes past the proud, formidable quarry master toward the distant spires. "Dovit, before you and I were lovers I was joined as a lover with the man who planned this treacherous scheme."

Dovit looked at her with surprise—and understanding. "And you still are."

"Yes."

"And yet," Dovit said, "you were armed for murder."

"Yes."

Dovit and Enzo shared a look. He hurt for Azha more than he hurt for himself.

"There was no other choice," Azha said. "He refused to hear arguments against it and is surrounded by too many influential people who will cover for any misdeeds," Azha said. "Of course, I threatened to take his plan to the others, to his people, but we both knew the truth: they would have descended on me like buzzing *punita* on the remains of the dead. That is why I had to try to stop this act the old-fashioned way."

Dovit looked at her with a blend of sadness and regret. "I wish you had trusted me. I and my lovers also have powerful friends."

"In the wrong places," Azha said. "Agriculture, tile masonry, seafaring, the stars . . ."

Dovit moved cautiously in the swaying basket to Azha's side, fresh urgency in his voice. He glanced back to the high stone tower from which they had departed a short sun-arc ago. "Listen to me. If you *are* telling the truth, and the Source isn't ready, then yes—it could take a great many lives! There are things, many things outsiders do not know about."

Azha gave him a look. "What things, Dovit?"

"The reach vents for instance, and the conduits have been expanded—extensive work that was done underground."

"Underground?" Azha shot back. "How was *that* accomplished?"

"In great secrecy and in remote regions," the Technologist replied. "We must go back."

Azha regarded the man with pity. "*Now* you reveal this."

"There are people I would protect too," he said.

Azha shook her head. "This frail vessel will not make it. Even if it could, very soon it will be too late." She paused, took a deep breath, and looked at the open sky. "Breaking exile means incarceration. I would rather die up here."

"Airships fall," Dovit said, indicating the ground far beneath his feet. "You will die down there."

"A figure of speech," Azha replied.

"Sister, many will die if we do not try!" implored Enzo.

"They brought it on themselves," Azha said coldly. "They wouldn't listen and there is nothing more to be said."

Silence fell upon them as the truth of her words and the fate of countless Galderkhaani settled on them like a heavy mist.

Azha pushed past her companions to the side of the gondola. Leaning far over and looking up, she surveyed the charcoal-gray surface of the balloon again. A huge ripple crossed the side of it.

Moving toward her, Enzo pleaded, "Please, Azha, let's turn back."

"To save lives, or so you can go back to your crazed mentor, to Rensat?"

"She is an enlightened soul," Enzo said defensively.

"She is a fanatic with a Candescent obsession."

"*She* is a fanatic?" Enzo laughed. "We have long believed that *you* are the fanatic."

"Isn't every expeditionary commander?" Azha shot back. "Do you think it is easy pushing the boundaries of our farming efforts farther and farther from the city where the winds and cold are—"

"That isn't what your sister means," Dovit interrupted. "Your well-known defiance of—"

"The Candescent Doctrine?" Azha cut him off, adding hand gestures to her words, small but emphatic arcs and angles.

"Farmers complained that you preached it on every voyage you ever took, while they were aloft in the ropes where they could not escape hearing," Dovit said. "'Seed the clouds with jasmine, don't search the tiles for bones. Embrace the breath of life, not the stones of death.'"

"Mine was a voice of moderation"—Azha poked her own chest—"something to balance the street-corner oratory of *all* your mindless followers. You and your kind are ripping us apart!"

"You talk of rigid pragmatism as if *it* were the only way," Enzo said accusatorily.

"It is *my* way," Azha said. "I accepted exile not only for my deed but because I've had enough! The Technologist Source may work, *some*-day, and perhaps so will the *cazh* of the Priests, *some*day." She gestured angrily to the sky. "But the Candescents? There is no proof that they are up there. There is no evidence that they are listening for you, or for you, Dovit. You simply believe, based on legends, that they are waiting to absorb you. And while you seek them, you miss life itself."

"The word of a naysayer is not evidence," Enzo said.

"How about the fact that they're *gone*?" Azha muttered. "Is that not evidence? If they ever lived at all."

"They lived," Enzo said. "And what is 'gone'?" Enzo asked temperately, before answering her own question. "Only their bodies. Only that."

"'Only their bodies,'" Azha sneered. "That's all? You're ridiculous."

"Azha," Dovit said gently. "That is not appropriate, or fair. And you know, I have always listened to *both* sides. I have advocated the Source and I have advocated the *cazh*."

Azha could feel her anger rising and she began making larger gestures to communicate that. She turned, shook her head slowly. "And that is why I love you, Dovit. You *are* a moderate voice."

The wicker basin shuddered. The trio looked up, out, and then back at each other.

"A deadly antique," Azha sighed.

Dovit smiled. "It is so old it smells of the jasmine fleet it used to lead."

Azha moved to the ropes, tugging in frustration, and cast her eyes with conviction and longing to the east, away from the city, toward a darkening horizon. "We must set down before long. It's strange but I have long wanted to explore the vast ice-locked eastern lands. The great birds of air and land survive somewhere out *there*, outside our great oasis."

"We will find it and learn to live as they do," Dovit said confidently.

"Eating fish, creating water from ice and sun, making clothes from the dead of the sea."

The balloon shuddered again and this time, it did not fully reinflate.

Dovit stepped behind Azha and embraced her. "Hope," he said, "has an enemy in unfavorable wind currents."

Azha looked at him, trying to smile at his soft candor. "Thank you, Dovit, for being here. I'm sorry I yelled at you."

Enzo regarded them. "Sister," she said. "Now that we are away from the state—tell me, who wishes to activate the Source?"

Azha turned to look at her. "Why? Why does that still matter to you?"

"Like Dovit, I chose to join you in exile," Enzo said. "I have given up everything. I want to know why . . . for whom."

Azha shook her head. "I will not say. I do not want this to color our lives in any way."

"It is a Priest?" Enzo said.

Azha regarded her suspiciously. "Why do you ask?"

Enzo looked back at the glimmering towers of Galderkhaan, the setting sun darting through the sharp spires. "Please tell me!"

Dovit and Azha both regarded the young woman.

"I will not!" Azha said. "Enzo, what is wrong?"

"What Dovit said about the subterranean tunnels," she said. "It will be a catastrophe. The Priests must stop this." Enzo's eyes were wide, helpless. "Please! Tell me the name!"

A shudder ran through Azha; it was not caused by the failing airship but by a sudden realization.

"Enzo, you came to *spy* on me? But—how would you have gotten the information back to Galderkhaan? You could not survive the journey on foot or make it in time!"

"I would not need to," Enzo replied. The woman smiled sadly as she regarded her sister. "Azha, I love you, even beyond death."

Azha heard the strange finality in Enzo's voice, the distant look in her eyes . . . a look that fastened on the fading, distant towers of their home.

Just then a loud flapping sound drew their attention up. Above, they saw yet another ripple in the skin of the dirigible, larger than before. Once again, the tube-shaped balloon failed to pop back into its correct structure. There was a lurch, and the airship began to drop, slowly at first. But they all realized it would pick up speed as it fell.

As Azha grasped the side of the gondola for support, she failed to see Enzo reach into her pocket and pull out a small, clear vessel filled with a yellow liquid.

"*Fera-cazh . . .* ," Enzo began.

Azha spun toward her sister with alarm. "What are you doing!?" she screamed. "Enzo, no!" Azha lunged at her sister, reaching for the vial and Enzo's throat at the same time. "*Glogharasor!*" she shrieked. "You doom us all! I'll throw you over before you set fire to my ship!"

But the ship heaved as huge repeating ripples made the balloon look like it was full of water. The three grabbed handholds as the gondola tilted and the shuddering, tipping airship fell faster from the sky. In no time at all they were seeing the sharp details of the rapidly approaching ice field below.

Enzo opened her vial and emptied the oil over herself. "Tell me the name of the one who betrays our people!" she shouted at her sister.

"*Don't do this!*" Azha implored.

Enzo dropped the bottle and regarded her sister. "Please—tell me!"

"Why? We're not—we *cannot*—turn back!"

"There is no need! I will remember it after—"

"After you *die*?" Azha raged. "You are too far from the stones—you won't be able to *tell* anyone!"

"Azha," yelled Dovit, "take my hands."

"No!"

"For once, *trust*!" Dovit pleaded. "Repeat the *cazh* with me! Believe that even if you believe in nothing else!"

Azha realized it was too late to save the airship or themselves and reluctantly called out the name. Despite the wind screeching all around them, Enzo heard it and began to chant.

Aytah fera-cazh grymat ny-haydonai pantar, pantar ida . . . Aytah fera-cazh grymat ny-haydonai pantar, pantar ida.

Dovit did likewise, firmly holding both of Azha's hands. Reluctantly, she joined him.

The ship lurched again and jolted until it was nose-down, plunging like a comet toward a gigantic crevasse.

And then the ice field seemed to suck the great airship into itself, bashing the gondola against the walls of the crevasse, shredding the deflated balloon. Screaming and barely holding on, Azha sought Dovit's eyes.

Enzo, bellowing her chant, exploded in flame.

And then they hit water, salt water, and plummeted down and down into its abyss. Enzo continued to burn within the sea. Azha refused to let go of Dovit and tried to kick herself up but the descending ship created a vortex she could not overpower. She fought with all her strength but soon she had to take a breath where there was no breath to take.

She was the last to drown but not the last to die.

• • •

Electrical engineer Jina Park drove her shovel down hard on the ice covering the miniature windmill that was supposed to help power this remote GPS station. She paused and looked up to see Fergal MacIan, who, having uncovered the solar panel that did the other half of the work, had tired of waiting for her to finish. He had mounted his snowmobile and was driving in circles around the vast white landscape like a teenager. Jina laughed and shook her head at the familiar sight. Three weeks into their posting, she had become the rational "sibling" of the duo and remained so throughout the Antarctic winter.

She lowered her head to the task at hand and felt a tiny pop in her nose. Tucking a gloved finger beneath her balaclava, she knew what to expect. The hyper-dry air had done it again: blood.

Then she smelled something. Not blood; burning plastic? Or sulfur? She looked down to see a bright yellow flame jump from the ice and engulf the left leg of her supposedly fireproof salopette. The other leg caught fire a second later.

"Fergal, help! *Help me!*"

Jina threw herself to the snow and rolled but the flames would not smother; in an instant she was consumed. She screamed and wailed as the pain tore through her, her clothes melting into her flesh as it bubbled and flaked.

Fergal, caught up in his manic figure eights, heard nothing over the roar of his engine until something caught the corner of his eye. Over his shoulder he saw a black and gold tower that seemed to dance in the polar wind, then topple over. He jerked the snowmobile around for a better view and, misjudging the arc, flipped the vehicle hard. With the full weight of it pinning him to the ice, he skidded for what must have been a hundred feet. Finally, with the engine humming helplessly, he and the mangled machine came to a full stop. With the last ounce of strength he could muster before losing consciousness, Fergal turned his eyes toward the diminishing flames and screamed, "Jina!"

But Jina was beyond hearing. She was beyond pain. She was deep within herself, observing her body as it burned away. In the distance she saw Fergal turn his head toward her. She imagined stretching a blazing hand toward him, touching his broken body, but he did not move.

Then Jina heard a voice . . .

"*Varrem,*" it whispered.

She turned her attention skyward and knew that something was looming above her. It was vast, unfamiliar, and overpowering. As it bore down she screamed from the depths of her soul. The Antarctic wind picked up, skipping with her ashes across the surface of the snow as everything grew very dark, very still, and very, very quiet.

PART ONE

CHAPTER 1

Caitlin O'Hara was lying in bed with her hands folded across her ribs. It was just after five a.m. and a weak, dark gray light was leaching into the black room through a crack in the curtains.

Predawn has always been undervalued as a witching hour, she thought. Midnight, in prose and poem, had gotten all the glory. At this hour, though, people had to gather their lonely, enervated willpower and make the first choices of the day. For that you needed raw courage. *Or crayons*, she thought with a smile.

Occasionally, when she was sitting in her office surrounded by diplomas, international accolades, and personal photographs from a life of world travel, Caitlin sharpened crayons. It was more than just mindless activity; her teenage clients frequently needed more than words to describe what they were feeling. Though new clients were often puzzled when she brought out the sketch pad and a sixty-four-pack of Crayolas from her desk, they quickly succumbed to the freedom of nonverbal expression, to the idea of reverting to childhood, to the comforting smell of the open box.

Right now, Caitlin was contemplating what she would draw if asked. Reluctantly, she stopped thinking and just imagined—a freedom she had been loath to give herself since the occurrences of a week ago because Maanik's trances, her own seemingly out-of-body experiences, the still-inexplicable visions, pained her. But for the first time since the night at the United Nations, like a child pushing off from the edge of the pool, she let her imagination roam.

She would draw herself in cerulean blue, turned to her right, and leaning into a small garden, smelling flowers. To her left, curving toward and over her, would be—nothing. A massive emptiness. There was no way to draw the muscular void she was imagining; she'd actually have to cut the paper into that curve.

Nearly half a lifetime ago, in her early twenties, she'd perceived a vacuum of any kind as an enemy. Blanks were a waste of time and elicited a deep unrest in her. Life seemed too short. Then, when she was pregnant, Caitlin had been expecting a tidal wave of hormonal upheaval, so she began working with a new therapist, Barbara Melchior. What she received when she left those sessions was internal silence, the deepest yet, and it scared her. There was too much information to process, too many threads to connect. Her brain, albeit NYU-trained, shut down.

Thankfully, Barbara had helped her see that silence didn't mean a void or failure. Silence was a symbol of something not yet understood, a placeholder until one's mind caught up to and embraced the new information.

When Caitlin's son, Jacob, was born deaf, Barbara had tentatively probed her about whether she felt a sense of irony.

"Absolutely not," Caitlin had said. "Irony is cheap. The universe—" She had hesitated, not sure where she was going with the idea. "The universe doesn't editorialize."

At the time, she wasn't even sure what she meant by that. It just came out. But it applied to her life now. Witnessing the strangely possessed teenagers in Haiti, in Iran, here in New York . . . her visions of the civilization of Galderkhaan . . . the universe had given those experiences to her without footnotes or context. They had just happened.

With Jacob, time allowed her to see his beauty, just as it did with each of her patients, one-on-one.

But this? she wondered, returning to the emptiness she was imagining. A world of strange sights, strange beings, and stranger philosophies. Where could she even begin to look for the connective tissue between the "real world" and this strange place called Galderkhaan? Her brain certainly wasn't providing answers.

So . . . crayons of the mind.

She lay still and breathed, feeling her joints and limbs slowly waking up. Her mind drifted to the imaginary crayon outline of herself within the chaos of flowers and color. It was as if her body *was* the garden . . .

A gentle tap-tap-tapping came at her door. When Jacob didn't immediately come in, she knew he was already wearing his hearing aid.

"I'm up, honey," she said.

He opened the door and scooched to her side, said, "Wakey, wakey," and put a finger in her ear. She jerked and squealed. This was a long-standing routine she wished would end but whenever she considered telling him she didn't like it, she realized that in the long run she'd miss it. It would end soon enough.

He placed a hand on her eyelids and said, "Don't look, Mommy, I'm going to walk you to the living room."

"Okay, not looking," she said as Jacob put his hands on her shoulders and tugged her upright out of bed. Grinning nervously and keeping her eyes closed, she allowed him to push at her back to direct her out of her bedroom. Caitlin immediately walked into the edge of the open door.

"Oof!"

"Sorry, Mommy. Okay, we're in the hall, go right."

"I know where the living room is," she said, laughing, and then suddenly stopped. One bare foot had landed in something slimy.

"Ew!"

Her eyelids barely fluttered open before Jacob ran his hands over them again. "Don't look!"

"There's something gross—"

"Don't look! Arfa threw up."

"Is that the surprise?"

"No! Don't move. I'll get paper towels."

Caitlin stood blindly in the hall on one foot. She listened to the sound of Jacob's feet retreating and paper towels ripping off the roll. He was talking to himself, muttering something about cat puke. He chuckled. The smell of coffee wafted toward her from the kitchen. She didn't think Jacob knew how to make coffee. Then she felt him wiping off her foot with the paper towels.

"Is it safe for me to stand yet?"

"One second, I'm getting the floor."

She could hear him rubbing the puke into the carpet.

"Okay. You can walk now."

Propelled again by her son, Caitlin put one foot in front of the other until she could tell by the blast of sunlight through her eyelids that they had reached the living room. Jacob positioned himself in front of her and said, "Open!"

Caitlin opened her eyes and saw, standing before her, her mother leaning over the dining room table with the coffeepot. A homemade chocolate Bundt cake was waving four candles at her, and crepe paper twirled from the chairs to the ceiling light to make a green and yellow tepee.

"Surprise!" they chorused. Jacob was so excited he started jumping, then stood on a chair near the cake, still yelling, "Surprise! Gotcha!"

"Hey, Jake," his grandmother piped over him as she poured fresh coffee into two mugs. "Derriere in the chair."

"I don't understand French!" he answered back.

"You understand Irish?" she demanded with a touch of brogue, pointing at the wooden seat.

He stopped hopping around and obediently went to where the no-nonsense finger was pointing.

"Were you surprised, Mommy?" he asked in a tone that was both giddy and sheepish.

"Well, I'm surprised I'm forty," she said, hugging her mother around the shoulders. "What the heck time did you leave home?"

"As soon as the bread rose," Nancy replied, patting Caitlin's hands. "Your father would have been here too but we had a no-show at the bakery so he had to fill in."

"I'll call him later," Caitlin said, sitting in the seat of honor. Quickly she glanced around for Arfa. The tabby cat was snoozing in sphinx position on an arm of the couch, obviously no worse for wear.

"Mommy, Mommy, Mommy," Jacob chanted, bopping up and down in his seat. "Make your wish!"

"All right," she said, though it was Nancy's stern gaze that quieted him.

Caitlin looked at the candles, thinking about being forty, about Jacob's having recently turned ten—

About Atash setting himself on fire, the flames leaping over his clothes . . .

My god, she thought, and quickly blew out the candles.

She vaguely noticed that Jacob was still leaning forward with expectation. An instant later the candles relit themselves. Jacob shrieked with laughter but Caitlin heard only screaming. She saw the man who burst into flame in the courtyard in Galderkhaan when she'd shared Atash's vision. Shaking, she blew out the candles again and of course the trick flames came back, now with all the souls of Galderkhaan burning and screaming and dying. Caitlin tried to keep it together, covering her nose and mouth with one hand, but she was visibly shaking. Jacob, unaware, was laughing and clapping.

Nancy O'Hara, who noticed everything, said to Jacob, "Now you get to put them out, the way I showed you."

Gleefully, he dipped his fingers in a small dish of water hidden under a napkin. He pinched each candle out with a *ssst*, the smoke wafting upward in tendrils.

Nancy occupied Jacob with helping her pull out the candles and then cut the cake into slices while keeping an eye on her daughter. Caitlin was breathing slowly, purposefully, through her nose, with her hands clasped in front of her face. She closed her eyes, checked her hands to see if they had stopped trembling, and took a few more shallow breaths.

Gradually, Caitlin normalized, nodded thanks to her mother, and sank a fork into a proffered slice of cake. With Jacob safely occupied by his own slice, Nancy murmured to Caitlin, "You're not done with that previous case?"

Caitlin didn't answer, and that was answer enough.

"But you're not going to be traveling anytime soon." It was pointedly a statement from Nancy, not a question.

"I—I don't know," Caitlin said quietly. "I never know."

"Don't do something dangerous and make me play the mother card with you, Caitlin. Grandparenting is enough."

"Mom, you didn't want me going to Thailand after the tsunami. What if I had listened to you? I wouldn't have met Jacob's dad, and you wouldn't be a grandmother."

"I was worried about your safety. You knew it was a dangerous situation and went anyway. And after your recent experiences, I am still concerned."

Caitlin sighed wearily. "Mom, you run a bakery—"

"Meaning what, exactly?" the older woman asked. "That I shouldn't have an opinion about how my daughter conducts her life?"

"No, I meant that our worlds are different."

"Caitlin, I meet more people every day than you do in a week—"

"I know. And you should be proud, Mom. *I* am, of you and Dad. I just mean that—"

"You think you know what's best for you, I know. I've heard it before," Nancy continued. "But here's my take. You're world renowned. You've 'made it.' What I'm saying, with a mother's pride, is, why can't you stop fighting so hard and enjoy that?"

"Enjoy? Mom, that's a word I apply to stepping in cat vomit because it makes my son laugh. Beyond that? I need to understand things, not just fix them. Sometimes that means going where the challenges are. Knowledge is worth the risk for me. Sometimes, like a week ago, things end without being tidied up or understood. Am I satisfied? A bit, sometimes. But I get no real peace or enjoyment. Don't take this the wrong way, but I can't run my practice like a bakery."

Nancy raised one eyebrow, took another bite of cake, and for a second everyone just chewed. Then she said to Jacob, "Don't forget the other surprise, kid."

"Oh, I almost did!" he exclaimed, crumbs flying from his overstuffed mouth.

Jacob leaped toward the silverware drawer and pulled out a tiny gift with an enormous pink bow and more tape than wrapping paper. As Caitlin struggled to open it—enjoying the moment, and proving it to her mother with a genuine smile—Jacob stood next to her with his hand on her shoulder, jiggling up and down. At last she got it open and found a key chain with a thin brass circle. There was a maze etched into the brass.

"It's a labyrinth," Jacob said, saying the word like he owned it. He pulled it from her hands and brought it close to her eyes. "It's medieval, Grandpa said. There's only one path." His pointer finger traced around the whorls of the maze. "See? You can't get lost. Whichever way you go, it gets you to the middle!"

She flashed back to the design she had seen in Galderkhaan, the swirls and crescents that left the center isolated, mysterious. She gave him a big hug and kiss and sent him to her bag to get her keys. She let him work on putting the keys on the new ring while she quietly apologized to her mother.

"Look, I didn't mean to come down so hard on you," Caitlin began.

Nancy hushed her. "I'm going to give you some advice from your grandmother, a miner's daughter. She once warned me that if you go too deep into something, you can lose your way or get buried. I resented the metaphor. Life wasn't a coal mine. But you know something? She was right. A person should have—a person *needs*—a full and diverse life. So," she continued, "when I hear your father say that he can't even start a conversation with you about your choice to go to Iran, it occurs to me that you need a piece of advice: if no one can even tell you no, if you can't even consider it, you're in a very dangerous place."

Caitlin thought a long time before answering, twisting ribbons of chocolate icing onto her fork. Finally, she said, "What did Great-Grandpa do each morning when the coal cart came to him, big and dark and very, very insistent?"

Nancy smiled. "He got in. But—and this is important, dear—not blindly and not alone. That's why he became a labor organizer, and maybe you've got his rebellious blood." Nancy's smile warmed. "How about a compromise?" she said. "Find yourself someone who you will trust now and then. Someone who can tell you the truth if you need to hear it, in a way you can take it."

"I've got this one." Caitlin thumbed at Jacob, grinning.

He held up the key chain, jangling the keys like bells and pursing his lips as if he were blowing a trumpet.

"I'm serious," Nancy said as she cleared the plates.

"I know," Caitlin replied, "and thank you. I will consider it. I promise." Then she immersed herself in another hug from Jacob and a comment about his wizardly key-chain ways.

It was soon time for Jacob to get ready for school and Nancy announced she would take him today; her birthday present to Caitlin was time for a long, hot bubble bath. They hugged warmly as they said good-bye.

And then Caitlin was alone in the apartment. She sat down again at the dining table, gazing at the cat and thinking about her mother. People didn't have to be the same. They didn't have to agree with each other. But they didn't have to judge each other either, simply support each other's choices.

Arfa twitched, stretched, and jumped down from the couch. He ambled to the table, rubbed his muzzle across her ankles, then sat back on his haunches with his eyes mostly closed, purring. Caitlin regarded him and realized that the tips of his whiskers were moving. Although it was hard to see, she was sure that all the fur on his face was blowing backward as if he were facing into a breeze.

She looked toward the window, which was shut against the fall chill. There was no breeze, no vent, no fan—nothing. Then Arfa stood up, walked around behind her, arched his back, and rubbed his side against empty space, as if it were someone's leg.

In the still, airless room Caitlin felt a sudden cooling in the small of her back, as if icy breath had been blown down her spine and pooled there. Simultaneously the cat turned to her, hissed silently, and hurried away.

Caitlin didn't blame her.

Something was here.

Something that didn't belong.

CHAPTER 2

At noon, the C train was mostly empty. Caitlin shared her car with only a few transit workers at the far end and a young Hispanic couple somehow cuddling around their backpacks.

Smelling of bubblegum—the only flavor of bath bubbles she could find in the apartment—Caitlin headed toward the Brooklyn International School, which offered eighth to twelfth grade for English-language learners. A large number of students were not just immigrants but refugees, many of them suffering from a wide range of traumas. Caitlin usually visited the school one afternoon a week to conduct individual therapy sessions but with all her recent trips, she hadn't been able to find any free afternoons. Earlier in the week she'd received an e-mail asking her to please come on an off day. One student in particular was proving especially difficult to reach.

Caitlin leaned her head back on the glass window of the train and stared at ads for a ministorage chain. Ordinarily, she'd have been rereading the e-mail from the school and thinking about the student, but she couldn't keep her mind off of Arfa and the presence they had both felt in the room. Most of the time his behavior could be passed off as random feline weirdness but the inexplicably rippling fur gnawed at her. The experience had blindsided her and filled her with a thought that stubbornly refused to go away:

Did I bring something back with me from Galderkhaan? Or, like an animal, has something sniffed me out?

Or was it neither of the above? Reason argued against those. But reason had too many enemies now.

Reality was suddenly very, very difficult to know and impossible to quantify. Souls from an ancient civilization had been stretching through time, trying to bond with souls in the modern day to complete a ritual. Caitlin had interceded, used a self-induced trance to place herself between then and now, breaking the connection. But it wasn't like an electric circuit where the lines were cut and the energy died. This was different. It had been like walking through a graveyard where the ghosts were visible, aggressive, and unhappy. Not even the great universities had literature to help her understand that. Caitlin was sure; she had checked.

Caitlin sat up straight and forced herself to focus on the present, on what she knew was real. She dug deep into her pocket for her phone and scrolled through e-mails until she found the one from the school. The boy in trouble was an eighth grader, originally a child soldier in the Central African Republic. Deserting one night, Odilon had managed to walk a hundred miles to the capital from his rebel camp without being picked up by any other militia. At Bangui, he hid in a hospital for a week until he passed out from hunger. Doctors Without Borders got him out of the country and now, through a generous line of supporters, he was living in a hastily converted meeting space in the basement of a synagogue in Brooklyn. He had seemed responsive during the summer school that guided the refugees through assimilation into American life. Now, in late October, he was beginning to isolate and was refusing to speak in class or out of it. The school's counselors suspected he was experiencing flashbacks but they couldn't confirm.

Caitlin looked up from her phone. A couple of college students had joined the car, both wired into music. She glimpsed several boisterous younger kids in an adjacent car, clearly skipping school. The rocking of the two cars made her aware of the reflections playing off the windows. Images collided with each other as the cars shifted or turned along gentle curves, layering the faces of passengers one upon the other. Her eyes traced the windows and their metal frames, the silvery poles and overhead handlebars, the yellow and orange plastic seats. The passengers and their reflections seemed to dance around the fixed structures as though they were figures around a maypole in some primitive ritual, complete with the transparent souls of the departed. She thought about the dead of Galderkhaan, the Priests trying to bond their souls together and ascend to a higher spiritual plane through the rite of *cazh*. The poles in the cars were like the columns of the Technologists, planted in earth, extending to the sky, connecting them both.

Her phone fell from her hand and bounced on the floor at her feet, apparently unharmed. She picked it up, squeezed her eyes shut, and shook her head out of its reverie.

Damn it, Caitlin, she thought.

There was a kid who needed her several stops away; she had to be ready. He wasn't another Maanik. He wasn't another Atash. This was a child, forced to be a man, who was having a perfectly logical reaction to the horror he had experienced.

She reached inside and drew on whatever latent strength she could find. Opening her eyes, she looked up at the ceiling, then out the window. The familiar world was all around her, the tracks carrying her along a station platform, the horizontal tiles of the walls, black and white signs between the columns. *This* was reality.

Yet almost as swiftly as it arrived the feeling of confidence dissipated. Down the back of her neck, along the backs of her arms, anxiety spread like a frost. It was an old, familiar, unwanted guest and she knew what it meant.

She was being watched.

Pulling into the station, the train came to a complete stop. She looked around. No one who joined her car was paying her even the slightest attention. A tall girl, probably a model, got on and folded into a seat, sliding a piece of gum into her mouth and opening a book. A teenager boarded with his bicycle. The train pulled away and Caitlin leaned forward to peer through the windows into the jostling cars ahead and behind. No one was looking at her.

She sat up straight again and pulled her shoulders back, but logic and posture weren't antidotes. There was absolutely nothing she could do to duck the fear, the feeling that eyes were upon her. There was no psychological foundation: she had never been prone to feelings of persecution or exaggerated self-importance. If someone, somewhere, were watching her, she could not fix that. And why should she? People looked at people all the time. Shoving the problem aside, she focused instead on her e-mails, which provided plenty of distractions to choose from.

Most of them, she discovered, were from Ben Moss. He had been combing through the videos of the Galderkhaani language in an attempt to construct a rudimentary dictionary. *Linguistic databases—ethnic dialects—Glogharasor*; her eyes skipped over sentence after sentence without letting any of the information stick. Then she landed on one she couldn't ignore: *I'm visiting my parents in Cornwall but I'll be back Tuesday. Would love to see you and celebrate your birthday.*

Tuesday was tomorrow.

She had reached her stop. Caitlin put her phone away and dug her hands into her gloves. She would deal with tomorrow, tomorrow.

Downtown Brooklyn was all thoroughfares and blocky buildings with few cafés or public indoor spaces to hang out in where she could take Odilon. But Caitlin knew that Brooklyn International had a Ping-Pong table. It was located in a dim corner of the cramped gym and even though one half of the table was an inch higher than the other and the net sagged, fifteen or twenty minutes of play could create enough of a bond before they moved somewhere else in the school to chat.

Odilon was short for his age and carried himself with the familiar sway-shouldered arrogance of many of the child soldiers she had met before. Handing him a paddle, Caitlin was prepared for him to shrug or sneer or refuse to play, but he did not. He gripped the handle as though it were the hilt of a machete and watched silently as she demonstrated the basics. He nodded to begin and then played without frustration or combativeness.

Forty-five minutes later he still hadn't spoken a word, laughed, or given her any glimpse inside. Caitlin was feeling exasperated, not with him but with the situation, though she was careful not to show it. She'd been reading him as he played. His gaze was uninvolved; his hand was studying the movement of the ball, muscle memory responding to something coming toward him, gauging how hard or how gently to strike. He did surprisingly well for a first-timer and did not become aggressive when the ball hit the net or missed the table. His mind and his heart were elsewhere. His dark eyes were steady, a good sign. It suggested memories shielded by time and distance rather than restless, current flashbacks. His soul was locked out, not in. She wondered how old he'd been when he'd first killed someone. Was it at gunpoint? At what distance? Had he cut a throat?

She realized she was impatient and that frustrated her. It was the tangible residue of Maanik and Gaelle and Atash. Those sessions had yielded quick results. How long would it take this boy to feel safe enough to actually play the game instead of working at it? Then add a few weeks to that before he would start talking to her. In the meantime, a thousand dangerous psychological and emotional wires could be tripped. Poor grades were a given since he wasn't talking in class, he could lose his makeshift bedroom in the synagogue, even a random altercation in the street—anything could seal him shut.

Caitlin wanted a shortcut with this boy too, as unrealistic as that was. She had five minutes left in the session and all they'd done was hit a little plastic ball while she affected cheerful encouragement. How could she give him a feeling of safety and continuity that would last until she came back next week?

Caitlin placed her paddle on the table and Odilon instantly tensed. The ball clacked past him. His eyes were on the woman as she walked slowly around the table until she was standing beside the net.

Caitlin's mind went to Maanik and Gaelle, the young women who had been in the thrall of the Galderkhaani souls. She remembered the contact she had made with them, and how, through movement-specific motions with her hands, she was connected with heaven and earth.

Unsmiling, Caitlin held out her right hand, palm down a foot above the table. Then she motioned for Odilon to do the same. He looked at her quizzically and then tentatively reached out his hand as though it were a Ping-Pong ritual he did not understand. She then flipped over her left hand, palm up, the fingers not quite rigid, as though they held an offering. She kept her eyes on his. He returned her stare, not defiantly but warily, in this moment more boy than soldier.

Sliding her open left hand four inches below his right hand, Caitlin instantly felt something leap within her palm, as if a stone had dropped into water and flung drops in the air. They both gasped. An immense cascade washed down her spine to her feet. She knew that this energy, strong and negative, was from Odilon. Instinctively she pushed her left foot hard into the floor to anchor herself, as she had in the conference room of the United Nations. The energy continued to pour through her.

Odilon broke their gaze and stared at their hands in disbelief. He then took an enormous inhale and suddenly backed away. He leaned forward, put both hands on his knees, and braced himself. She could hear him, see him taking long breaths in and letting long breaths out. Caitlin lowered her hands, turning her right hand down in the process, and she could feel the energy discharging through her. Her own spirit lightened. When Odilon straightened there was moisture in his eyes and, after a moment, he smiled faintly with relief. Holding his right hand before his tearful eyes, marveling and uncomprehending, he turned it toward her.

Caitlin stepped toward him and, this time, very lightly, she gave him a high five.

The session had lasted an hour. The final part of it had taken less than thirty seconds. It had bonded and impacted them both.

And for Caitlin, it lasted. She felt jubilant as she walked from the high school onto the noisy sidewalk. The traffic was louder than when she had arrived, the fall air suddenly warm, her shoulders no longer compacted. Whatever portal she had opened, she wedged herself firmly into it, not wanting the joyful freedom to close. She laughed, grateful to be reconnected with *this* place, *this* time. She hadn't felt so content in weeks.

Underground, she boarded a slightly more crowded train headed into Manhattan. She had a corner bench to herself and let the cacophony of the subway wash around her, observed the solid and translucent images without becoming unsettled. Now, she thought, was the time to go through Ben's e-mails.

Oh, Ben—he overexplained his thought process for each linguistic discovery, and second- and third-guessed himself for nearly every translated word. On the one hand, his linguistic mapping of Galderkhaan had confidently identified the two main groups: Priests and Technologists. The Technologists were largely scientists, though the words "faith" and "myth creation" appeared frequently in connection with both groups—a puzzle that suggested they came from the same root beliefs and had somehow diverged.

Ben had other discoveries to share, but all of them had the proverbial asterisk since a diacritical hand gesture could skew the interpretation one way or the other. Maanik had made similar hand gestures when she was under the control of the Galderkhaani soul.

Caitlin lifted her eyes from the phone as the train stopped at a station with a jolt. Several passengers entered the car, looking for places to sit. When they swung into seats, their eyes found hers.

A fresh wash of ice cascaded down her spine. The departure bell sounded but the train stayed in the station. Caitlin looked around, shocked that the fear had found her again and determined not to let it get the better of her.

She then did what she had done with Odilon: turned her right hand down and emptied herself, raised her left hand palm-up to receive, and let her fingers guide her mind. Away from herself, through the car, outward, farther—

In the car ahead, Caitlin noticed a woman with black hair and a deep suntan. She was the reason for the train's delay: her backpack was between the doors, preventing them from closing, and she was looking at Caitlin. Suddenly the woman, in a small gesture, wiped the air with her fingertips.

Images flooded Caitlin's mind. Unfamiliar faces, all bronzed, all frozen as if in snapshots—some laughing, some crying, some screaming. They came rapidly, one after the other, faster and faster until they seemed to move: one body with hundreds of expressive faces. Caitlin's body felt overcome with turbulence, white-water rapids. She tried to raise a hand and couldn't. Effectively blind, suddenly nauseated, and panicking, Caitlin struggled to shut her eyes, to shut out the images.

And despite those unwanted images she realized she still had some control, her mind still worked, and she thought to herself: *You are here, now, in the train, going home. When it starts again you will feel the car swaying, hear the wheels on the tracks. Picture it. Anticipate it.*

What was it she heard Jacob's art instructor say once, the phrase that stuck with her? "If you can visualize it, you own it"?

And suddenly, it worked. Caitlin felt as if the visual aura of a migraine had suddenly dissipated. When she opened her eyes again the doors were closed, the train was rolling forward, and the woman was gone.

That's what it was, she told herself. *The onset of a migraine from the stress of what you did with Odilon. That's all.*

But though normalcy had reasserted itself, something of the assault remained: an unsettled, bordering-on-urgent feeling deep inside her that was somehow familiar. It had all the earmarks of mild anxiety but with a difference:

Caitlin felt the woman's eyes still upon her, still very near, invisible, somehow watching her.

CHAPTER 3

"Senator Cooper, we don't have to represent it that way to your constituents."

Flora Davies forced her voice to stay pleasant and charming on the phone as she pried the Control key from her laptop with a fingernail. An aggravated Flora always meant damage to the nearest object in her office.

"But," the senator started in his infantilized lilt, "what if the other side finds out about my support for the increased funding you've requested and starts spreading rumors that I now believe in global warming or climate change—or whatever they're calling it now?"

Flora calmly countered, "Then our colleagues, who are numerous and well connected, will simply answer back in the media that the funds you want to study the Antarctic ice melt have nothing to do with the environment. It doesn't have to do with dying polar bears or rising sea levels. It has to do with your fear, the Group's fear, that the Russians or the Chinese can expand their presence there and pose a threat to our nation from this new and wide-open platform."

"I see," he said. "I like it."

"Everything is a public relations battle these days," she said.

The senator sighed. "It *is* a muddle," he agreed. "I liked it better when we either did or did not support abortion, without all the debate about this month, that trimester, or which state you are physically in. When we supported human rights across the board, not this for gays or that for women or something else for some other group."

"You are a true humanitarian."

"Thank you," the senator said.

"Which is why it's important to let your colleagues and constituents know that supporting *and* supervising the expenditures for our work will allow you to make sure less money is spent on faux science, like whale massage and meditation for schizophrenics."

"Faux science," he said. "Yes, I like that phrase. It sounds like 'foe,' as in 'enemy.' "

"Yes, Senator," Flora said, rolling her eyes. She popped the Control key.

This, thankfully, would be the last phone call she'd have to make this morning. Well, early afternoon—she surmised the time when she heard mail drop through the slot in the front door of the Group's mansion on Fifth Avenue. Three new senators supporting her publicly acknowledged Antarctic research. Every dollar helped. That was quite an accomplishment, almost as impressive as getting her Berkeley colleague and Group member, Peter, to send her a new science associate even after telling him about the dicey experiment now taking place below her in the mansion's heavily secured basement.

With Senator Cooper happily burbling away about press releases and news spots, she let her mind wander back to that experiment until it was necessary to answer a question.

"Say, Dr. Davies," said the senator, "does this mean I can get a trip to Antarctica? My daughter would love to see penguins."

"Yes," Flora said, "the Group Science Foundation will be thrilled to give you a junket in Antarctica." She did not mention that half the continent's penguins had left due to the ice event that only her aide had witnessed.

They ended the call convivially. Flora used both hands to massage her face out of its scowl, then headed downstairs to the basement corridor, now crammed full of destroyed deep freezers. She really had to figure out a way to dump those unobtrusively. Opening the door to the smallest lab, she encountered the glare of what had turned out to be the best and worst part of the bargain with Berkeley: Adrienne Dowman, a reportedly brilliant if contrary young scientist, newly arrived the day before, who refused to exhibit even a veneer of social grace, from manners to lip balm to deodorant. She looked as if her lips bled every night.

"How's it coming?" Flora asked as pleasantly as she could.

"It's not going to work," Adrienne barked.

"Well, Peter sent me quite the optimist, didn't he?" Flora whipped back.

"You asked for my opinion."

"I did not," Flora replied. "I asked for a progress report. Let's be clear. While you're working with me, which will be for the rest of your career, you have an 'on' button but not an 'opinion' button. Got it?"

"It's never been done at this scale," Adrienne said, undeterred. "That's informational, not an opinion."

Flora gave up, for now. "When are we starting?"

"In a few minutes."

Adrienne turned back to work on the room, which had been emptied and its soundproofing tripled in the last forty-eight hours. Flora had made it clear to Peter that the scientist doing this favor for the Group would be hers permanently in order to keep a lock on the Group's "proprietary information." Peter had leaped at the chance to offload his least-favorite associate. On the plus side, Adrienne was a profoundly gifted physicist and tech. She had installed eight black panels in the room: two large ones fixed on floor-to-ceiling columns and six smaller but still sizable panels on rotary devices by the walls. A viper's nest of wires led outside the room to the Group's private generator and to a control box that looked like the kit of a DJ. On the platform fixed to the floor sat the last stone Mikel Jasso, one of the Group's field agents, had brought back from the Southern Ocean. Flora had privately dubbed it "the Serpent" because there had been no trouble at all in her garden of relics and finds until this one showed up. Since its arrival there had been a succession of ruptured, melted deep freezers and her researcher Arni Haugan had been found dead on the lab floor, his gray matter liquefied and pouring from his ears. This experiment had to work or Flora would have to seriously consider throwing the artifact back in the ocean. Success here would be preferable.

"Ready for nothing," Adrienne grumped. She handed Flora headphones with an embedded communication device and placed a set on her own head.

"How audible is this going to be if the soundproofing fails?" Flora asked. "I do not want to be aggravating my neighbors."

"Nobody's going to hear it," Adrienne snorted. "Including us, unless you have canine ancestry."

Before Flora could respond to the dig, Adrienne flicked a switch and said, "But ultrasound decibels can do damage too."

Flora most certainly felt the sudden hum of electricity. But far more importantly, the Serpent stone jumped four feet in the air and hung there, at the exact midpoint between the floor and ceiling panels. Flora laughed out loud. To date, the heaviest object to be acoustically suspended was a metal screw. Now they had lifted something magnitudes larger.

Adrienne was not indulging in a celebration. The stone was bobbling wildly and she was quickly but lightly turning knobs, nudging the side panels into different angles. The stone stabilized for a moment, then two—then suddenly flipped upside down, and Flora gasped. Its crescent carvings were now facing the ceiling, the object quivering.

"Huh?" said Adrienne.

"You weren't expecting that?" Flora said over the hum.

"A stone shouldn't suddenly become bottom-heavy, like a water balloon."

"Magnetism?" Flora suggested.

Adrienne glanced at readings on a laptop, shook her head. She bent over her console, turning a knob with a feather touch Flora would have thought impossible from her lumpen personality. In the center of the room the stone returned to its previous equilibrium.

Adrienne stood still, watching intently.

"So . . . ?" Flora asked, pondering.

"That should have been impossible," Adrienne replied. "I knew there would be minor fluctuations, but in order for an object to flip like that, the sound wave on one side would have had to overpower the other, which would have destabilized the levitation. The stone would have dropped to the floor." Adrienne peeled her eyes from the major milestone she had just achieved, which no one would ever hear about, and looked at her new employer. "What the hell is this thing, Dr. Davies?"

"A very ancient relic with properties we do not understand," Flora said. "Yet."

"You already told me that," Adrienne said. "What *aren't* you telling me?"

Flora's implacable expression caused Adrienne to snort in frustration and turn away. As she did, her eyes shifted to the door, beyond which sat the destroyed freezers. She looked back at her new boss.

"Flora, did it try—to get *out*?" Adrienne asked.

"Not exactly," Flora replied. "Lord, don't go imparting intelligence to it. It's just a mass of nickel and iron."

"And uranium is just silvery white metal," Adrienne said. "This thing has all the hallmarks of being very, very dangerous."

Flora glanced at the levitated stone. "Not anymore."

Adrienne turned a little scarlet. "Christ, you could have told me. What did it do?"

"Hopefully, nothing it will do again," Flora replied. "In fact, now that you've tamed it, why don't we see what *it* hasn't been telling *us*."

CHAPTER 4

Andreas Campbell pulled his mail cart west on Ninth Street. He stopped outside the Augustine Apartments and switched off the audiobook on his iPhone. Elizabeth Bennet was just telling Mr. Darcy he was the last man she'd ever marry. Leaning over his cart to retrieve the building's bundle of mail, Andreas suddenly doubled over with pain. The stabbing in his gut was so sharp, he had to transfer his full weight to the cart, and the pain kept coming. He felt a spike of blinding, searing heat rocket to his head, as if his body temperature had just soared to triple digits—which it had.

Looking down the street, he saw people near Sixth Avenue and called weakly, trying to get their attention. He waved helplessly at the lobby beyond the glass doors of the Augustine. The doorman was chatting with a maintenance man, not looking at the street, and the security camera was pointed in the opposite direction. Andreas fumbled for his phone in his pocket.

As the next assault of pain lunged through his kidneys, he fell to his knees, clasping his stomach and then screaming at his own touch. His midsection felt like it was exploding outward in every direction. He vomited on the sidewalk, trying to scream through his convulsing throat. Then the heat came again and he screamed so hard that blood vessels burst in his eyes.

The doorman finally caught the strange and desperate image through the sliding glass doors and he and the maintenance man ran down the steps to help. There they found the mail carrier lying on the sidewalk, blood pooling around his body, vomit sprayed around his head.

"Call 911," the doorman yelled, loud enough to attract attention from passersby on Sixth Avenue. He knelt next to the man, hands hovering over him, not knowing what to do as Andreas continued to claw at the pavement, his voice losing force.

A crowd began to gather, gawking and gossiping about the nice man who had worked in the neighborhood for years as they captured the tragedy on their cell phones. In the background the maintenance man attempted to describe the scene in broken English while pleading for an ambulance. Finally they heard a siren in the distance, coming nearer.

"Hold on," they told Andreas. "Hold on!"

• • •

Flora Davies was heading from the basement up to her office when her phone chimed with an alert. A week before, when rats had inexplicably stampeded from Washington Square Park to the basement entrance of the mansion, she had set a dozen tracking systems to alert her if anything unusual happened nearby. These were a confluence of social media platforms that fed her data based on keywords and GPS locales. An algorithm used by the NYPD starred potentially disruptive events. There had been surprisingly few alerts: a couple of muggings, a police takedown of a sword-swinging nut on Bleecker Street, and tiresome celebrity sightings. Now there was a stream of tweets with photos and exclamation points.

"Probably a rock star," she muttered irritably. Then she noticed the sprawl of a body, and the blood. It was in front of the nearby Augustine. She moved rapidly through the tweets and, yes, someone had snapped the carrier's ID and posted his name. She knew him, she thought, though she could barely recognize his face.

Flora called to her assistant, "Erika, look up Andreas Campbell, male, late forties, early fifties."

"Andreas? Our mail carrier?"

"Yes. Start with pharmacy records."

The Group had long ago established methods for consulting the medical history, bank statements, and credit reports of virtually anyone in America, and they were working toward global access. Any individual would be fairly well delineated with just those sources.

Flora rushed from the building, the front door slamming behind her. Down Ninth Street she heard a siren abruptly shut off. By the time she got to the Augustine Apartments the ambulance doors were closing, Andreas Campbell behind them. She grabbed the nearest bystander, an older man walking his Yorkshire terrier, who was straining toward the blood as far as its leash would allow.

"Did he die?" Flora asked.

"We don't know."

"What was it, what was the matter?"

"Something bad," the man replied. "I heard a paramedic say it looked like he bled out half his body."

The crowd watched the ambulance drive away and then slowly, conspiratorially dispersed.

"Leave it, Bisco!" the old man snapped as the terrier growled and strained toward the mess. The man yanked definitively on the lead and the two of them walked away, leaving only Flora and the maintenance man to contemplate the remains. Flora crouched down on her haunches as close to the vomit as she could get without contaminating the pool of blood.

"Ma'am, what do you think you're doing?"

Flora quickly stood and transferred a twenty-dollar bill from her pocket to the maintenance man's hand. She then pulled out her debit card.

"Whatever you're going to do, do it quick before the cops come and turn this into a crime scene," the man said.

Holding the edge of her suit jacket over her mouth and nose, Flora used the tip of her debit card to sift through the puddle of vomit. It was filled with one-inch, pale, squirming objects, hundreds of them, if not thousands. Flora stood up just as her phone rang. It was Erika.

"Our friend has friends, Dr. Davies. He's got a prescription for albendazole, which is—"

"I know," Flora said. "Intestinal parasites."

"Yes. Herring worms, specifically," Erika said. "How did you know?"

"I think his pals just ate him from the inside out."

Erika made a gagging sound as Flora hung up. She used a tissue to wipe off her card.

"You all done here, lady?" the maintenance man asked.

"Yes, I'm quite through with that," she said, motioning at the ruddy mixture. "Make sure you tell the police to bag it and use disinfectant. Don't let them hose it into the gutter."

"Why? Is it dangerous?"

"Only if a dog or pigeon or some other unfortunate ingests it."

The man looked at her in disgust and gave a short nod of his head. "Whatever you say, lady."

As Flora walked back to the mansion, Arni, the dead researcher, was heavy on her mind. Upon entering the building she asked Erika if there had been anything else special about Andreas Campbell: mental irregularities, any psych meds?

Erika reported nothing unusual about Campbell, ruling out a potential link to Arni, who was a synesthete.

Flora sat at her desk and flipped open her laptop, calling up a map of her neighborhood. Then she remembered Andreas had just been at the mansion. She had heard the mail slot flap open and shut. Fifteen minutes later he was falling catastrophically ill two-thirds of a block away with parasites that *never* caused that much damage that fast. Yet it had happened, in the brief time that Flora was—

In the basement. With Adrienne and the Serpent.

First Mikel came back with the stone, then the rats stampeded, then Arni literally melted, then intestinal parasites went wild. By no reasonable yardstick was this a coincidence.

She switched to an advanced mapping program and drew two vectors, one from the Augustine to the mansion, the other from the mansion to the arch in Washington Square Park, the origin point for the rats. Her skin crawled as she remembered the undulating mass of clawing, twitching rodents that had covered the arch before they ran down and past her.

Like the grid of New York, the two vectors on-screen made a right angle crossing at the mansion.

All right, so what? she thought. Then she caught herself. The Group's mansion wasn't important. It was the *stone* that was important. Quickly she looked up the e-mail from Mikel that explained approximately where the Serpent had been collected in the Southern Ocean. She expanded the map and drew a vector from the Serpent's origin point to the mansion. Next, she marked the location where Mikel said he saw the iceberg calved from the Brunt Ice Shelf, with an airship lodged inside, and connected it to the mansion as well.

What else, what else . . . Mikel's albatrosses. Uruguay; hadn't it been near the Montevideo airport? She added that point to the map, then descended on Erika, demanding immediate research for any unusual animal behavior around the world over the previous couple of weeks.

"Whale beachings, haven't we been seeing reports on that?"

"A slight uptick—"

"Penguins leaving the Antarctic, we saw a lot of that. Look up any other weird flocking, dog or cat attacks, maulings at zoos, anything."

Erika's research was limited by what the media considered newsworthy, but within an hour Flora had virtual flags all across her map, with a line drawn from each to the mansion. A nexus of whale beachings in Hudson Bay. A dolphin *attack*, of all things, on a motorboat near Sea Gate. A man who lost his flock of homing pigeons when they dove, apparently in a mass suicide, into the ocean off of Breezy Point. An increase in jaguar attacks in Amazonas and parrots falling from the sky, already dead with no known cause, in Rondônia, Brazil. A sea lion reserve in Necochea, Argentina, that lost a third of its sea lions when they attacked each other.

Flora sat back in her chair. The lines drawn to her mansion were as obvious as the spokes of a fan, but she leaned forward and drew in the most important line anyway—the edge of the fan, the vector connecting all of the incidents, including the arch and the points where Mikel found the Serpent, where the iceberg broke, and where Andreas died.

Of course the line looked curved on the globe, but Flora triple- and quadruple-checked. It was a path as straight as a sword leading from the research station Halley VI to the stone's current resting place.

However, there was one giant anomaly. The albatrosses in Montevideo missed the vector by nearly two hundred miles.

She picked up her phone and dialed Mikel's number.

• • •

Bored out of his head at a pub in Stanley on the larger of the Falkland Islands, Mikel picked up on the first ring. His mind was foggy, directionless, wheels spinning in the mud. Two whiskeys had failed to sharpen it.

"I was just about to call," he said. "You'll need to arrange this one."

"Mikel—"

"Look, there are no ships going anywhere near the ice shelf and the only flight is the British Antarctic Survey. I've tried with them but they're suspicious as soon as I start talking."

"Suspicious of you? What have you been saying?"

"No, it's got nothing to do with me. They're petrified of something."

Flora took a restrained breath. "Mikel, what do you think it might be?"

"If you got me on that flight I'd be able to ask them, wouldn't I?"

"I will overlook your tone, Mr. Jasso."

"Sorry, I'm tired—"

"And I will arrange your transport. It seems we've more reason than ever to get you to Halley VI."

"Why? Something else going on?" he said, ignoring the last of the whiskey in favor of something—finally—more interesting.

Flora described the vector of animal madness.

Mikel sighed. "So you claim the stone I brought to you is interacting with something in Antarctica—never mind the total implausibility of that—but it's also affecting humans and mammals along a global route?"

"Yes. And I am extremely interested to see what is lying on the Antarctic section of that route, close up."

"But with the ice moving up to half a mile per year now, and who knows at what rate in the past, and with Galderkhaan existing millennia ago, then—"

"Whatever the other point of this vector is, it *has* to be under the ice." She added, "Not far from that research station."

"As the crow flies, you mean. Halley VI is on the moving ice sheet, nearly forty miles from the coast of the mainland. And to get to the ground, I'd have to do god knows how much tunneling down through hundreds of meters of snow and ice. Dr. Davies, even if you sent me with a team of experts and the British government falling over itself with permissions and assistance, it couldn't be done."

"That's true," she said, "but only if you never start."

"Don't give me that 'every journey begins with a single step' line."

"I'm not. I'm only asking for your best effort, Mikel."

"Flora—"

"Your best, which I know is considerable. One other thing. Your incident with the albatrosses was not on the vector."

"Wait," he said, "how is that possible?"

"Precisely," Flora said.

Mikel considered what she implied. "Your calculations must be off."

"They're not," Flora assured him. "I'm wondering if you actually experienced what you think you did."

"Are you questioning what I saw?"

"That's not what I said. You told me yourself that the flight attendant didn't seem to know what you were talking about."

"Yes, but what I said happened, happened," he barked into the phone.

"So what does that suggest?" Flora asked.

"I don't know."

"Think about it," urged Flora.

"I am. Nothing's coming."

"Now you're just being lazy," she said. "What if you saw the albatrosses as they were, but in some other time?"

The words cut sharply through the whiskey. That was new. And a little unnerving. But remotely possible? Mikel gazed across the bar as if he were looking through the wall at the birds themselves.

"Mikel?"

"I'm here," he said. "I think."

"Touché," she replied.

"But crap," he said. "Arni."

"What about him?"

"Maybe he got hit with the same 'something' I did, only his synesthete's brain magnified it. Maybe I'm lucky I'm not so advanced."

Flora let the thought sit a moment. "Look, I think it best that you keep track of what you experience *with* and *without* supporting evidence. Both are valuable but keep them separate in your reporting. Clear?"

"Very," Mikel said, and he meant it. He felt as though the grunge had suddenly been cleared from his brain and a universe of possibilities had opened.

CHAPTER 5

As Caitlin hurried from the subway to her office, she left a message for Barbara asking for an appointment as soon as possible. So much had blown in on her in the last few hours that she felt unable to prioritize which questions and feelings she should heed first . . . which were real, which were intuited, and which might be wholly imagined.

She was certain the exchange with Odilon was real. The rising power she felt in her hands, the look of amazement on his face, and the sudden well of emotion; those were all completely honest.

That's the place to start, she decided, *the part you* know *is true.*

The question she couldn't answer was how far to take it, how much to tell Barbara.

Maybe the choice wouldn't be hers. The feeling of openness and expansion had not returned since she'd seen the dark-haired woman on the subway.

What happened?

Had Caitlin shut the power down? Maybe there was a mental off switch in her brain that she'd stumbled onto blindly. Maybe it wasn't off but simply sleeping.

And then there was that woman herself. Was she just a convenient, innocent figure? Or did she open the power? Had Caitlin's mind, overloaded, grabbed at a meaningless gesture and ascribed power to it? Was she developing paranoia? Imagining that someone was watching her was certainly a first step.

She was unclear about everything, except for the surprising but unmistakable welter of sadness that had risen since that moment on the train when Caitlin had shut the cascade of faces down. It was a form of mourning, of suddenly losing this new and frightening but *vital* window on the world . . . perhaps on several worlds. She imagined her mother chastising her, but there was no way she could let this be.

Caitlin felt suddenly, strangely defensive when she received a text from Barbara confirming an availability the next morning. What if Barbara wouldn't understand and judged her?

Caitlin was relieved to have scheduled patients that afternoon. More than once in her individual therapy sessions with the high school and college students, she longed to try a repeat of the conduit she had manifested with Odilon.

But these students didn't need a drastic assist. They were doing the long, slow slog through their psyches, identifying old patterns, accepting their entrenchment, learning and trying and failing and trying again to deprogram from the distortions, succeeding by increments. It was steady, honorable work, made possible by the relatively stable lives they were living. Odilon was different. He'd been on the edge of a cliff and unable to ask for help. These kids faced challenges but no immediate danger. To interrupt their process would have impugned their responsibility for themselves.

After Caitlin's last session, though, the grief washed back into her so powerfully she put her head in her hands. Thinking was a burden she no longer wished to bear. She needed to talk to someone who wouldn't need a preamble. It was four thirty here; in Cornwall, Ben would probably still be up.

She checked Skype first and there he was. She hesitated, wondering if he might be talking to someone. *Ow*, she thought. And her heart floundered when the call resulted in silence. But it was only a delay, and he blipped on-screen with the biggest smile and a warm "Hi."

"I only have half an hour before I have to pick up Jacob, I'm sorry," she began.

"I'll take it," he said, continuing to smile.

"But if you want to get a late dinner tomorrow, if you're not too blown out from the flight back—"

"I won't be," Ben replied. "I want to take you out for your birthday." She smiled, but he must have seen the hesitancy she felt because he quickly switched subjects. "Okay, half an hour, counting down. What's happening?"

"A lot," she said, looking away from him. "I can't even begin. Can you do me a favor, Ben, would you mind going over what you've learned about Galderkhaan from your translations?"

Ben laughed, and she knew it was a "things never change" laugh.

"Caitlin, it's in the e-mails I sent—"

"Yes, I know, I read them, but I'd like to hear them from you. It's just—it's how I'm thinking these days. Human to human, not soliloquy to soliloquy."

He grinned and said, "Firstly, that's commendable. And secondly, can I begin with some new bits first?"

"Wherever you like," she said.

"Until last night," Ben said, "I was focusing on the three videos we have of Maanik and the one I took with my phone at the UN when you—when you saw Galderkhaan."

Caitlin noted his careful choice of words. Not "visited," not "witnessed" or "experienced," but "saw," which could mean "imagined." Clearly, he still didn't completely believe her about that night.

"So what've you got?" she asked, trying not to lay on the affected cheerfulness too thick.

"Okay. First, I dove into something basic: volcanoes in Antarctica," he replied. "Galderkhaan must have been located on the west side of the Antarctic Peninsula. Or possibly north in the Scotia Sea. Those volcanoes are submerged now and there's been quite a bit of earthquake activity there. That wouldn't be unusual but they really are very distant from the continent. So the west coast is far more likely."

"Isn't the west coast the part that's melting the fastest?"

"Yes, several studies have confirmed that all the western glaciers are going to melt and the whole ice sheet could follow."

"I wonder—"

"And that's a yes as well. A couple years ago they found an active volcano under the western ice sheet. If it blows a fissure, the whole area could come out looking like Iceland, all hot springs and thermal vents. Only more melty and less therapeutic. Geologists are pretty sure earthquakes around the volcano line are contributing to the big meltdown, although they're not the only causes."

"There's also idiocy and arrogance."

"Whether it's global warming or deep and latent magmatic activity or just a big nasty climatic cycle, the west side is our place. There are no known volcanoes around the other coast. Now, Antarctica being covered with snow and ice, that means that our Galderkhaani friends had to have some impressive tricks for making their city habitable. I've started assuming geothermal engineering to an unprecedented degree. Actually, to an unantecedented—" he stumbled over the word a few times until they were both laughing. "To a degree unmatched to the present day. They were oasis builders, Caitlin."

"Huh, okay . . . could they have built more than one oasis?"

Ben *hmm*ed noncommittally. "That jibes with a particular word I found: '*ida-ida*.' Caitlin, I can't tell you how unusual this word is—half hour, you said?"

"Yes, sorry, Ben."

"All right, then, to the chase. The word means 'building,' but not in the sense of a single structure. It's more like building something that's ever expanding, sort of like 'fulfilling'—dare I say, a manifest destiny."

"Is it related to the Technologists or the Priests or both?"

"Just the Technologists."

"Ben, is there anything about expansion in an—*internal* sense?"

"I don't follow. You mean like a soul?"

"More like an expanded consciousness." She stopped there, unwilling to say anything that might lead to a discussion of why she was asking. Ben was a friend, but not an uncritical one. The kind, in fact, her mother wished for her.

Ben studied her for a moment. "A psychiatrist walks into a bar," he said, grinning, "and sees herself sitting on a stool."

She smiled back. "Cute." It was an old joke of theirs, dating back to their college days. Ben used it whenever he had to pull her from what he called her "Hamlet reflections."

"To answer the question—seriously—there's no talk of their inner lives, except for the *cazh*, which is really about an outer afterlife. Maybe this wasn't a very inward-minded people?"

"I doubt that," said Caitlin.

"Why? We don't know if they had art, songs, poetry—"

"They loved," she replied. "It wasn't just physical love. I felt it when I eavesdropped on their lives and relationships."

"Quite possibly," Ben agreed. "Then again, we did keep encountering them in crisis mode, which would explain an outward focus."

Caitlin fell into a sudden depression. Earlier, she had thought something might have come back with her from the past; she wondered now if it weren't just the opposite: that something of herself had stayed behind, connected to these people, *hurting* with them.

And then, just as suddenly, she came out of it, as cold poured down her spine again as it had at the apartment. She forced herself to focus on the screen. That's where reality was, she told herself.

"Cai," Ben said, "I see my time is running down and I have a more important question."

She looked at him expectantly but when he didn't respond to her cue, she raised her eyebrows, further encouraging him to speak.

"When we have dinner tomorrow night," Ben said with a direct gaze and a light tone, "how romantic should I make it?"

Caitlin glanced away but had to look back at him. She adored his sweet face, she truly did. But he had the most inelegant way of transitioning between topics she had ever experienced.

"I don't know, Ben. Can we wait till we're together to see?"

"Human to human," he said, nodding.

"Yes, human to human," said Caitlin.

Ben only broke their gaze for a second and then he was back to his buoyancy. "All right," he said. "I've got another few minutes and I'm gonna use them. Gaelle—over the past day I've been studying the recording of her when she was having her crisis in the marketplace. In Maanik's episodes, *she* seems to be talking about the Priests and Technologists equally, as if she's caught between them. But Gaelle—the camera didn't capture much of her, only a few sentences, unfortunately, and she spoke exclusively of the Technologists."

"That fits," Caitlin said. "I mean that Gaelle would be talking about them, since in her vision she died trying to leave Galderkhaan with them. Physically, I mean. Not spiritually."

"Which brings me to this," Ben said. "When you were—back there, while we were at the UN, did you see anything in the air? In the sky, I mean."

"Like what?"

"I don't want to feed it to you."

"Okay." She shut her eyes and carefully, tentatively drifted back to that night. It was all instantly real again and she snapped herself back.

"Cai?"

"Yes," she said. "I saw clouds, the moon, volcanic ash spreading, and of course the rising souls, though I wouldn't quite describe that as *seeing* them, more like sensing them."

"That's it?"

"Well, yeah. No birds. Also the columns of the Technologists, which were tall, very tall, and wide. They reminded me of the towers of the Brooklyn Bridge. That kind of stone, I mean."

"Hm. Well, there's a word in Gaelle's video that—trust me, I have doubted this and struggled to prove I'm wrong, but it's unmistakable. '*Aikai.*' 'Ship of the air.' "

Caitlin sat up straight.

"What?" Ben asked.

"Like zeppelins!" she said. The thought had occurred to her before, when she'd considered how the Galderkhaani might have mapped the region. "Ben, the Technologists' columns were absolutely tall enough for that."

"For what?"

"To be docking stations. Remember, like they tried do with the Empire State Building right after it was built?"

"They did?"

"Yeah. Just like the columns, it was low enough to use stairs to disembark, yet not high enough to get clocked by upper-level winds."

"But you didn't actually see any airships?"

She shook her head. "Not one. Besides, if they did have airships, why wouldn't they have tried to escape on them?"

"Maybe they could only fly at certain times?" Ben suggested. "Or they were being prepared, perhaps enlarged, for the coming catastrophe? Remember, the eruption seemed to come earlier than anyone expected."

"Maybe," Caitlin replied. "Then again, I wouldn't necessarily want to fly through air filled with rocks spewing from a volcano."

"Good point," Ben said. "Better to die trying to outrace a pyroclastic outpouring."

"People's instinct is to outrun something. That's animal, human nature. Like with the tsunami. I heard it in Thailand over and over, 'I thought I could run faster than the waves.' Some of the Galderkhaani might have been running to the sea to try to escape."

"That does make some sense," Ben agreed. "Anyway, before you go, here's what set me off on this, Caitlin. Gaelle says the word '*tawazh*.' The Norse had a god named Tiwaz. A sky god."

"The Norse again?" The prow of a Viking ship had been one of their first clues about the existence and potential reach of Galderkhaan.

Ben nodded. "It doesn't mean that someone escaped on an airship, but maybe part of the language made it out somehow."

"Meaning people did," Caitlin said. "By sea."

Ben nodded again.

Caitlin considered the repercussions of what he was saying. "That's a big thought. Living descendants."

"It's a possibility," he said, correcting her.

"Yes, but there's something else. Remember, the earliest I saw of Galderkhaan was just an hour before it was destroyed. They could have been sending airships anywhere, any time before that. Maybe some of them never came back."

He grinned.

"What?"

He laughed devilishly. "Are you conceding that I might be onto something?" Before she could answer he continued, "Remember the Varangian Rus? The Norsemen who traveled east as far as Mongolia?"

"A little," she said.

"Well, listen to this: those Norsemen also traveled south, and they became some of the most trusted guards and soldiers of the Byzantine emperor. Most of them started their careers in the navy before they moved into the palace. And on their ships, they used what was called 'Greek fire'—a substance that burned on water as well as land. It would burn just about anything anywhere, and we still can't figure out what it was made of."

"I don't follow," she said . . . and then she did. All the people she had seen erupt into spontaneous flame—she forced herself to push away images of melting flesh. "But, Ben, didn't the Greeks—"

"Invent it? Who says history's always right?"

She answered without thinking, "Those of us who actually witnessed it."

"Cai . . ."

The certainty of her answer, the conviction, stopped Ben hard.

"Hey, I have to pick up Jacob," Caitlin said. "Safe trip—I'll see you tomorrow, okay."

Ben managed a wary smile before she shut her laptop.

CHAPTER 6

When Caitlin and Jacob arrived home, she suggested they cook something that neither of them had made before. Jacob was always game for new things and right now Caitlin needed a distraction that had start-to-finish directions.

The result was a frittata that nearly made it out of the skillet intact. They laughed as they poured the runnier parts into their mouths and for a moment, Caitlin forgot everything that wasn't egg, cheese, ketchup, and her son. After dinner she shooed Jacob off to do his homework. He went gleefully, eager to return to Captain Nemo and find out what had happened to the troubled submariner.

Just as he was about to shut the bedroom door, Caitlin knocked on the table and called out to him. Jacob emerged again into the hallway to catch her question.

"What do *you* think will happen to him?"

Jacob shrugged, obviously content to let Jules Verne do the heavy lifting.

"Isn't he out there sinking ships with his submarine?" Caitlin asked.

"Yes, but people hurt his family," he signed. "He's mad."

"Angry or mad?" she asked, making the loopy sign beside her head.

Jacob scowled. "He's pissed, Mom. Very, very pissed." With that, he shut the door.

The initial question hadn't been answered, but Jacob seemed to be in Nemo's corner. She supposed he could have worse father figures in his life than a brilliant scientist who was sick of war.

Jacob finished reading and then asked her permission to watch a movie in his room. Caitlin considered joining him despite her work overload. Alone, she felt overwhelmed. She didn't want to think, didn't want to answer e-mails, didn't want to communicate with anyone. She wanted temporary oblivion. She walked into Jacob's room, gave him a kiss good-night, and walked straight to the bathroom to pop half of a sleeping pill, regardless of the early hour. She pulled the shades in her room. Then, lying in bed with headphones on and the sheet pulled over her head, she listened to Pachelbel—less familiar than Bach, more focus required to stay with each note—until she slipped into unconsciousness.

As she slept, there was a drumming on the wall. It was slow and low at first, then grew louder. The cat jumped on the bed and slunk low across Caitlin's legs, its tail dragging like a chain. Arfa mewed, stopped just beside her knee, then pawed at the air.

A cool wind rustled the tissues in a box on the night table, blew across the cat's low back, swept under the door and into the hallway. It moved like a low mist, rolling out, surging unevenly toward Jacob's room.

It entered.

The drumming grew louder, more insistent.

"Ma. Ma. Ma."

Jacob's voice was a dreamy monotone, like exhaled breath that somehow formed the same word with each cycle.

"Ma. Ma. *Ma.*"

The drumming grew more desperate, like someone trapped behind a door with something they had to escape—

The cold mist unfolded toward the boy's bed. It stopped and slowly rose up, towering above Jacob with a slow, writhing presence that stirred the drawings pinned to his walls and rippled through the open pages of Verne on the bed, then it stealthfully lay across him.

There was a whisper, a breath warmer than the rest. It touched the boy's cheek and the knocking slowed, then stopped. A word swept into his ear.

Tawazh.

• • •

At breakfast, Jacob was grumpy. "Did you take a pill last night?"

"Half of one. Why?"

"You never hear me knock when you take those."

"Jacob, you're always asleep when you drum on the wall."

"Uh-huh."

"Sorry, kiddo," she said. "Really, I am." She got up and crossed to hug him but instead tickled him out of his grump.

"I heard something in my sleep," he said.

"Oh? What was it?"

"A word," he replied.

"What word? 'Nemo'? '*Nautilus*'?"

"No," he answered. "I can't remember. But I heard it," he insisted. "Inside my ears."

"A dream," his mother said, kissing him on both ears.

After a relatively cheery breakfast and warm good-byes at the school gate, her mood quickly reverted to unease. She was eager for her morning appointment with Barbara and headed straight uptown to arrive early.

Barbara's apartment was one of the high-ceilinged gems hidden above Manhattan's flower district, though only a handful of shops there still sold potted trees and orchids. Six floors up, with wood-paneled walls and tall, sun-filled windows, the apartment always reminded Caitlin of an old but beautifully restored ship. The impression was inevitable, given the number of intricate knots displayed around the room—in table legs, fabric runners, throw pillows, and various media framed and mounted on the walls. Barbara's first career had been as a mathematician specializing in topology. Her friends and family had decided that knots were her thing, and despite the fact that it had been ten years since she'd changed professions, they continued to gift her display-worthy examples for her collection.

Barbara had a round, open face with a strongly pointed chin and sculpted eyebrows. But what everyone noticed first were her crystal-blue eyes. If you stayed with them, they shone like hopeful, helpful lights.

The women embraced warmly at the door before Caitlin found the familiar comfort of the armchair across from Barbara's. Concise and controlled, she then told her everything that had happened, from the first trance with Maanik to the "journeys" to Galderkhaan to Odilon's energy to the strange woman on the train.

When she was finished, Barbara smiled warmly. "How many times did you rehearse that in your head?"

Caitlin laughed. "Twice on the way here. I wanted to give it to you as objectively as possible."

"Well, you tipped the narrative into clinical. In your ten minutes left, are you prepared to tip back into the personal?"

Caitlin looked at her watch. "Yikes," she said, suddenly feeling anxious that she wasn't going to get what she needed before the session was over. She took a deep breath and pressed her back against the chair, uncrossed her feet so they were flat on the ground, and placed her hands cupped one inside the other on her lap. "Okay, Doc. I'm ready."

"All right, let's start with something big and basic. Which concerns you most: the idea of new, expanded abilities—"

"Am I crazy to believe they're even *possible*?" Caitlin blurted.

"I'm asking the questions," Barbara reminded her.

"Sorry. Right."

"Which concerns you most: the idea of expanded abilities, or the belief that Galderkhaan existed and in some way you might be linked to it?"

"Oh god, Barbara. Both. I feel—stupid. Really stupid. And afraid. The lady who runs into disaster scenes is cowering in a closet. Why aren't I exhilarated? Why aren't I . . . I don't know. Taking charge? Writing a paper about it or . . . ?"

"Didn't you do that with Maanik and the others? Take charge?"

"Yes, but when it's just me I can't . . . think myself out of paralysis."

"Is there something specific you are afraid of?"

"Oh yeah," Caitlin said. "That with all the evidence that's piling up—"

"Each scrap of which is still circumstantial or has an alternative explanation, as far as I can see—"

"Fine," Caitlin said. "Fine. I'm still very afraid that everything I've experienced is *real*. I scared myself last night, Barbara. I told Ben unequivocally that I'd witnessed history that's long gone. Not imagined it, not dreamed it, *saw* it. I was so sure. Yet even that doesn't scare me as much as the fact that someone will find out and decide I'm losing my mind."

"You aren't," Barbara assured her.

"I'm not so sure," Caitlin said. "If we buy that I self-hypnotized at the United Nations, what if I'm doing that unwittingly, over and over, in small bites—on the subway, remembering people and places that may be fiction, imagining the cat brushing against people who aren't there?"

"Cats were wiccan familiars for a reason," Barbara said.

"What, you're saying I'm a witch?" Caitlin laughed.

"No, no—I'm saying cats are unexpected little creatures. That there are explanations for everything, including unremembered dreams surfacing when you're awake and post-traumatic stress triggered by people making strange gestures in your direction, like Maanik did."

Caitlin sighed. "Maybe. Maybe. But what if what I'm doing, and the time I'm taking to do it, causes me to lose my job? What happens if the decision makers happen to see or hear and label me a quack?"

"And if you didn't look at the negative? These experiences have been liberating. I see a change in you, Caitlin. What about Maanik and Gaelle and the other people you have helped and will continue to help?"

"I know, and maybe that's ultimately what I'm afraid of," Caitlin said. "That all my training goes out the window and . . . like I said, I become the crazy lady who does some weird semaphore thing with kids."

Caitlin moved her arms willy-nilly but what was meant as a joke hit her in a very different way. It felt comfortable, like she was communicating something very personal.

"Let me take this in another direction," Barbara said.

"Please do."

"Are you afraid you'll start having episodes like Maanik?"

"No," Caitlin answered without hesitation. "This is different. I mean, I don't feel in danger of causing physical damage to myself or anyone else. But taking this further—" She swallowed a lump in her throat, paused, and breathed deeply. "For the sake of argument, whether this is real or imagined, what if I fail to recognize *my* reality anymore? The one I'm in with my son, and my work? What if I explore in here"—she said pointing to her head—"and I get to a place where I can't go back to normal?"

"Again, you're anticipating what may never occur," Barbara said. "You're creating the perfect storm for a self-fulfilling prophecy. Whatever is going on, might this just be a phase?"

"Jesus!"

Barbara started. "What?"

"I thought you said 'aphasia,' like I had a mental dysfunction."

"Caitlin, I said 'a . . . phase.' "

Caitlin fell silent and Barbara gave her the space to calm. She forced herself to breathe. "You know what's sad? All this talk and thinking and heightened emotions and 'powers.' God, it might actually be easier if I *were* crazy. Easier for me to deal with, easier to fix."

"I don't agree at all," Barbara said. "What's more, in my professional opinion you are quite sane. And I think you know it. Which is not a bad thing," Barbara pointed out. "You retain the capacity to be there for everyone who needs you. Focus on that. Stop playing with these ideas like they're all loose teeth."

"Easy for you to say. You don't speak Galderkhaani."

Barbara smiled strangely. "No, but I came close."

Caitlin looked at her in shock. "Wait, when? How? What?"

"No. This is your session, not mine."

"My session ended five minutes ago—I was watching the clock. What are you saying, Barbara? You can't just let that drop."

Barbara sighed and leaned back. She dropped her professional mask. "It was while I was doing postgrad at the University of Virginia. I agreed to a past-life regression for a neurobehavioral class.

"With about two dozen people as witnesses, I was hypnotized and led back to some time and place when I could make click consonants like the Xhosa people in South Africa, though I was speaking in a language no one recognized. I did that for about ten minutes, then came back through my own life—speaking English."

"What did the professor say about it?" Caitlin asked, fascinated.

"That either I went back through racial memory or it was a past-life experience—someone's, if not my own."

"Someone's?"

"I shouldn't do this."

"Why?"

"Because I don't want to prejudice your perceptions or my own."

"Too late," said Caitlin.

Barbara shook her head. "The professor said some schools of thought believe that when we are hypnotized we slip into a kind of astral 'pool' of experiences, if you will. We just grab one, or it grabs us, and for that time the experiences merge."

"An astral pool," Caitlin said thoughtfully. "Like the transpersonal plane some Hindus believe in. I like that—the idea that under a controlled, scientific situation you had a remotely similar experience." She then stood up, shook out her arms and legs, flexed her fingers, rolled her neck, and sat down in her chair again, feeling lighter, feeling finally ready for her day.

"I have a suggestion," Barbara said, just as the bell rang to signal her next patient's arrival. "Don't worry, it's Simon, he'll understand." Barbara buzzed him into the lobby and continued. "When was the last time Jacob saw his aunt Abby in LA?"

Caitlin smiled at her friend. "Nice carom shot, Doctor. *I* haven't seen her in a long time either."

"Go out there," Barbara said. "Get some family time embedded in your body and your brain. You never know when you might need it as a reference, a touchstone."

"Okay, maybe. Once I'm fully back on track with my regular clients."

"All right. How's everyone else in your life?"

Caitlin ran through the short list, starting with her parents and ending with Ben, their night together, and how it was better that they were proceeding as friends.

"That's a good thing, isn't it?" Caitlin said, convincing herself. "For now."

"For now," Barbara said, nodding in agreement. She then took a meaningful beat. "Speaking of 'for now,' want to schedule another one?"

"Probably a good idea," said Caitlin. "Strike while the iron's hot."

While Barbara walked to her desk, Caitlin let her eyes drift around the room and ended up gazing at a lamp stand, amazed at how brass could be twisted so extensively, with such precision. Suddenly, she wasn't thinking about the lamp. With eyes still on the brass, she slowly brought her hands together, her right hand slightly curved below her left hand, a few inches away from it. Instantly she felt energy coil in her chest, and her sight changed into—vision. The brass began to move. Just as the silvery metal poles and bars in the subway train had come alive with reflections, the shining patches of sunlight on the brass flared. They began to extend in the same curious geometry, reaching toward and running through her. She felt herself expand mentally, emotionally, and physically. Optimism, ebullience, pure joy surged back into her.

She slowly looked around the room and Barbara's multitude of knots was magnificent. They were all pulsing as the light side of each rope strand pushed against the side in shadow, and their loose ends extended past their frames through the air. Caitlin laughed in her throat and turned to take in more of them.

Suddenly, the room flashed white, as if an old-fashioned reel of film had snapped and there was just a bare, brightly lit screen. Only it wasn't entirely opaque; Caitlin could see a turquoise color swirling toward her from behind the white, and there was sound—several quick thuds, a pause, more thuds. They were amplified to the degree that Caitlin could feel them in her chest, in her back. There was an echoing quality to them but no actual echoes, just thuds.

The rest of her senses, she realized, had vanished. She tried to raise her arms and step forward, to find something to hold on to in the whiteness. The motion was almost impossible, as if she were moving through mud. Using every ounce of her strength to push against the arrhythmic thuds, she managed to stretch out her hand. Then something darkened before her, a shape. Was it shoulders and a head?

Caitlin thought she heard her name called, thin and wispy beneath the thudding. Slowly, she managed to pick up a foot and move it a couple inches ahead of her. Suddenly, her chest went empty with horror. She recognized the thudding. This drumming with no consistent beat was Jacob, drumming hard with his fingertips on the wall between their bedrooms.

She tried to scream, tried to curve her hand into knuckles so she could knock back, if there was anything to knock against—but her mouth and her hand would not—

Jacob! she yelled in her mind. *Where are you? Who is with you?*

"Caitlin!" she heard again, to her left, louder and sharper. "Come back!"

With monumental effort, Caitlin moved two of the fingertips of her outstretched hand slightly to the right, as the woman in the subway had done.

At once, the whiteness and the thuds vanished. Caitlin fell back into the armchair, causing Barbara to pitch forward.

"Oh my god," Caitlin said, "Oh my god, Jacob."

Barbara crouched so they were face-to-face with her hands firmly placed on Caitlin's shoulders. "Caitlin, what just happened?"

"I went away. Somewhere. White clouds, or whitecaps on water, everywhere white. And drumming. I couldn't find Jacob. Was he . . . were *we* drowning? Flying?"

"Neither. You were right here," Barbara said. "You didn't go anywhere."

"Oh no," Caitlin said. "I was *not* in this room."

"Caitlin, you were. Listen to me: are you tired?"

"What? No! Barbara, it wasn't petit mal. I didn't have a seizure."

"How do you know? Perhaps we should schedule an EEG."

"That's not it!" Caitlin said, pushing herself from the chair, making and unmaking fists. "No dizziness, muscles working fine. Not sweating and I wasn't twitching, was I?"

"No . . . ," Barbara said, rising to face her. "Caitlin, at least sit and talk it through. Simon texted and said he could use some more time to make a phone call."

"I can't," Caitlin said. "I have to go."

"Caitlin, do you know where you are?"

"Yes!"

"Where are you going?"

"To check on my son," Caitlin replied, heading toward the door.

"You should go home."

"No," Caitlin replied. "I have to make sure he is okay."

CHAPTER 7

Caitlin was too electrified to sit in a cab.

She began the crosstown trek to Jacob's school. She did it power-walking, burning off energy, pushing into the fear, into everything that was roiling inside. The session with Barbara had opened doors to . . . what exactly?

There was no more dodging or denying this *new* reality.

She continued to walk.

Despite everything she had said to Barbara, Caitlin realized that she was fighting herself. She was a scientist who took rational steps, one at a time. Now she was forcing herself to jump into areas for which there were no reliable textbooks, no maps. There was just one consolation, something that hadn't been present when she was working with Maanik and Gaelle: *I'm not facing the same threat.*

But she was facing the mysteries of Galderkhaan and the feeling of awful terror when she thought Jacob was knocking in that opaque blank nothing place.

Caitlin had just taken out her phone to call Jacob when the phone rang in her hand. It was a local number, elusively familiar. She answered and it was the vice principal of Jacob's school.

"Dr. O'Hara, is Jacob with you?"

Nothing from the past few weeks equaled the cold fear that smashed into Caitlin now.

"He is not with me," she said tightly. "Is he not at school?"

There was the tiniest of pauses during which a well-trained educator kept himself from cursing in the ear of a parent.

"Dr. O'Hara, we have lost track of your son. We think he may have walked from the building about half an hour ago but we aren't sure. However, we have looked everywhere . . ."

Caitlin had no idea what the man said next. She couldn't hear him over her internal screaming. She stood on the street shouting into the phone for a few minutes but it felt like years. Then somehow she said to herself, beneath the screaming, *Where would he go? Start there. Somewhere near school?*

Caitlin hung up on the vice principal, saying only, "I'll call you back." She glanced around, registered where she was, then started sprinting with a stamina she didn't know she had.

Her peripheral vision grayed out. Looks from the people she passed hardly registered. Vaguely she wondered whether she should try to reach for Jacob using this new power. Was it even possible? But the thought was a bare blip in the total urgency of running. She lunged across the street before traffic had fully stopped. Horns honked, someone yelled, she heard nothing. Her lungs started to beg for a pause. She didn't notice.

And then she was on Twenty-Seventh Street. Her phone buzzed in her bag while she was pounding up the stairs but somehow she knew and didn't bother picking up. She shoved open the door to the lobby of Jacob's cooking school and the receptionist stood up, the phone to her ear.

"Oh thank god, Dr. O'Hara, we were trying to—"

Caitlin ignored her and looked around, gasping. No sign of him. She hurried past the desk and bashed open the door to the long, bright test kitchen. At the far end of the room Jacob was on his hands and knees on the floor. He looked like he was vomiting.

The receptionist rushed up behind her. "He just wandered in here, he was talking but he wouldn't respond to us—he kept saying something that sounded like 'towers.' "

Caitlin was already diving across the floor to him, her feet and then her knees skidding across spilled sauces and fragments of food. Large bowls were scattered everywhere. A small cluster of people surrounding him drew back as Caitlin reached him. His small back was arched and he heaved hard, but nothing came out but a horrible rasping. There was no vomit on the floor in front of him.

"What is he trying to throw up?" Caitlin shouted, placing her hands on his back. "What did he eat?"

"He didn't eat anything," someone said. "We were watching. He came in and he was spasming, walking and spasming. He looked like he was reaching for us but his arms were all over the place, like he wasn't trying to knock things over but . . ."

"We've sent for an ambulance," the receptionist said.

"Not now," Caitlin said. "Everyone get out. *Please.*"

The receptionist hesitated but then gestured for the staff and onlookers to leave them be. The door swung shut behind them and the room grew muffled, quiet, still, dead. There was only the mother and her son.

And whatever the hell was preying on Jacob. Caitlin knew it was there, cold and possessing.

"Jacob, it's me, Mom," Caitlin said, trying to modulate her voice. She leaned down to look at his face. His hearing aid was still in but he didn't turn toward her. Then he screamed, and it was like nothing Caitlin had ever heard, not from him, not from the souls in Galderkhaan. Her boy made a sound like aluminum being ripped apart by a high wind.

"Jacob, I'm here," Caitlin started. She kept up a long murmur to him, hardly knowing what she was saying. It was the sound of her voice that mattered, the tone, not so much the words. Jacob still didn't acknowledge her. He crawled forward, grasping at the tiles with his nails—but scratching the floor was better than scratching his forearms, as Maanik had done, Caitlin thought with a shudder. His back heaved again but still nothing. Caitlin tried to cup his chin in her hand and turn his face to her. She caught one glimpse of his eyes passing over her face. There was so little of the normal Jacob there that a fresh sob climbed along her throat.

He kept turning, looking over her shoulder and then he forced himself up, to standing. He reached to the counter for support and another bowl overturned, something milky white flying across the surface.

"Fire," he said and signed. "Fire. Fire below me."

Christ, no!

Caitlin continued speaking to him. "Jacob, I'm going to start counting now, I want you to count with me. One . . . two . . ."

She kept going but he wasn't listening. Her hands were on his shoulders, which were damp with the sweat rolling down his face and neck. She wasn't restraining him but hoped that his body would register the weight and familiarity of her touch. She didn't want to take that away to sign for him, and he wasn't looking anyway. He was looking at a stove.

Jacob started making sounds and Caitlin's flesh chilled in anticipation—but it wasn't Galderkhaani. It wasn't English either. They were animal sounds, like he was a toddler again learning to use his voice, but with the pacing and pauses of English. Jacob pulled himself away from her toward the stove and Caitlin thought of Atash setting himself on fire in the library in Iran. Jacob reached for a knob on the stove, his mouth still working around the same odd nonlanguage. Caitlin grabbed him with one hand to stop him, and at the same time she reached out with the other hand and began knocking on the counter, re-creating his tapping on their shared wall at home. He showed no sign of hearing. His fingers were on the knob but they kept sliding off in an odd way, as if the knob were covered with oil, though Caitlin could see that it was dry.

Suddenly, Jacob's head jerked in an upward, backward swing that was not normal—still human, but not normal. His head turned so quickly that his shoulders and torso followed, and now he was looking at her. There was a chill in the air around him, something that had no apparent source, something that moved when he moved.

"Twenty-seven, twenty-eight, twenty-nine . . ." Caitlin kept going, her voice rigidly calm over her fear. Her hands dropped to his elbows, placing pressure there but not squeezing desperately the way she wanted to.

The curious sounds died away and Jacob was just looking at her. For one moment, Caitlin thought she saw his face shift away from his face. She shivered with terror. It was as if his face were momentarily displaced. Underneath were other eyes . . . dark eyes.

"Jacob!" she screamed, and shook him.

And then he spoke. Not animal sounds, not English, and not "towers."

"*Tawazh*," he said with a voice that sounded like gravel.

He turned very slowly away from her. Again, he reached for the knob. Again, Caitlin stopped him as gently as possible. She did not want to shock him but she watched carefully, closely. He fought her and she held him more firmly. She didn't wrest his hand back: if she were to know how to treat him, she had to know if he was in the same situation as Maanik and especially poor Atash, who had burned himself to death. The small fingers reached out, tried to turn on the flame.

"No," Caitlin said softly. "Jacob, you mustn't touch that."

The fingers wriggled, tensed, then dropped limply. A moment later, so did Jacob. The cold around him exploded away, like a fever breaking. He was warm again, and Jacob was back. He became alert, suddenly, as if he'd been daydreaming.

"Mom," he said, and turned to her. "I could hear!"

Caitlin checked his eyes, then wrapped her arms tightly around him and felt his arms circle her back and hold on. After a moment of deep relief, she looked up to see students and teachers peering through a glass panel by the door. Caitlin led Jacob out through the onlookers, took him away before the EMTs arrived. She already knew there was nothing they could do for him.

In the cab home he didn't say a word.

Caitlin hesitated but asked, "Jacob, did you feel like something was—"

He pulled the hearing aid from his ear and handed it to her. Then he closed his eyes and burrowed deep into her side, pulling her hand until her arm was tight around him. By the time they arrived home he was asleep. She hated waking him but he was too big for her to carry up the stairs. He trudged with heavy feet and heavier eyelids up the steps, leaned on the wall while she unlocked the door, then walked straight to his bed and climbed in without taking off his coat and shoes. Caitlin carefully slipped them off, pulled the blankets over him and sat quietly, gently stroking his head. She couldn't help but wade through all of Maanik's episodes. This event with Jacob was not the same, but it was too close; Caitlin was vigilant lest her own post-traumatic stress return.

She spent the rest of the afternoon there, watching him sleep, seeing and sensing nothing abnormal. She called the school, learned that Jacob had left the building with a group going on a field trip but had never boarded the bus. The vice principal assured Caitlin that there would be an investigation and that—if she allowed Jacob to return—he would be watched constantly.

"How? With an ankle bracelet?" Caitlin asked irritably.

"Nothing of the kind," the vice principal replied. "He isn't a prisoner."

Caitlin calmed, knew she had just been venting.

"We'll watch him and use your son's cell phone GPS, if you agree, Dr. O'Hara," the official went on. "I'll monitor him myself until we understand what happened here."

Caitlin agreed. She heard it all through a thick mental gauze.

A few hours later she called Ben, intending to cancel their evening.

At the sound of his voice, she ended up pouring out the entire story of Jacob's . . . whatever it was; his disappearance. Her voice was shaking by the end of it. He listened, sympathized, and didn't put her through the third degree about symptoms, for which she expressed her gratitude. He refused to accept a rain check, however.

"Are you insane?" Caitlin said. "I can't leave Jacob. Ben, he said a Galderkhaani word!"

"Maybe he heard you say it."

"He didn't."

"Or maybe he was saying just what the receptionist thought he said: 'towers.' You heard what you wanted to hear."

Caitlin didn't believe that. But she had to admit she was hardly an impartial observer.

"Anita," he said. "See if she'd be willing to watch Jacob. That serves two purposes, no?"

Dr. Anita Carter was Caitlin's coworker, the psychiatrist who filled in for her when there were emergencies—of which there had been quite a few, of late. So many that Anita had joked she wasn't making any plans until she knew that Caitlin was "back." Ben was right but Anita could actually fill three roles here: standby babysitter, analyst, and role model. African-American and originally from Atlanta, her no-nonsense approach to problem solving was: acknowledge the problem, solve it, file it, and go to dinner. She knew how to handle emergencies and she might just be the impartial observer that Jacob—and Caitlin—needed.

Caitlin put Ben on hold and called Anita. She laughingly agreed to be there, seven o'clock.

"Another new patient?" Anita asked.

"Yeah," Caitlin told her. "Me."

"What's going on?"

"I need a little air," she said. "But I can't go too far—"

"Jacob?"

"Jacob. He's been having nightmares. I don't want to hover—"

"I understand," Anita said.

Caitlin decided not to tell her the details about what had happened. If Jacob's symptoms recurred, Anita would call her and handle them her own way. Caitlin could use that right now. Smothering Jacob with attention, even passive attention, wouldn't give either of them a chance to breathe. But there was a larger issue. For her, right now, all roads seemed to lead to Galderkhaan. She had to get some input on that, some understanding. Some *solutions*. And as long as she was just an elevator ride away . . .

Caitlin told Ben that he should meet her downstairs at seven; she'd pick the place. In the meantime, she decided to see if Nancy O'Hara's classic anger management technique worked just as well for her daughter as it did for her: she cleaned her apartment. At the same time she scrubbed her mind, her mood, her loss of perspective.

You are here, in New York, with your son, in the present, she said as if it were a mantra.

Galderkhaan was a project but Barbara was right. All of the manifestations had individual solutions. They could be treated separately. She had to take precautions but she also had to live her life.

By the time Caitlin was folding a load of laundry with a second one rolling in the dryer in the basement, the miasma of frustration and temper had evened out enough for her to sing Motown songs to Arfa. The feline usually sniffed Caitlin's mouth as she crooned, as if he were confused, trying to figure out what the hell was happening and whether he should seek cover under the bed.

Not this time. Arfa crouched behind the laundry basket as though waiting for a mouse. Maybe there was one, not a wandering soul, a ghost. Funny how she would have welcomed that right now, a real-world problem with a quick, sane solution.

As Caitlin folded the second load, she came around to accepting her new realities with her customary courage instead of fear. She would take the approach that Jacob's sociologist father Andrew Thwaite had advised when they were helping survivors of the tsunami that had caused unthinkable destruction in Thailand: *"If you can't run from the beast, embrace it."*

Caitlin did her hair and dressed as if she were going to a World Health Organization fund-raiser: a warm, double-lapel zip-trim crop jacket, velvet cropped ankle pants, T-strap pumps. She put on makeup—not a lot, but more than the little she usually wore.

Anita was impressed.

"If I didn't know better, I'd think faculty and trustees were part of your dinner plans."

"Nope," she said. "Just Ben. I needed to feel . . ." She sought a better word than "human," settled on, "normal."

Anita's expression was warm and understanding and she gave Caitlin a hug as she grabbed her purse and headed out.

She arrived in the lobby before Ben did, impressing the doorman and refusing to look at her cell phone while she waited. She stood near the door, watching life and traffic, ivory clouds against a darkening sky, people moving north and south and plugging into their own intangible, invisible worlds of thought and wireless conversation.

I shouldn't be here, she thought with a welling of guilt. She glanced back toward the elevators, felt the pull. She started back, fished in her purse for her cell phone . . . then stopped herself.

No. You're right downstairs. Jacob will be fine. You need this, need to get out, grab distance, perspective.

A cab pulled up and Ben charged from it like Pheidippides announcing that the Persians had been defeated at Marathon. Either he was running from his day or—

His expression as he came through the door settled the question. He stopped inside, stunned to immobility. Ben's mouth was the first thing to move, forming the widest grin she'd ever seen. He was very happy to see her.

"Crap," he said.

"Just the word I was hoping you'd say," she told him.

"No—no, Cai, you look amazing! That's what that meant. Not 'crap.'"

She smiled, smelling her own lipstick . . . and smiled a little wider. She walked toward him, hugged him. They continued to hold each other, moving aside only to get out of the way of other tenants.

"You're going to get through this," Ben said in her ear. "You and Jake."

"I want to believe," she said.

"Then do. We understand the nature of the problem, if not the specifics. The solutions are out there."

"Ben, my son was—possessed. That's the only word that applies."

"No, it's a convenient label that conjures up all kinds of negatives," he said. "What happened is something ancient, something Galderkhaani, and that's our new business: understanding that world and its processes. We've done pretty well so far, I'd say."

"You would," she said. "You've been studying it . . . I've been living it."

Ben drew back slightly. "That's not fair. I've been there every step. I've seen how 'possession' affected Maanik, how it affected you. That wasn't easy. I wasn't just an observer."

"No, you weren't," she agreed. "I'm sorry."

"Apology accepted, and I'm going to tell you now what I've said before: we are in this way too deep to be objective. We have to regain some of that."

"I know."

He stepped back a little farther and offered his arm. She had been sobbing, just a little. She dried her eyes with the sleeve of his jacket.

"Nice," he said.

"You better mean that."

"I do!" he said as she hooked her arm in his. "I also want you to know I feel underdressed."

"You're not," she said, finding a little laugh. "You look—Ben-ish."

He made a sour face. "Is that good or bad?"

"Sartorially neutral," she replied. "It's the man in the clothes that matters."

He took her arm and held the door open with the other. They walked into the cool night, amid but apart from the throng.

"Jesus," he said, shaking his head. "Cai, you really are beautiful."

"Thanks."

"I feel like we should be going to the opera. Well, you should, anyway."

"There was a time," she said, "when people dressed for dinner . . . every night."

"Only people of means," Ben pointed out. "Servants like my ancestors, we ate around a butcher-block table in the kitchen."

Mention of ancestors threw a chill into Caitlin. Ben saw it, put his free hand on hers. "Cai?"

"It's okay," she said, putting on a smile. "I'm discovering that there are shiny new trip wires in my life. Got to work around those." She squeezed the fingers on top of hers. "Let's eat."

She gave his arm a tug and headed to the corner, turned west—toward a halal food truck with ten people in line: single men and women, some with dogs; a female cop; and a group of teenagers.

Ben stopped hard when he saw it. He was thrown back to their college days, grabbing street-corner hot dogs before their next lecture. This was classic Cai.

"Zero romance," he said, raising a hand in surrender. "Just us."

She grinned. "Just us."

He chuckled, so did she, and they settled into the line. The cop and a man from her building noticed her, looked partly away as the line moved forward a few paces.

"We don't have Washington Square Park to sit in," Ben noted, "no guitars or drummers or hip-hoppers with boom boxes."

"We have my building's courtyard and the playlist on my cell phone, if you want. All eighties, all the time. Besides, we may not have many alfresco nights left," she went on.

"Winter's around the corner—frost on your rivets and ice in your nose," Ben said.

He twitched his mouth like his beloved fellow Brit Charlie Chaplin and Caitlin smiled, then hugged him. She held him closer, harder than she expected. He wrapped around her and they just stood in the hug, ignoring the world, the grid of skyscrapers, the impatient horns of taxis jerking across the intersection. Finally, the big guy behind them told them to move up, and they stepped forward with their arms still around each other. Ben gave Caitlin a peck on the top of her head and she disengaged.

"So how are you?" he asked.

"We'll get to that," she replied. "How are *you*?"

Ben laughed, and despite her anxiety over the afternoon's events, Caitlin smiled too as memories—her own—flooded back warmly, the repetitive, stalling *Alphonse and Gaston* bits they sometimes stumbled into.

"It's good to be home," Ben said to avoid the logjam. "Obligatory question number one: how are you?"

"Better, for the moment," she answered truthfully.

"Glue or spit?"

"Glit," she replied. That was something Ben used to ask her before an exam: did she know the material or was she winging it, was she held together securely with glue or tentatively with spit.

God, our past is good, she thought.

"What's obligatory question number two?" she asked.

"Hold on, woman. I don't consider 'glit' an answer."

She whispered, "It's Galderkhaani for 'I'm going to take whatever the world dishes out, even if it takes some time and adjustment.' "

"I don't remember that one," Ben said.

"You'd have to have been there," she said sheepishly. "In Galderkhaan."

Ben laughed out loud.

"That's my Cai," he said. "Just walk right over to the eight-hundred-pound gorilla in the room and kick him in the stones."

"Question two?"

"Us. In English, please."

"Specifically?"

Ben looked around. "Since our sleepover," he said delicately.

Caitlin shoved her hands in her jacket pockets. "I don't know how you're feeling about our night together, and I'm not completely sure how I'm feeling about it either. I don't have the first clue about going forward, I just think that we should—"

She stopped as she noticed that Ben was not just grinning but chuckling.

"What?" There was annoyance in her voice but she couldn't help smiling.

"Oh, I've got you. I've totally got you."

"Care to elaborate?"

"This is going to *kill* you. Caitlin O'Hara," he whispered into her ear, "it's only been a week and change. And I'm a guy. And there *you* are, getting deep and intense about it—"

She narrowed her eyes at him in mock offense, then chuckled and shook her head. "Damn, I'm doing the Girl Brain thing."

"Like you're in high school," he chortled. "You have a crush on me, a crushy crush!"

She swatted him on the arm. "You might speak a dozen languages but modern slang is not one." Then she laughed wholeheartedly for the first time in days. It felt good.

"Move, ya lovebirds, before I crush ya," said the construction worker behind them. "The man's waiting for your order."

"Sorry," Ben said, though he continued to mock her while their food was being prepared. They stood in silence and then headed toward the small courtyard behind her building. Caitlin couldn't wait and took her first bite as they walked, exclaiming how good her dinner was.

"Note to self," Ben said, "she's got Girl Brain *and* she's a cheap date."

"Note to self," Caitlin echoed, "watch out. He's making noises like he's planning for *some* kind of future."

"Not true," Ben replied. "I know better. I wish I didn't."

They allowed the relationship discussion a respectful moment to die before moving on.

"All right then, Ben," Caitlin said. "Back to the gorilla. Give me the good stuff."

He looked around puckishly. "What, here, in public?"

"Grow up. What new translations have you done?"

"Oh."

"Yeah, oh. I'm assuming you worked during your flight."

"Guilty. My astonished cries woke the man sitting next to me. He looked at me funny."

"You should be used to that."

"Seriously, no exaggeration, I did actually vocalize at one point. Galderkhaan. Galder. Khaan. Remind you of anything?"

"No."

"Old Norse and . . . ?"

Caitlin stopped chewing, then stopped walking. "No way. That obvious?"

"That obvious. I have no idea what the '*Galder*' is but '*khaan*' means the same thing as the Mongolian word—a title for a lord and master."

"Who used it more," Caitlin asked, "Priests or Technologists?"

"Very clever, you. First thing I checked. It wasn't the Priests."

"That's surprising," she said. "I would have thought they'd be the ones into the 'supreme being' thing."

"You're thinking like a modern person," Ben pointed out. "Things were different then and there."

A long, relaxed walk later, Ben guided Caitlin into Paley Park, a small courtyard that had more benches than trees. They had the courtyard to themselves. The views were mostly of brick, with an oblong of sky above. But it was quiet, save for a freestanding wall at the back lit in russet gold and covered with long, beautiful, gently melodious rivulets of water.

"So was this *khaan* a god for the Technologists or a great ruler?" Caitlin asked.

"I don't know. My guess, based on nothing but intuition, is that the volcano was the *khaan*, given their focus on geothermal energy. Think Vulcan, Hades, the gods of the underworld."

Caitlin made a face. "Somehow I'm reluctant to ascribe that kind of primal mind-set to them."

"Why? It was good enough for the Greeks, Romans, and just about every other culture, including ours. Is modern religion any different? How many people believe in the 'fire god' we call Satan?"

"Okay, point taken," Caitlin said. "So with *khaan* in the name of the city or whatever Galderkhaan was, does that mean the Technologists were in power?"

"Shared and equal power, as far as I can make out, but with increasing hostility between them. Not physical hostility; there was a reference to banishment for anyone who used violence. Anyway, the two groups did split the place."

"Geographically?"

"Nothing formalized"—Ben nodded at the pieces of the Berlin Wall that were displayed on one side of the park—"but each had their sector and there they lived."

"Glogharasor and Belhorji?" Caitlin couldn't believe she was casually pulling names from one of her trances as if they were "Manhattan" and "Brooklyn."

Ben regarded her. "Yes. Jesus."

"Don't do that," Caitlin said. "I'm trying not to freak *myself* out."

"Sorry," he said. "Sorry. The Priests lived in Glogharasor. They used the root word '*Glogharas*' when they spoke of themselves—the 'dawn seers.'"

"And Belhorji?"

"Don't know yet," he admitted.

Caitlin returned to her food. She wasn't very hungry but needed something to do. Saying those two names had caused something strange to happen inside her.

"Cai, are you okay?"

"Hmm? Yeah. Yes. Why?"

"You looked like you went somewhere."

"No, there's just—an idea. A thought. I don't know why I had it."

"Speak," he said encouragingly.

"Galderkhaan," she said. "If there's anything left of it, we should find it."

"I'm all for that, but how? And why, specifically?"

"Maybe it's not as strange and remote as we think," Caitlin said. "How do we know that things haven't been found and misidentified and hidden in museums and universities somewhere, the way meteors and fossils have been for centuries?"

"I'm glad to hear you say that," Ben said. "I had that idea myself. While I was in London I took a turn through the British Museum, looked at the relics with fresh eyes, peered here and there for Galderkhaani writing, wondered the same thing. I couldn't find anything, though."

He stared at her as she munched. She looked at the fountain.

"Cai?"

"I'm here," she said as she glanced at her phone and saw that there were no text updates from Anita about Jacob. "Do you mind if we walk some more—maybe just around the block?"

"Not a bit, if those heels of yours don't care."

She smiled a little as they stood and left the courtyard, binning their food containers on their way out.

"The frustrating thing is I'm running out of things to translate," Ben went on. "I only have about twelve minutes of tape from all those sessions. And I'd really like to know why there were several mentions of agriculture in the sky."

"You're sure it says 'in' and not 'under'?" Even as she asked it, she regretted it.

"Caitlin, this is me. I've checked it a dozen times and it's unmistakable. Of course it's nonsense, unless they were doing something on a mountaintop or caldera—but then they would have said 'mountaintop' or 'caldera' and not specifically used the word 'sky.'"

"Right. These people were pretty specific about things."

"Lots of words, very little nuance when the hand gestures were added."

She chuckled. "Sounds wonderful."

"What does?"

"A civilization without nuance. You're this or that, a word is that or this. Understanding was instant and absolute."

He put a hand on her arm to slow her to a stop.

"What?" she asked.

"Where would I fit? In that language, I mean?"

She looked into his sweet smoke-colored eyes. And because she couldn't answer him, she kissed him. She kissed him until she knew that when he asked, she would say yes.

Caitlin briefly considered staying where they were. She discarded that idea, though; she might have felt like a college kid again but being spotted in public could cost her her job. There was the laundry room—but then, she decided, she was just being ornery for the sake of it.

She called Anita.

"How is Jacob?" she asked.

"Fine," Anita replied. "You don't have to check every hour—Jacob is sleeping peacefully."

"Actually, I'm coming back," Caitlin said. "*We're* coming back."

"Oh!" Anita said. "Reaching for coat as we speak."

Caitlin ended the call and they went upstairs. Anita greeted them on her way out.

"Halal?" she said, sniffing once.

"From a cart," Ben said. "*Not* my idea." He added quickly, "But *perfect*."

"Thank you," Caitlin said as Anita slipped past them.

"Happy to help," she replied, pulling the door shut.

As they moved into the apartment, neither of them reached for a light switch. They went to Caitlin's bedroom, where they circled each other, peeling clothes, turning slowly closer and closer to a window full of distant, scattered lamplights. Falling onto the bed below, pressing into him, Caitlin felt like she was inhaling Ben's skin. The sensation felt full of nostalgia and promise, and almost relief. She bathed in the perfection of normality for a long while. Then, still touching him as completely as two bodies can, she let their linked limbs flow like the brass in Barbara's Celtic knot.

"Oh god," Ben breathed, and she knew he was feeling the vastness too, dropping down and reaching into and through them. It was utterly, wholly *dark*. A darkness never seen on Earth—but not threatening. Not in the least frightening. An ancient and serene darkness.

And then something happened to Caitlin. Something more potent and longer lasting than she had ever experienced.

• • •

Later, as Ben was getting dressed, he attempted to put words on it.

"No," she cut him off. "Let it be what it was. You *got* it. You don't need to translate it."

His arm went around her waist and she felt again the wild joy of having both touch and—beyond touch.

"Words are what I do," he half-apologized.

"Yes? And what did *I* do?"

"I don't follow."

She squirmed against his arm. "That wasn't—like before."

"No." Ben smiled as he let go of her and looked dreamily out at the lamps across the blocks of Manhattan. "It was great, beyond great, and we can leave it at that."

Caitlin smiled as she watched him leave in the dark. She was glad he agreed, because she didn't want to explain what she really meant.

That toward the end, something indistinct had appeared in her mind, silhouetted against the light and dark in its own changing pattern. Something dimly familiar, vitally alive.

Ben was not the only one with whom she'd been joined. Someone else had been reaching toward her from beyond and that someone was not a man.

CHAPTER 8

Seated in a tiny red Twin Otter plane, Mikel couldn't recall a bumpier, more unnerving flight. Every thrust of turbulence jostled him up, down, and to the sides, often in rapid succession. Nonetheless, he kept his cheek pressed to the window and his eye scanning the ice as they headed to the Halley VI base.

The dozen others on board were mostly British Antarctic Survey scientists. The only one who seemed not to fit—besides Mikel—was a young man sitting across the aisle, Siem der Graaf. Prior to takeoff, Mikel had overheard that he was half Dutch, half Kenyan, with British citizenship. Siem wasn't a fellow researcher, which meant he was maintenance, which meant he was a replacement for either the dead or the missing staff member at Halley. The scientists weren't rude to him; they just had other things to discuss, data to review, topics of mutual importance to mull over in huddled secrecy.

Mikel had not learned much more than the fact that troubles at the base, and momentarily favorable weather conditions, had caused the flight to be moved a week ahead of schedule. The scientists had tolerated Mikel's presence only because Flora had pulled some strings with the Royal Air Force; although *what* strings Mikel was not privy to.

At some point over the Weddell Sea, Siem—his six-foot-seven-inch frame wedged with miserable discomfort into his narrow seat, head barely clearing the bulkhead—gave up waiting for a friendly chat that never came and plugged his ears with music while he reviewed documents on his tablet. The music leaking from his headphones was heavy metal, especially slow and grim, probably from Finland. Mikel knew he could use this man. Now all he needed to find was his target.

Just a half hour or so out from the base, still over the Weddell, Mikel identified it. Mentally noting the location using landmarks, he said nothing to the other passengers.

There was one other outsider on the flight, Ivor, a garrulous Glaswegian who was getting on just fine with the scientists because he had information they needed. At different times during the eight-hour flight he had walked them through laptop training sessions about the eight main modules of Halley VI and the outlying buildings, dressing for the weather, the components of a climbing kit, and driving a Ski-Doo. Mikel paid as much attention to all of these as discretion would permit. He'd learned his survival skills when he traveled to McMurdo Station in Antarctica a few years back, but a refresher was most welcome. The Glaswegian made the scientists parrot back what seemed like six hundred safety concerns and precautionary measures, and couched everything in terms of potential damage to the base and the machines, not the people.

The plane landing was lumpy, skidding, and as backbone-unfriendly as the flight itself. The passengers zipped and buttoned their coats, donned tinted goggles against the near-perpetual brilliant daylight, and hurried to the nearest module.

Mikel was taken to a guest bunk but did not stay there. Instead he kept close to Siem as the young man oriented himself to his new surroundings. Finally, Mikel found his moment to approach Siem in the large red modular building that served as the social heart of the base.

He and the replacements were being served one of the additional meals that enabled Halley VI residents to ingest the six thousand calories a day required for the climate. In the dining area, the Glaswegian placed his tray as close as possible to the pool table and challenged one of the female scientists to a game. Siem walked carefully across the blue carpet, trying to avoid building up static, though he'd been told it was a futile effort in Antarctica. He stopped at a table full of red chairs and maintenance staffers and almost as a body they found excuses to stand and leave.

When Mikel sat opposite him he saw that Siem's nose was bleeding. He handed the young man a tissue and smiled.

"Those are fairly standard around here," Mikel said, slicing into his passable version of chicken cordon bleu. "Cold, dry air, increase in blood pressure—bad combination."

"So I've heard," Siem mumbled, stuffing shreds of tissue in both nostrils. "What do they think, that I've got a disease?"

"No, I'm sure they're used to it."

"Then why—?"

"It's their version of a hazing," Mikel explained. "You're one of them when you don't bleed or get debilitating earaches. Didn't you get briefed?"

"Briefly," Siem joked, "and not about the social customs. This was all very quick."

"So I've heard."

Siem turned to his own plate, began slicing. "Where are you from?"

"Pamplona, originally."

"You're not a scientist, though? You weren't in on the discussions."

"No, I'm not part of the cabal," Mikel laughed. "I'm an anthropologist with a strong streak of archaeologist."

"A sensible combination. What are you studying here—are there ancient igloos?"

"It's independent research newly underwritten by the US government about Bronze Age magnetic fields and their effects on early civilization."

"That's not something I'd think politicians would care about," Siem said.

Mikel leaned forward conspiratorially. "It is, when it's supported by big donor constituents."

"Ah. 'Money makes honey,' as my father used to say."

"Very true. So I'm here to collect rock samples when I can find them, and spend the rest of my time on readouts, like everyone else."

"Very, very heady."

The cover story was not entirely farfetched. While Mikel was still in the doctoral program at the University of Córdoba, he had published a paper on the impact of the geologically active Ring of Fire on early Asian society. That study caught the attention of Flora Davies, which was how he came to be employed by the Group.

"I'm always looking for grand answers," Mikel went on. "I get that from my grandmother's side of the family. She was very religious, believed there was a kind of sticky fluid substance that bound everything in the universe to every other thing. Called it 'the Adur.'"

"What kind of religion teaches that?"

"It's a Basque pagan faith from before the fourth century. My grandmother was Catholic, devoutly so, but for many Basques the old ways were an inseparable part of their culture."

"Do you believe in that?"

"I don't know about the Adur, exactly, but I want to believe that there's still a little bit of wonder out there," Mikel replied. "You find similar concepts in many, many cultures—the Chinese, the Navajo and Cheyenne of North America, the Polynesians. These and many other people had no contact with one another yet they came up with the same ideas, the same archetypes."

Siem made an approving sound. "So what makes the Basque idea special?"

"Good question," Mikel said. "The Adur connected not just objects to objects, people to people, and people to objects, but all things to their names. One of the major evolutions of the human brain was its leap to symbolism, to understanding representation."

"Like cave paintings?"

"Exactly like that, whether it was depicting a battle or drawing a map to the nearest hunting ground. Euskara is arguably one of the oldest languages of *Homo sapiens*, and in it the Basques had made that crucial leap in cognition—object and name, one and the same. And they actually named the leap itself."

"You mean that 'Adur.' "

Mikel nodded. "My grandmother had been raised on the universal, all-encompassing importance of this concept. So she read everything she could find, talked to every priest she met, never stopped searching." He leaned in slightly. "I'm the same. It's why I started researching ancient cultures, to learn what they knew. To rediscover what the world has forgotten."

Siem struggled with that, but nodded. "I hear what you're saying, but I don't think I could chase phantoms. I like to work with things I can feel and fix."

"Oh, I do a lot of that," Mikel said. "There are no phantoms, but there are always relics, ancient tablets, buried cities, tombs."

"And magnetized rocks," Siem said.

"Everywhere," Mikel answered. He waited a moment, did not want to seem too eager. "Actually, that's one reason I want to look at the site of—the incident."

Siem lost interest in his food. He pushed his tray away and tended to his nose.

"Sorry," Mikel said. "Perhaps I shouldn't have—"

"No, I've been wanting to do the same," Siem said. He looked around. "It's been very frustrating. Everyone here has been avoiding it because it's so horrible. Strange."

"Which one of the two are you replacing?" Mikel asked, loading his voice with kindness.

"The woman," Siem said, lowering his eyes.

"The missing one."

Siem nodded.

"Do you mind talking about it?" Mikel asked, just to be sure.

Siem shook his head slowly.

"I heard they haven't found a trace of her," Mikel said.

"Nothing," Siem replied. "They checked for a couple miles around her Ski-Doo. There were no crevasses, no piled snow or ice. Just—nothing."

"Any idea what happened to the other one? Sorry, what was his name?"

"Fergal, I think."

"Right, right," Mikel said, subtly collecting as much information as possible. Familiarity helped to construct subterfuge. "His Ski-Doo flipped, right?"

Siem nodded. "He broke his neck. During the briefing in Stanley, they said he was probably careless, maybe racing to the woman."

"Yes, but it's strange. Ski-Doos only flip on rough ground. They're hefty objects; they don't turn over for just anything. Wasn't he on a smooth surface?"

"Yeah, I'm supposed to get out there and look at that," Siem said. "They have big fat holes in their reports. They're also having a problem with the GPS unit, which stopped working again. My first job is going to that site later today with one of the researchers."

Siem took another bite but he was force-feeding himself now.

"What do you think you'll find there?" Siem asked.

"Sorry?"

"At the accident site?" Siem said. "You're not going to find rocks. Steam vents or something?"

Mikel chuckled. "Who knows, right? Vents would leave a molten residue but—I was actually wondering if all of this could have something to do with the edge where that berg dropped a week ago." Finally he'd found a chance to sneak in his real question. "Did they tell you about that calving?"

"I saw something mentioned about it," Siem told him. "But that was dozens of kilometers away."

"True, but I was thinking that underground liquefaction might have impacted the site where the woman went missing."

"Huh. You mean a kind of quicksand effect—with snow? When they went looking for her, the surface was undisturbed."

"I've been around all kinds of primordial geologic events that destroyed societies and buried all trace of them. In Pompeii, for instance. People just evaporated. It might be worth getting over to the source, see if there's anything that compromised the underlying landmass."

"That's a little outside of my job description," Siem admitted.

"Of course," Mikel said. "Hey, do you see any problem with me tagging along today?"

"I don't see why not," Siem replied, shrugging. "The Survey's anxious for answers. The more minds working on it, the better for everyone, right?"

"Exactly."

"You had better check with the boss of field ops, though," Siem added.

"And that would be . . . ?"

"Dr. Albert Bundy, a.k.a. Dog Alpha. He was the one who ignored us most on the flight."

Mikel smiled. Flora had furnished him with a list of personnel being rushed to the station.

Outwardly, Mikel started up a conversation about survival skills. But inwardly, he was smiling with satisfaction as he neared accomplishing one of his goals. After this short trek with Dog Alpha, it would be that much easier to tag along on future trips to the ice shelf edge. His other goal—getting forty miles inland and then through the ice to the ground—was exponentially tougher. But he figured that after a few days here he could steal a Ski-Doo . . .

When Siem left to take a pre-excursion nap, Mikel approached Bundy about the reconnoitering mission. The deal was easily sealed and the run was set for two hours hence. Mikel spent some time refamiliarizing himself with extreme-weather gear and a climbing harness, and asked Ivor to reacquaint him with snowmobiles.

At zero hour Mikel tied himself to his Ski-Doo and tied his Ski-

Doo to Siem's. Siem's machine was tied to Bundy's, so that if any of the machines fell through a suddenly breaking snow bridge, the snowmobile—and the man—would only dangle instead of plummet. As this was Bundy's seventh summer at the base, he led their small convoy southwest across the ice.

They traveled in sharp sunlight; at this time of year the Brunt Ice Shelf saw only an hour of darkness per day. Once watching for cracks in the white surface had become automatic, Mikel's mind began to drift. The vast blue and white landscape could not hold his attention; landscapes never did. That was one of the major reasons he got out of Pamplona, with its big skies and endless plains. Even as a child, Mikel had chafed against the place. The only two mildly interesting things about the region were the fact that the residents of Navarre windfarmed the hell out of it, beating even the Germans at renewable electricity, and a strange blip of mountainous desert that looked like it had been airlifted from the American West. Mikel had done a fair bit of rock climbing there but not to enjoy the landscape. Choosing the right grip on a cliff face was an intellectual game for him, high-stakes chess.

His thoughts were interrupted when he noticed Siem waving at him. Mikel was slightly off course and if he kept going in this direction the rope would jolt his Ski-Doo. He veered. Siem continued to wave his arm—now he was pointing in the distance, toward the left. Mikel saw a collection of vertical sticks that would have disappeared in a landscape less stark. There was motion at the top of one of the sticks. He squinted and caught sight of the turning blades of a windmill.

Didn't Siem say the GPS station was broken? Why are they turning?

The next instant, Mikel was looking at the sky as he fell backward. The seconds that followed seemed slow and endless. The whine of the Ski-Doo surged into a scream as it lost its grip on ground. The surface beneath the rear of the snowmobile vanished and as the machine slipped backward, the snow dropped from under the front as well. At once, Mikel felt the Ski-Doo fall out from between his legs. He lost his grip on the handlebars and the Ski-Doo crashed against the sides of the crevasse. The shocks traveled up the cable catching him, while the nose of the Ski-Doo pointed to the sky, which was a now a fathom away and very, very small.

Mikel slammed against the dangling Ski-Doo as the rope to Siem's snowmobile jerked taut. He tried to grab it but he tumbled over it instead and fell away from the Ski-Doo as his own screams echoed in his ears. Flailing at the walls of the crevasse, his thickly gloved fingers clawed uselessly. The vertical cliffs were far beyond his reach; this was a big goddamned hole. Then the ropes wrenched at his waist and groin and jerked him backward till his feet flipped higher than his head.

Mikel swung on his back, gazing at the undercarriage of his machine. Far beyond that, against the tiny patch of sky, he could see a black object intruding on the light like a partial eclipse. The back of Siem's Ski-Doo had nearly dropped into the crevasse as well, prevented from doing so by a swift turn.

Mikel had to force himself to stop hyperventilating lest he pass out. And then there was silence—pure blue silence, for that was the color all around him. An impossible blue, ethereal and hollow.

My god, he thought, even in the midst of his desperation. *It's beautiful. And peaceful.*

"Mikel!" he heard reverberating around him. "Mikel, are you all right?!" Siem's calls shocked him back to reality. Mikel yelled back with every ounce of strength left in him that he was fine. He was told that they would set up a rig to hoist him up but it might take a few minutes. Mikel imagined how Siem's blood must have been running cold right now. He could not be the replacement for one presumably dead colleague and lose another the day he arrived.

Silence came again, vast and embracing. Mikel looked around at all the blues layered like petals, the vertical striations of the ice and great fist-sized nubbles extruding from the walls. He noticed one horizontal slice—a ledge. He could fit half of each foot on that he thought.

Gently, so gently, he swung himself inch by inch closer to the wall, as the Ski-Doo turned above him. His toes reached the protruding corner and he managed to grab two nubbles, first with his fingertips, then, once balanced, with his entire hand.

When he felt secure he let go with one hand and pulled his ice ax from a pocket on the leg of his salopette. He thwacked the stainless steel tip into the ice as hard as he could and it stuck fast. Now he had three secure points. He looked down again at the cold, crystal cathedral vanishing into darkness below him.

Without thought, Mikel unstrapped his helmet, took it off, and refastened its strap with one hand, holding it still against the wall with his chest. He slung the helmet back on his forearm out of his way, reached up, and pulled his fur-lined hood over his head. Then he rested the side of his head against the wall of ice and just breathed. He heard nothing—a total absence of sound. But on the wall, right at eye level, a drop of liquid water caught his attention. Covering his mouth to make sure that he wasn't melting the ice with his breath, he peered closer. There were a number of drops.

The Adur, he thought, not entirely in jest. And as he stared, he realized with a jolt deep in his gut that he was witnessing the droplets of water slowly trickling *upward*, like rain blown against a pane of glass. He held his breath and remained very still to make sure he wasn't causing the motion. The droplets continued to travel up.

He peered below him and saw nothing but blue upon blue. He certainly couldn't feel anything through his layers of cloth. Staring at the drops again, he almost willed them to stop in their tracks. If they somehow did, it would make his life simpler.

Flora would be angry with that, he told himself. "Mysteries are clues," was her constant refrain.

A rope descended from the small, distant sky and the clamp on its end thwacked against Mikel's hood, then his shoulder and back. Siem shouted for him to attach himself to the cable, then detach from the Ski-Doo connection.

Mikel looked down again. How many of Flora's "clues" lay deep in that abyss? Maybe none. Maybe the water was full of sun-seeking microorganisms, colonies of them. Or maybe the cause was wind stirred by something otherworldly. How had the Old Testament described the force that opened the Red Sea? "A blast of God's nostrils" or some such?

Regardless, right now, by ascending he risked giving up everything—not just important data but his very concept of what it meant to be a researcher, a scientist, a member of the Group. What if he left and couldn't return?

"Are you all right?" Siem called down.

Mikel pulled an ice screw from a pocket and tapped it into the wall of ice. When it was secure, he detached from the Ski-Doo rope and reconnected—not to Siem's line and certain rescue, but to the crevasse.

"Hey! What are you doing?" Siem cried out.

Maybe Mikel had just sentenced himself to an early death, but maybe before he died he would find out what, below the surface of Antarctica, caused water to flow uphill.

CHAPTER 9

Dangling in the crevasse, Mikel pulled spiked crampons from his backpack one at a time. He heard Siem calling down to him, his voice echoing like a distant foghorn, but Mikel did not answer. He was too busy concentrating on the task at hand. Carefully, he latched the crampons to the soles of his boots knowing that dropping even one of them would end the journey before it began.

Hooks on, he arranged his ropes, then pushed away from the ice wall and down. For the next few minutes, Siem continued to call out to him. Then silence. Mikel looked up at the tiny bright hole to the world and it was empty. He thought he could hear muffled noises over the ridge, but with his next swinging descent that sound disappeared and Mikel heard only his own rapid breathing and the rasp of the ice as he thrust his spikes into it.

He felt that he could be mesmerized by all the shades of blue in the ice but losing focus might cause him to lose his grip, his life. So he focused on the water droplets instead. There were never many of them, but always enough to confirm that their upward motion was neither temporary nor a fluke.

Soon he had descended deep enough so that the darkness of the crevasse forced him to fish the head lamp from his backpack and turn it on. Mikel was not enamored of flashlights. They were necessary things but they limited his view and threw off the true colors of a surface. They illuminated dust particles, flecks of ice, and other distractions. Just now the shifting circle of light made everything pop from the surrounding darkness, like it was all pressing in on him. The place felt even more claustrophobic than it was. The creak of the rope seemed like a voice and the shadows seemed to creep.

Damn it.

He stopped moving and took a deep breath. Now was not the time to start imagining things. The crevasse was daunting enough as it was.

Focusing again on the tears running up the ice, Mikel became aware that the cold was not one of his challenges. The temperature certainly wasn't balmy but at this depth he should have had to crack some hand warmers at least. Instead, the air felt about as cold as the surface and no more.

He tugged at his rope to test the latest ice screw, then pushed out and down.

The Brunt Ice Shelf was only one hundred meters deep on average but this crevasse seemed deeper. As if to confirm that, Mikel reached into his pocket for another ice screw and came up with nothing. He checked all his pockets hopelessly, knowing he'd put all the screws in one place. With a very strong grip and cautious movements, he held his backpack open while he searched through it. No luck. He was out.

A wave of anger swept through him. He shoved his backpack over his shoulders again, dangled in the air a moment, then kicked at the wall, hard. Cursing, he spent the next minute jerking his stuck, spiked foot back out of the ice. Then as he tugged his balaclava down for a breath of fresh air to clear his head—he felt it. A subtle, gentle, but unmistakable breeze.

The propellant for the water droplets.

Excited by his discovery, Mikel Jasso did something incredibly stupid. He used one ice ax as an anchor, reattached his ropes to it, descended, and used the other ice ax as another anchor descending as far as he could go into the darkness.

Literally at the end of his rope, he peered down into the maddening hole. His flashlight beam disappeared into nothingness. He glared at the ice, the *running water*, looked down again—and caught his breath. He'd seen a flash of green.

Tiny, just a spark, but familiar—he slowly swept his head lamp over the diameter of the hole. Then he stopped sharply. There it was again, and not just any green. If he was extrapolating correctly through the yellow of his light, this was olivine green, the same as the crystals in the last stone he'd picked up for Flora, the stone that caused them so much trouble.

Mikel lowered his goggles and squinted. There appeared to be a surface he could stand on about twenty feet below him. He couldn't be sure; it could have been just a shadow. But if he hesitated, if he started to think, he would be paralyzed. Finding cracks in the wall of ice that he could fit his fingers into, he unhooked from the rope and slowly, very slowly, climbed by hand and spiked foot down the wall. Then he hit a spot where there was nothing to grip. Mikel closed his eyes and rested his forehead on the ice. He had to continue, no matter what the cost. He jerked one foot out of the wall and, gripping his last handholds, jerked the other foot out. Lowering himself by extending his arms, he let the spikes on the soles of his feet search for purchase—

Suddenly, he lost his grip and with the claws on his crampons screeching against the ice, he slid. The drop lasted no more than two or three seconds, though it felt like ten and ended with him landing hard on solid rock. His ankle twisted beneath him. Whether it was a ledge or the bottom of the crevasse didn't matter so much in that moment.

I'm breathing, he thought. *Why the hell am I breathing? This should be ocean down here.* He didn't even hear the sea.

Gingerly, he curled over and got up on his hands and knees. He looked around, no longer damning his head lamp, and froze.

The gray-black rock he was on looked *tiled*. It was all hexagons fitted perfectly together. His mind leaped to ancient peoples, their carvings, but reminded himself more rationally that, under certain conditions rock could form hexagons by itself. Slow lava could harden and fracture into six-sided columns if it was cooled by contact with ice, and if ice sheets moved across the surface for years it could smooth the rock to this even expanse. He would begin with that sensible assumption—well, it was sensible if he conveniently forgot the fact that there are no volcanoes on the east side of Antarctica.

He was kneeling on a long lump of rock. He paused, questioning his judgment—was this really a lump of rock? He searched through his pockets for the first expendable item he could find, which turned out to be a pencil. He placed it on the rock and it rolled haltingly to the left. There was a slight curve here. Could he be on top of a lava tube?

He then cast his light over the ice above him.

There were moving water droplets here too. Could something have melted all the ice that once filled this space?

Mikel noted the direction the water droplets were blowing and began to crawl toward whatever was blowing them. *Could something have melted all the ice that once filled this space?* he wondered. He had not moved more than half a body length, before his hand knocked against something. He backed up and pivoted his neck so that the head lamp hit the spot.

A human fist was protruding from the rock.

With a stab of horror, Mikel scuttled backward but kept the light on the hand. The fist did not move. Finally he crawled close again, taking off his head lamp so he could direct it more easily. To his relief, the fist was not human. It was rock, purposely sculpted to look like a human hand. And it was not the only sculpture—adjacent was another wrist that ended in a differently shaped hand, one with two fingers pointed outward, the other fingers curled in. A bar, like a scepter, was in another hand, pointing up. Mikel was too stunned by his finding to think about what it was he was seeing, to process the enormity of the discovery. He tugged on the object but it was stuck fast.

Edging forward, Mikel stopped again almost immediately. This time he swept the light over the whole surface. What he saw did not seem possible.

It was like finding Pompeii. The basalt rock held dozens of objects. He recognized a knife, bizarrely twisted; a bowl; a carving of the face of a baby. A huge rock thrust from the surface was in front of him and it was tessellated with a mosaic of olivine-green crystals. The archaeologist in him trumped all else and he pounced forward. He approached it with joy bordering on rapture. When he touched the stone he felt it vibrating.

No. Humming.

Mikel yanked off his glove, and as he gripped the stone, a wave of red broke across his mind. The world skewed, exploded, filled with a sulfurous smell like he was back on the airplane at Montevideo—

Then a weight fell on his left shoulder. Mikel screamed, turned, and skittered backward. When his light finally landed on his target, and a string of curses flew from his mouth with the speed and duration that only a Basque could deliver, there was Siem kneeling on the rock next to him, stunned and shaking. He was still reaching out with the hand he'd placed on Mikel's shoulder, but his gaze was on the protruding objects all around them.

"What *is* this?" whispered Siem. "*How* is this?"

"Shut up," Mikel snapped.

Siem closed his mouth and just looked at him, scared.

Collecting himself, Mikel sat up and waited for his pounding pulse to subside. Siem had pulled him back—but from where? *Damn it*, he thought, now he had a witness. "How the hell did you get down here anyway?"

"I . . . rappelled," Siem said, following the glow of his own head lamp. "There was an argument. Bundy didn't want me to follow you but I made him see we couldn't let you—I mean—we already lost two people out here."

Mikel had to make a decision quickly. If he allowed Siem to see this, then Siem had to die. Mikel could make it happen, regardless of the man's six-foot-seven frame. But he was just a kid, and scared, and he trusted Mikel. So the archaeologist moved to block further inspection with his body.

"Siem," Mikel said, "get back up to the surface."

"Why?"

"Somebody has to tell them to move Halley VI off the ice shelf."

Siem started to ask why again but changed his mind.

"Because it's melting," Mikel answered anyway. That much was true. "These objects, probably from an old shipwreck, will be gone soon. You will be too if you don't go."

"But what about you?" Siem asked. "I saw the rip marks in the ice. It looks to me like you fell."

"I climbed down," Mikel answered. "Not elegantly, but I made it . . . and I'll make it back. I really have to examine a few of these objects before I follow you. But you—you might be saving some lives if you leave now. They'll need time to make evacuation plans."

Siem almost turned to go but stopped. "Climbing down is easier than climbing up. I'm not sure you can make it."

"I'll make it," Mikel insisted. "Thanks for the concern. Truly."

With a sigh, he turned to go. "I hope it's worth it," he said as he started back up.

Mikel watched him disappear into the blackness, then looked back at the olivine mosaic and thought, unequivocally, *If anything is worth dying for, this is it.*

CHAPTER 10

Mikel didn't move for at least ten minutes after the last scuffling sound drifted down from Siem's ascent. He just stared at the olivine mosaic with a feeling of almost physical hunger.

Each of the olivine tiles embedded in the rock had been etched. Each had an ethereal, internal glow that he could not explain other than through some kind of phosphorescent content. The characters showed a predominance for snakelike crescents and S-shapes, resembling those that comprised the triangular symbol on the troublesome artifact he had brought back to New York. But these were more complex and had many more variations. He was definitely looking at a written language. Seen in aggregate like this, it was obviously more advanced than the artifacts the Group had collected over the years had led them to believe.

Mikel's hand strayed to his radio. The Tac-XI unit was international, keyed to either general radio receivers or specific programmed phone numbers. His impulse was to contact Flora. But of course, the radio wouldn't work this far down. Not unless there was a direct opening to the surface. His hand dropped and he felt almost grateful. There were no hoops to jump through, insufficient explanations that would feel like silt in his mouth compared to the magnificence of what lay before him.

Where to begin?

He moved with caution, remembering the incapacitation he'd felt on the airplane as that small artifact had hummed through the camera case into his chest, how his mind had reeled and possibly hallucinated. He could have been setting himself up for far worse than that now.

So what are you going to do? he asked himself. *Scurry back up with Siem?*

Practically in slow motion at first, then with a bold thrust, Mikel reached toward the stone, his fingers opening like fronds. His hands hovering over the stone, he felt the humming without touching it. It reminded him of a tuning fork, soothing rather than disturbing. After nearly a minute he let one hand drift down and grasp the mosaic.

A red flood rushed into his mind so vigorously that he felt as if he were falling over. He cried out and clutched at the olivine-studded stone with his other hand. A rank odor rose toward him, the smell of sulfur filling his nose and throat—making him gag. He could feel the hum of the stone growing more vibrant, as if it were using his entire body to amplify itself. Afraid that it would shake loose his grip, he leaned forward, resting his head in his hands and gripping the stone as tightly as he could. The mosaic was fading now, though it was still there, still tangible.

And then suddenly, he was looking at a room. It was all around him but he wasn't in it—his hands were still on the mosaic and his knees felt like an extension of the rock. He willed himself to look around the hallucination, the vision, whatever it was.

He saw a tall chamber with smooth but fantastically twisted walls, all dark gray. *Basalt*, he realized, but no lava flow he'd ever seen created such spirals or—his eyes traveled up—a latticework dome. The grid held glass and above that, thin smoke drifted across a bright blue sky.

This was the work of artisans.

Of Galderkhaani.

His heart pounded against his chest as he peered incredulously into the living past. The latticework, a complex of knots, had an overall counterclockwise spiral shape that was mirrored by the floor, which held an enormous double-armed spiral. One arm of the spiral was the same smooth basalt as the walls but made simply, without twists or adornments. The basalt also provided a solid center to the spiral. The other, recessed into the floor, was filled with clear water. Every few feet, a cluster of flames seemed to float mysteriously upon the water's surface with no materials or gas pipes feeding the small fires.

These fires had to be decorative he thought. Nothing about their strength or position suggested they were used for light or heat. Nor was there direct sunlight anywhere in the chamber. He believed he could make out a walkway just below the dome that sported flames dancing in stone braziers built into the wall—or did they protrude from the wall?

Everything seemed to have the same regular texture, like plastic poured in a mold. Below the walkway, the walls were sculpted in the shape of shelves. Panes of opaque white quartz enclosed the shelves, but enough of the panes were open for Mikel to see stacks of parchments, hundreds of them, piled in no particular order. This had to be a library, but the librarian would not have met Flora's meticulous standards.

Flora.

It was a real-world thought reassuring him that at least he still had some control over his own mind. And, yes, he still felt the stone in his hands and smelled sulfur. This *was* merely a projection of some kind, like a hologram. Suddenly, he was staggered by the realization of where he could go, what he might learn, if he figured out how to "drive" the mosaics.

Returning to what he could actually see with his eyes, he surveyed the room. A second, wider walkway directly beneath the first provided access to the shelves as well as space for furniture, which seemed to bubble from the rock. Small tables held stone cups with steam rising from them. Suddenly, the smell of sulfur lessened, replaced by the gathering scent of—what was that?

It was jasmine tea.

Stone couches and chairs cushioned with bright, gem-colored pillows stood near the tea tables and as Mikel's eyes adjusted to the dimmer light here, he saw that there were a few dozen people in the room.

Not just people: citizens, he thought. Adults, all. Proud and rich with *purpose*. They had the carriage of women and men who belonged here. He longed to catalog all the detail. He was so accustomed to taking cell-phone images that recall, mental snapshots, was a nearly forgotten craft.

Don't try, just let it in, he told himself.

And then, curious, he lightly squeezed his fingers on the transparent tile as if on a touch pad. The flames froze. So did the people. The shadows were all locked in place.

He *could* control this. Tightening his grip froze the image. No doubt it could be rewound, replayed. He relaxed his grip and the display resumed.

On the whole, the citizens did not appear relaxed. Only a few were sitting down, their yellow and white robes draped around their feet. They were drinking tea with curiously coordinated movements: when one reached for a cup another always did the same. Then each person inhaled steam from the other person's cup while maintaining eye contact, and usually smiling, before drinking from their own. It was something like a toast but more intimate.

The more restless citizens were standing and talking urgently to parchment bearers. The parchments were changing hands with nervous movements and gestures and hastily scrawled signatures.

That's not paper or papyrus . . . it's too malleable. Vellum? No, it's too fine for animal skin. At least, the skin of animals known in the modern day. The writing implements—fish bones, possibly. Or teeth mounted in wooden or stone styluses?

Hands touched hands as the swaps were made, fingers trailing in lingering, comforting gestures. Everyone's faces were lost in downward looks so Mikel couldn't see their expressions. He could not hear them nor see what was on the parchments. He let his eyes wander through the many shadows.

For a library, the chamber was remarkably ill lit. One could retrieve parchments from the shelves, then move to the upper walkway to read them, but that would require holding them dangerously close to the open flames in the braziers. Below, there seemed to be no way to read closely at all. Perhaps the ink glowed, Mikel thought, like the olivine in the stone he was holding. Maybe they had a phosphorous content that glowed when exposed to light?

Or perhaps the parchments weren't the point. Along the floor-level walkway, statues were arranged among all the furniture. Mikel's eye had skipped over them; he'd assumed they were decorative. At second glance, he realized that the furniture was oriented toward the statues, regarding them. He studied the figures more closely with rising excitement. They were all black basalt human forms but they were not paeans to the elegant musculature and shape of the human body. The asexual torsos and arms were exaggerated in size, while the rest of the bodies were carved wearing long robes that seemed to cling only occasionally and only at the bottom to indicate the position of the feet.

Why the feet? And the hands? The hands were oversized, and they displayed a wide variety of different positions and gestures.

Mikel moved closer without changing the position of his hands. He felt like a kid with his nose pressed to the candy store glass. He wanted more.

The easiest statue for Mikel to see in the dim space stood straight with the robes hiding its feet. The left arm was close to the torso but the left hand pointed away from the hips with all fingers parallel to the floor. The right arm was crossed diagonally over the chest and the right hand pointed with all fingers across the left shoulder. Mikel felt that he'd seen this placement of hands before but he didn't have time to rake through his memories. Absently, he moved a thumb as he tried to lean closer still.

"Damn it!"

The tableau jumped ahead. There was suddenly more light in the room. Was it earlier? Later? Mikel had no way of knowing. He remained still, not wanting to miss anything. There was so much to see.

Excitement washed over him as he left his hands splayed wide and let the drama play out. A tall man with Dravidian skin and rugged features unfolded himself from one of the couches. By his undeniable sense of belonging, Mikel guessed this was the librarian.

"Egat anata cazh . . ."

"So, we attempt the ritual . . . ," the tall man was saying.

Somehow, Mikel understood the words. *But wait, the tiles couldn't have been translating; English hadn't existed then.* There was some other mechanism at work.

But before he could put his mind to it, a door banged open, wood against rock, and a short man with a splendidly curled white beard hurried into the room. The man left the door open and Mikel could see to the room beyond. Like a horde of red ants, glaring red-orange lava was inexplicably moving *up* a trellis forming a spiral not unlike those on the library walls. Pale yellow fumes were quickly pulled away from the growing column by a mechanical process that sent the smoke floating out of the building and across the blue sky.

"Pao," said the tall man.

The man with the beard quickly retraced his steps and shut the door, commenting as he went, "Vol, why are we doing this *now* with all that's still going on in the next room?"

Vol smiled. "Why don't you read our declaration. It's quite—"

"I'm asking *you*," said Pao.

Vol's smile faded. "We must know if the ritual works."

"But how can you know unless you *die*?" Pao asked.

"The soul lives even when the body dies," Vol replied. "There are risks in everything a person does. That's why *we* have all signed a declaration." His emphasis seemed designed to remind Pao that he had not affixed his own signature. "My friend, don't you think the Technologist plan has risks?"

"Of course," replied Pao, "But there are controls built into *that* process."

"So we're told," Vol said. "Does anyone outside the elite core know what those are?"

"We know these people well," Pao said. "They are honorable. This ritual—we just don't know what it will do, what it *can* do."

"Which is why we must try it," Vol replied patiently.

"I don't agree. It's premature," Pao said, stroking the rolls of his beard. "I've been watching the Technologists' project. It shows promise."

Vol smiled. "You know the saying: 'Give all a chance, but trust your instincts.' "

Pao frowned. "That wasn't a saying. It was from one of my poems."

"And wise words they were," Vol said, nodding. "My instincts, our instincts"—he indicated the others—"tell us that this is the right path. Come back to us, Pao. Come *with* us. Help us to find out."

The two men stood like the statues. Then the tall man extended his arms. The bearded man accepted them and the two men linked forearms, lightly, the shorter man seemingly fearful of a tighter embrace.

"We loved, once," Pao said. "Was that not a bond greater than the flesh?"

"You know it was," Vol replied. "But the body was a part of that, an important part."

"That is an understatement," his companion replied.

Vol smiled. "True enough. Now we must know if that flesh can be shed."

"*Votah!* Inevitably we *will* lose our bodies, death will see to that," Pao said. "Why be impatient?"

"To learn," Vol said. "To see if we can become Candescent."

Pao's face twisted unhappily and he released the arms of the other. "That is Rensat's influence, my friend. She still lives on the myths of the past. Legend will not save you . . . but the Source might."

"So might the ritual that you yourself composed," Vol said.

Just then, at the command of one of the women, half of the people in robes and carrying parchment moved through the room and filed through the door. The others appeared to be trying to see over their shoulders but were not allowed beyond the entrance.

"Pao, Pao!" an older woman called as she passed through the doorway.

Pao looked up to find her, but a moment later she was barely visible as the other parchment bearers swept into the room beyond.

Vol tilted his head at his bearded friend with blatant judgment. "We said no physical attachments before this test. You know this, Pao. The connection must be *solely* of the spirit. When we achieve that, without distraction, then the body can be trained to move aside at will."

"I tried to create distance," Pao said, "but she comes to me—"

"And your focus changes to the physical."

"Of course."

Vol gripped Pao's arms. "I cannot blame her, or you," he continued sadly. "It tortures *me* not to have a physical connection with my lovers. A complete connection, to accompany the spiritual."

"Then *make* that connection with whomever you wish," Pao said, urging him. "But give *this* up, at least for now."

Vol deflated. He released his friend and turned away. Then he stopped and looked back.

"Pao," the librarian said, pressing him, "you once had more faith than any of us. Yet now you want to put your trust there?" He pointed toward the door.

"Not trust," Pao said. "Hope? Optimism? The point is, we *don't* have to decide that now, which is why I ask you to wait."

Vol eyed his friend carefully. "Tell me. Do you truly believe in what the Technologists are attempting to do? Or is it that you lack faith in the alternative, in us?"

"Both," Pao admitted. "More study is required on both sides."

Vol regarded his friend silently. The door was shut and the remaining dozen people had now gathered loosely around the two men. Vol turned from Pao and began to walk around the basalt arm of the spiral.

"Pao," a woman called and took several steps toward him. "Do not let Technologist propaganda cloud your eyes."

Pao regarded her with fondness. "You have no fear about what we do?"

The woman's eyes grew stern. "I *am* afraid, yes. To die, to ascend, but not to transcend—eternity on earth, immaterial and alone? That frightens me more. But there are other views, even among the Technologists. The earth is restless, the ice moves, the animals are fearful. We may not have time to explore alternative rituals as much as we would like."

"Certainly not if we continue to debate the topic," Vol pointed out, turning to Pao.

Everyone was silent.

Vol walked toward the woman and took her arms as he had taken

Pao's. "I will be honored to go forth with you, Rensat, but I do not want to take you from him whom you love."

"I love you both," Rensat told him. "Ultimately, however, I love the Candescents above all. If I cannot have that, no life, no love, is worth possessing."

Her words had an impact on Pao. He moved closer to the other two, and Mikel could feel their energy shift. "I have spent my adult life looking at existence from many viewpoints," Pao told her. "That is why I have written—not just to share ideas but to see them as if they belong to someone else, to consider them impartially. And I have come to believe some of what we believe but also aspects of what the Technologists believe." He faced the other members of the Priesthood. "There are basic questions that remain to be answered. I say wait."

"What questions?" Rensat asked.

"The question of infusing ourselves into the cosmic plane."

Vol released Rensat and waved with disgust. "The Technologists are not planning an 'infusion,'" he said. "They are planning to *break into* the highest plane, like thieves. Never mind the animal violence inherent in that—by what logic can anyone think of overpowering limitless power? No." He shook his head. "Our souls must bond. Together we must *present* ourselves to the infinite. We must merge with the cosmos. That is how the Candescents survived their obliteration."

"You think *that* is what they did," Pao said. "You believe that based on stories passed down since the world was young."

Vol stood strong, wordlessly defending his faith.

"And you are wrong about the Technologists," Pao said, correcting him. "They look to target a point in the cosmos, not to crack it or assault it." Pao looked out at the others. "My friends, think about your approach. Even bonded souls may bounce from the cosmic plane like light from polished metal. One soul, a dozen, a thousand—it may not matter."

"The Candescents proved it does," Rensat retorted.

"And you suggest that rising like a geyser-powered stone on molten rock will achieve that goal?" Vol asked.

"I don't know!" Pao confessed. "I don't. That is why I say we must wait. The Technologists have built a device that may give us the opportunity to ascend. Even the legends tell us the Candescents rode into the cosmic plane on an inferno."

"The word is *haydonai* and no one is sure what it meant," Vol reminded him. "The ancient Galderkhaani may have meant 'great glow,' not 'fire.' The great glow may have come from luminous souls working together, not a column of fire. It may be figurative, not literal."

Pao smiled thinly. "All I am asking is that we save, for later, the one option that might kill everyone here—and then prove too weak to allow us to reach any of the planes beyond death."

"And I say again, there are risks inherent in all things," Vol said. "*Your* thoughts and words and poetry were instrumental in creating the *cazh*. Do not abandon us now."

Vol studied Pao's reluctant face. Then he made a little open-handed gesture, as if to say, *Join us*.

"I do not wish to," Pao said at last. But then he looked long and openly at his two former lovers. Their faces were so familiar, so dear, that the thought of living without them was unthinkable. "And yet I cannot abandon you," he said.

With an encouraging look from Rensat, Pao finally nodded. Vol clapped the man's shoulders joyously, then turned and pulled a parchment from its display on a wall and followed Pao as he strode without another word around the spiral toward its center. The other dozen arranged themselves along the basalt path so that they were evenly spaced, close to the fires floating on the water. Pao sat cross-legged in the center. Vol placed the parchment in Pao's lap, then stood behind him.

The bearded man looked around. He still seemed uncertain.

"These are your words," Rensat reminded him.

Pao looked at the parchment. It was a gesture, no more, but he placed his name on the document. Then he took a dramatic breath and bowed over his knees, exposing the nape of his neck.

Vol stood before him with his feet shoulder-width apart and closed his eyes. His breath became tremulous. The others held a respectful silence. Vol opened his eyes and extended the first two fingers of his right hand to point exactly at Pao's neck. He raised his left hand above him and pointed those first two fingers at the lattice dome. Then he looked directly into Mikel's eyes and smiled.

"Welcome, all," he said. "In the name of the Candescents, we commit our spirits to wherever the ritual takes us!"

Almost at once, an invisible surge began to manifest itself, a shock wave that grew in power until it was no longer rippling but forcefully expanding—

• • •

Mikel jerked back in terror. His hands recoiled from the mosaic and the vision ripped away from his mind. Almost simultaneously, a massive fireball exploded nearby.

• • •

Three hours by plane, northeast of Halley VI, on the north coast of Antarctica, the commander of the Norwegian Troll base pushed his way through a huddle of scientists to get a full view of the jagged lines on the computer screen they were all staring at. He had NORSAR, a geoscience research foundation, on the phone and the phone to his ear.

"We've never seen seismic activity like this," he said in awe.

"And no aftershocks?" asked the seismologist on the phone.

"Just that brief burst," the commander said. An inveterate fidgeter, he began to drum with his fingers on the desk. As if he were reading music, he tapped the long and short lines from the Antarctic bedrock's seismometer, but the resulting beat was far too arrhythmic to be music.

There were two people in the world who would have recognized the sound.

A psychiatrist seven and a half thousand miles away and her ten-year-old son.

CHAPTER 11

A cat woke from a nap on the Upper West Side of Manhattan and lightly descended from the couch to the floor. He stretched his shoulders, then stood for a moment, still half-asleep. Then he ran at full speed out of the room, down the hall, out of sight.

Caitlin and Jacob O'Hara sat at the table having breakfast, watching Arfa's impromptu sprint. Caitlin was tempted to go find him but Jacob was in the middle of a dramatic reenactment of what it must have been like to be the chef on the *Nautilus* and refused to be distracted. He was so fired up he'd been holding a glass of almond milk for at least five minutes despite occasionally sloshing it onto his hand.

Suddenly, Jacob dropped the glass on the table. Raising both fists in the air, he threw his head back, eyes squeezed tight, a picture of frustration.

"Jake, honey?"

Caitlin knelt by his chair, suddenly worried that perhaps Jacob's recovery from the episode at the cooking school was really just the eye of a storm.

"*En . . . do . . . ,*" he said, as though he were struggling to form words. "*En . . . dovi . . .*"

Caitlin reached out and touched him lightly on his face. Jacob reared back as though repulsed by human contact.

Then he brought both fists down on the table. It was a tense but controlled movement—not in a rage, not aimed at anything, more like trying to gather himself—except that the table met his fists with a massive thump. The impact startled him, as if he'd forgotten the table was there. His eyes jerked open and Caitlin, horrified at what she was seeing, realized that Jacob was suddenly himself again. Which meant, even more terrifying, that for those few seconds he had not been himself.

Jacob looked at his hands, looked at the table covered in milk, looked at his mother, and began to cry.

For more than ten minutes, Jacob continued to writhe in Caitlin's arms.

First he would twist away so he could sign with both hands, then he would turn to his mother to clutch at her neck. Signing was his default, emergency mode, and though he was wearing his hearing aid, he wasn't responding to anything Caitlin was saying. She didn't want to break the embrace to face him and sign herself. He was only signing one thing.

"I want to go to bed . . . I want to go to bed."

Caitlin stood, hoisted his legs around her waist, and carried him. Any other time she would have felt the burn in her legs under the weight of a growing ten-year-old, but not now. She walked quickly down the hall, feeling Jacob's wrists move against her back as he continued to sign, clutch, sign.

But as much as he wanted to go to bed, he was not quite ready to be left alone. As if he were three years old, Jacob wanted the comfort of the full bedtime routine, including help from Caitlin taking out his hearing aid and changing into his pajamas. He even demanded to floss and brush his teeth, something he typically disliked. Finally, with his head on the pillow and the sheets and two blankets pulled up to his chin and perfectly smoothed over his chest, his stuffed, fraying whale from the Museum of Natural History under his left arm, he sobbed his last sob and calmed. Caitlin slipped her left hand under his right hand and he slapped her hand away.

"No talking, Mommy," he signed. "Hug."

She curled over and hugged him tight. Then, sitting back, seeing that he was still gazing at her, she finally signed, "What happened?"

"It didn't work," he signed back, his eyes downcast.

"What didn't work?"

"There was sky and then there was ice and water that was on fire."

The mention of fire sent a shiver up Caitlin's back. This was the second time he'd had a vision that included fire. Her whole experience of Galderkhaan involved fire, and then there was Maanik and Atash, the latter of whom had died from it.

"What are we talking about?" she asked with slow, patient gestures. "Can you tell me that?"

He shook his head, then signed, "I have to sleep now."

She wanted to ask if he was alone, if he had seen people, heard them talking, felt something, but she didn't want to put any ideas in his head.

"All right, honey," she signed. "You sleep."

Caitlin was reluctant to leave it at that but knew that Jacob didn't do his best when pressed. She kissed his forehead.

"Sleep," she signed.

"Sleep, Mommy," he said in agreement.

He turned over, curled in the fetal position, and put his forefingers in his mouth. He hadn't done that in six years.

Caitlin closed his door behind her and stood for a moment with her hand on the doorknob. *Have I brought this on my son?*

She stalked back down the hall to the sunny living room, awash with an anger and guilt she had never felt in her life. She couldn't keep her thoughts straight, couldn't sit, couldn't control her breaths and didn't want to. The memories were battering into her brain—Maanik screaming, squirming in bed, barely making sense before descending into gibberish, then screaming again. Was Jacob taking his first steps into that same cycle? If so, why? She had stopped the assault, over a week ago. Those souls were *gone*.

Caitlin whipped back and forth across her living room cursing.

Her phone rang. She let it go for a couple of seconds, then crossed the room to grab it from her purse. The screen said it was her father and she thought, *Not now!* as if she were yelling at him. She flung the phone onto the table and returned to the living room.

What if those Galderkhaan souls are back, somehow? If they didn't die before, I'm going to make sure they do this time. And where the hell *is the cat?*

Had Arfa sensed something in the apartment again? Was that why he ran out of the room before Jacob fell apart?

Caitlin felt something rising inside of her, something dark and ugly that wasn't just a protective parent, wasn't simply outrage. It rose up her back like molten rock, turning every nerve to fire. She had to fight to keep from breaking something.

At that moment the cat entered from the hallway, ambling at his usual pace. He walked straight to his food dish by the archway to the kitchen and settled on his haunches for a long chow down. Still frustrated and wanting to scream it out, Caitlin got close to him to test his responsiveness. He didn't even twitch an ear. Nothing amiss there.

So this isn't the same as Maanik and her dog, Caitlin thought. *This* is *something different.*

Because life wasn't strange enough, it had to get stranger. And endanger her son.

She jumped when the phone rang again. On autopilot, she grabbed it from the table. This time it was Anita. She rejected the call, dropped the phone on the table, and hurried back into the living room. She needed the wider space around her, needed to think, but she couldn't. Nor was there any reason to think: she *knew* what she had to do.

She had to get back to Galderkhaan to see what, if anything, might be causing this. But then she remembered the horrible white ice trap she'd traveled to last time she tried, where she'd heard an invisible Jacob knocking for her and she couldn't reach him.

Stark fear saturated her anger. Was there a connection? *Had* she done this to him?

The more she thought about it, the more it made sense. What if she tried to go back there and only caused things to deteriorate further?

You left me without a bloody guidebook! she screamed at everyone who had brought her to this moment—herself above all. She wished she could take a week off and pick the brains of Vahin, the Hindu cleric she'd met in Iran, and Madame Langlois, whose Haitian Vodou world was as vivid as it was foreign. They had provided such strong insight with Maanik's case.

But this was Jacob. She couldn't leave him and she couldn't take him with her. She didn't even know if she could get back into Tehran now.

She paced to the hall and listened for anything from Jacob's room, but all was silent. For a second she sank onto her heels and put her forehead in her hands. Almost instantly she stood again, unable to be still. Staying there by the hallway, she closed her eyes and ground her left heel into the floor. She stretched her left hand toward the chair Jacob had been sitting in and extended her right hand toward the floor, willing herself back, back, back, to Galderkhaan, to *any* place that wasn't here—

Nothing happened.

Damn it!

She opened her eyes, shook out the stance, then looked at the nearest piece of curved metal, her coffeepot on the table. Again, she willed herself into the alternate mind stream or whatever the hell it was—and again, nothing happened. She cupped her right hand under her left palm, not touching, but she didn't even feel the centering that had been occurring regularly for weeks.

Whatever power she'd discovered had died in her. She was dead.

Why? How?

She had shut it down in the subway. Had she willed that to happen again?

Anger and fear cascaded over her again. The ignorance and uncommon stupidity in her skull made her want to tear at her hair.

Then the apartment intercom buzzed. She grunted with frustration, paced to the screen, and saw that Ben was outside the apartment building. She punched the "talk" button.

"Not a good time, Ben."

His face turned to the fish-eye camera. "That's why I'm here."

"Ben—" she said, resisting.

"Let me up, Cai. Just let. Me. Up," he insisted.

She hesitated. She wanted to say no but realized that this could after all be what she needed. Not Ben but whatever gifts Ben bore. She buzzed him in.

A minute later he was at the door, having taken the stairs two at a time. He looked drawn and pale and was speaking before she had a chance to.

"I felt you," he said.

"What?"

"I felt something snap—*wrong*," he explained. "I don't know how, whether we're still entangled on some level or something from the United Nations, but it was stronger than just an intuition, something I couldn't ignore."

He reached out to pull her in but she backed away. She had noticed that Arfa was sniffing Ben's ankle—the same way the beagle, Jack London, had done in the Pawars' apartment.

"Cai?" Ben said.

She shook her head several times. *Not here. Not the same situation. Not in* my *home.*

"Cai!" Ben said more insistently.

She motioned him in, shut the door, and launched into a description of Jacob's episode, speaking so quickly even the UN interpreter could barely follow. Finally, he interrupted her.

"What were the words he said?"

Caitlin thought back. "*En. Dovi.* I think they were two words. He struggled a few times to get them out."

"Probably just fragments," Ben said. "He didn't get to finish."

"Right. I should have let him just scream it all out."

"I didn't say that," Ben said soothingly. "Where is he now, can I see him?"

"Why?"

"If I knew, I'd tell you," he said. "More information, he may say something else—I don't know."

Reluctantly, she walked him down the hall. When she opened the bedroom door, Jacob was visible in the bed, his stuffed whale cast to one side, his fingers no longer in his mouth. For a moment there was only the sound of his deep sleep breathing.

No, it wasn't just his breathing. There was a sound like . . . wind? Breakers on a beach? It was distant and indistinct but it was *not* his breath.

She tugged the sleeve of Ben's jacket and they backed into the hall. Caitlin shut the door and waited until she was back in the living room to speak again.

"It's Galderkhaan," she said. "I have to go back and I haven't been able to. But with you here maybe I can try using the *cazh*."

"Whoa," Ben said, cutting her off. "The chant you went into at the UN? The ritual that talked about you going 'Hundreds of feet in the air, I want to rise with the sea, with the wind'?"

"Yes."

He looked at her with surprise and she started when she realized why. He had quoted it in Galderkhaani and she had understood him. The sound of those very elements seemed to creep in around them. Behind them the cat was curled under a chair. Its fur rippled faintly.

"Holy shit," Ben said.

"Yeah. There is something going on," she said. "Do you disagree?"

He shook his head.

"All right, then. At the very least, going back will help me to establish whether the souls are somehow still in this goddamn spin cycle, whether they're still trying to use that final *cazh*."

"I'll be damned if you'll do that, Cai," Ben said. "Wherever it took you, it's a dangerous tool."

"No, this is perfect, Ben. You've seen the process, you'll know if you need to stop it. And you're familiar with everything Maanik went through so if Jacob wakes up, if he—" She stopped herself. "If he needs anything, you'll be here to give it to him."

"And you? What happens to Jacob if you get lost in Galderkhaan or inside your head somewhere?"

"Inside . . . my *head*?" Caitlin's fury flared out of her. "You're still not convinced *any* of this is happening, are you?"

"Something is going on, I just don't know what!"

"Didn't you just say you got a 'ping' from me, miles away!"

"Maybe it's ESP, or a strong sixth-sense animal instinct, absolutely worth exploring *with controls* . . . but not something to jump headlong into. And I have to say it: why are *you* convinced this stuff is absolutely, no-question, for real? You're the psychiatrist, the scientist! We had the language, Maanik's fits, the power of suggestion they created—"

"No," she said. "Ben Moss, don't you dare do this to me."

"Do what, exactly? Caution you? Think, Cai! You used that chant as a last resort to save a life. Maanik was literally generating fire in her body."

"Another strong indicator that this is real, wouldn't you say?"

"Pyrokinesis, spontaneous combustion, I don't know," he said. "*Please* listen. Jacob is down the hall, asleep. For right now, he's perfectly okay. And from what you described, whatever he experienced bore no resemblance to any of the other kids' experiences. Besides, you can't know for sure that going back won't exacerbate the problem. Tell me one reason you should go jumping into some self-induced hypnotic state that may not have an exit strategy!"

"Because Jacob wasn't here, Ben. For a couple seconds it wasn't him. *That* happened with Maanik too, you saw it. And let's not forget yesterday, at the school, he went away somehow."

"But what he did was totally different."

"No." She pointed at the almond milk still covering the table. "It was violent and angry."

"Show me."

"Why?"

"Because I want to see what you saw."

With a cringe, Caitlin sat in Jacob's chair. She mimed the dropping of the glass, then re-created the two fists in the air, the arc of them downward. "That's when he hit the table," she said. "It seemed to jar him out of the episode."

"Yeah, well, I don't see anger there, Cai. What I see is frustration, pure and simple." He read her doubting face, motioned for her to stand. He sat in her place and re-created the sequence. "Which way do you see it, now that it isn't Jacob?"

She half-turned, nodded, then released a huge breath. "Okay, not anger. Not wrath. Something more like . . . disappointment? Resignation about *something*? I . . . I don't know but he was affected by something."

"Regardless, not worth risking your mind or life for. Not yet."

She gazed at him mutely and at last shook her head no. "But I have to *do* something, this is Jacob! So what the hell am I going to do, Ben?"

"I don't know yet but you can't go about it like this," he said.

"I know, but I am so angry," she told him as she flopped onto the sofa. "And my apartment's already clean, so housework therapy is out."

"Well, my apartment's not."

She smacked him in the arm.

"Not bad."

"What?"

"If my UN stress counselor were here, he'd tell you to throw a couple punches at a pillow."

She made a face. "Bad Psychiatry 101."

"Mommy?"

Caitlin's head snapped toward the hallway. Jacob was standing there, smiling, with Arfa prancing toward him. He waved at his mother.

"Hey," she said, forcing a smile as she signed. "What happened to your nap?"

"It's done," he said, brushing his hands against each other.

"Did you have any dreams?"

"Yes," he gestured excitedly. "I was flying."

"Sounds fun," Caitlin said, still pretending to be calm.

"*Tawazh!*" he spoke aloud as he ran forward.

Ben and Caitlin exchanged quick looks. Ben was visibly surprised to actually hear the Galderkhaani word, to know that the boy wasn't saying "towers." She hugged him and he hugged her back in a long "normal" embrace.

"He said it," Ben whispered. "You didn't imagine it."

Caitlin nodded over Jacob's shoulder. "Thank you."

"And it didn't come from me or from you."

She shook her head.

Ben stayed where he was, studying Caitlin. He noticed that her eyes were wet, and that not all of her tears were from relief.

PART TWO

CHAPTER 12

Mikel flung himself back against the lava tube, trying to keep distance between himself and the red-orange flame. A lone tendril of fire reached along the stone ceiling and for a moment dipped toward his boots, then it vanished and the echoes of the cracking boom faded to silence.

Hyperventilating, he forced out a big exhale, and it emerged as a horrible, choked shadow of a laugh.

"Christ almighty," he said aloud, as much to check his hearing after the blast as to vent some of the lingering terror. His ears were fine, though the subsequent quiet was far more discomfiting. His vision had temporarily blanked after the glare but was already returning. He fought a desperate urge to strip off some of his layers of clothing. The suffocating heat was going to dissipate rapidly and then the cold would lunge back at any exposed skin.

He took a deep inhale now and realized two things: that there was no odor associated with the blast, which seemed impossible, and that he was breathing far more air than he should have been after an explosion had just gorged itself on the oxygen in this cramped space.

Quickly taking advantage of the residual warmth, he tugged down his balaclava, pulled off a glove, licked his fingers, and held them to the air to determine the breeze's point of origin. It was in the same direction as the fireball.

Mikel ignored his brain warning him that another fireball could explode at any moment. It could easily have been a solitary incident, right? Or one that occurred, what, every year or two, at the most? Every decade? Every century? There was no way to tell, judging by the lack of old charring under the fresh scars on the walls.

Maybe old Vol had a point, he thought. *Nothing is ever learned or discovered by caution. My very presence here is evidence of that.*

Mikel pulled on his glove, his hand already starting to feel the chill, and wriggled into a crawling position facing the source of the breeze. One hand nearly landed on the olivine-studded rock and he jerked away from it.

If I'd stayed with the projection, or whatever it was, what would have happened to me? What happened to them*?*

"Projection," "hologram," "vision"—they all seemed too mundane for what had just occurred. And the fire he'd experienced had been no vision. The dripping sounds that reached his ears were evidence that the heat had been very real. Eyeing the basaltic rock anchoring the olivine mosaic stone, he assured himself he'd come back to reengage if necessary.

I know where you live, Vol!

Mikel moved cautiously through the tunnel, though his hands bumped and brushed other half-buried objects, Mikel did not experience any unusual sensations.

The mosaic tiles. The artifact I brought to the Group. All one. But one what? Phosphorous needed oxygen to glow, and that luminosity was definitely coming from *inside* the stone. No oxygen there. It was not porous.

The crawl was ludicrously short, only about fifteen feet. There at the end of it was something that looked like the top of a chimney, with a generally circular shape that extended down at least twenty-five feet, with a hole at the top four feet across. This structure too was of basaltic rock but it was not continuous with the lava tube. Where the tube had fractured into hexagons while in contact with ice, this projection was as smooth as the walls, shelves, and furniture Mikel had seen in his vision. Inclined at a forty-five-degree angle to the tube, it looked like the lava had hit it, broken it, surrounded it, and then locked it in place as the flow cooled and solidified.

Mikel stopped short. As he shone his lamp ahead into the angled structure he saw stairs.

Not a chimney, he thought. *I'm at the top of a tower. A hollow column of some kind.*

He bared just a wrist to test the air and felt a stronger breeze coming from within the tower. Had wind from this tower extinguished the fireball? Or had the fireball issued from it?

He crept forward a little. Narrow spiral stairs bubbled from the inside of the tower going down. A direction his gut told him not to go.

A tingling sensation filled him, not from without but from within. Fear. Now that he had stopped, now that he was undistracted by physical stimuli, terror had purchase in his atavistic core. It wasn't the geographic isolation; he had been in caves before, in tombs.

No, the fear came from his sharp awareness that he was not alone. There were no hidden lions or snakes here, as in the African veldt or the deserts of Egypt. Nothing that might spring at him. This was worse. It was something enormous and eternal, possibly good, possibly not. And he was stumbling through it like a child. The destruction of his body he could live with—so to speak. But a tormented immortality?

That is hell.

Indeed, for all he knew, that statement might be more than figurative. He trembled as he considered how much an educated, experienced man like himself did *not* know and for that reason, he could not turn back. To live with his ignorance was a worse fate than destruction or damnation.

But then as soon as he took a step forward, the strange, subterranean wind suddenly seemed to have a voice. It was a new voice, a woman's voice. It seemed to whisper a single word:

Gene . . . gene . . .

"What?" he said through his mask.

The wind was just wind again. And then it wasn't.

Gene . . . ah . . .

"Oh, God," he muttered. "Lord God."

The voice was saying "Jina." The name of the Antarctic researcher who had gone missing. Was she now, somehow, part of this place? Was her mind, her soul, *her knowledge of English* now present in the tiles? Is that how he understood what was being said?

"Release . . . me . . . please!"

The utterance was followed by a blast not unlike the one he had heard earlier, only this one was much nearer. It rocked the world around him, on all sides, shaking pebbles from above, and brought with it a fireball that blazed toward him like a hot, red comet until it suddenly came apart. It didn't explode; it simply seemed to come apart, as though it lacked cohesion. There were no embers raining down; the flaming fist simply vanished, taking the ghostly voice with it.

Mikel's first thought was that there was some kind of gas leak down here, and that he was hallucinating. His second thought was that he had to get out, whether it was to get answers or to escape, he just had to move. He adjusted the lamp on his head and, holding the rim of the tower's mouth, lowered himself in.

At a catastrophic tilt, the stairs no longer functioned as such, so Mikel clambered down them using both hands and feet. He moved very, very fast, concerned about being trapped with any additional fireballs. His peripheral vision caught glimpses of olivine tiles on the walls but this wasn't the time to stop and look at them.

Minutes later—maybe a hundred feet down, Mikel propelled himself through the first opening he found. Pressing himself against a wall and briefly shutting his eyes, he was relieved to find solid ground. When he reopened his eyes, he let out a little laugh. He was inside what looked like a man-made tunnel, not a lava tube, and he could feel that the movement of air was stronger now, even through his balaclava.

The tunnel seemed sculpted, because the walls and arched ceiling were smooth except for two long, raised parallel lines that ran along the rock ceiling like tracks—though he couldn't imagine why tracks would exist anywhere but a floor. They appeared to have bubbled from the overhead rock, as though vacuuformed, and there was a spiral twist to them, like a corkscrew. Had they suspended carriages of some kind?

No, he thought. *Spiral tracks don't make sense.*

Still looking up, he realized that the basalt he'd crouched upon above must have, in its molten state, simply flowed along on top of this tunnel. Was this part of a system that once fueled the Source that they were discussing . . . poured molten lava from one place to another?

He stood upright and was about to step forward to search for the origin of the breeze when an inner voice stopped him. Over the years, he had learned to listen to that voice. This time, though, it insisted. He stayed by the wall and looked around for whatever was causing the internal alarm.

Just over an arm's length away was a mass of olivine tiles placed in the wall roughly at eye level, and a small bubble of rock like those he'd seen in the chamber. The olivine was glowing. With half of his body still edged to the wall, he stepped to the mosaic. To the right he saw an arched entrance, clearly a designed opening and not a lava crack. However, the opening was sealed shut with a mass of basaltic stone—hardened magma.

That didn't make sense, though.

If lava flowed over the tunnel, it should have kept flowing, poured down, and filled much more of this space. Instead, it simply stopped with a curious edge as if heaped against something—but there was nothing to heap against.

Maybe there was a barrier that has since collapsed? he thought. *But what kind of structure could have withstood volcanic heat, other than volcanic rock itself?*

The olivine mosaic was just as mysterious—not just its chemistry but its design. Given the position of the tiles on the wall, Mikel thought they bore a distinct resemblance to an exit sign in a theater—a cautionary or emergency notice of some kind. Could it have been put there by the mysterious Source-tapping Technologists just in case something went wrong? He was habitually on guard against the unscientific impulse to assume one's own culture could automatically explicate another. But upon closer examination the drawings etched into the olivine clearly showed *gestures*. If he was interpreting the drawings correctly, it looked as though the viewer or reader should retrieve something from the bubble of rock and put it on their face.

Mikel touched a small quartz panel on the bubble of rock. The arched entrance immediately opened like the door of a cabinet. Inside, he found a row of hooks holding four sagging, beige bits of what appeared to be remarkably well-preserved cloth masks. He set his teeth against the cold and pulled off a glove to touch one. It didn't feel like fabric. The swatch had an unrecognizable smoothness, definitely not plastic. He would have compared it to skin but it didn't move like skin when he lifted it. Somehow it felt flexible and then oddly structured, but the structure disappeared as soon as he moved it again.

Technologist gear? he wondered.

As Mikel pulled down his balaclava and cautiously placed the mask to his face, its edges cinched themselves to his skin. With some effort he could pry it loose again, but it was designed to be airtight, and suddenly Mikel felt why. His lungs felt full and remained that way, holding a flex like a bodybuilder ballooning a muscle. The mask hadn't appeared to *do* anything—yet what else could have caused this?

He tried to stay calm, rational, as he contemplated the truly foreign technology . . . something so alien it was beyond his ability to analyze or understand. He reminded himself that he was here to catalog and move on. Perhaps the larger picture would help to explain these magnificent parts.

The olivine mosaic provided no other clues. Their pulse seemed slightly faster than before, but he had no way of quantifying that. Mikel carefully turned to face the tunnel again. He could see that several feet ahead there was a larger, closet-size panel with the same olivine design, yet this mosaic was dark and could not be read. Inching himself along the wall, he reached out to open it and discovered within upright stacks of what looked like bobsleds made of Persian rugs, ribbed with some kind of wicker.

Flying carpets, he thought jokingly, reaching for one of them. But who could say whether or not this was where the legend began—carried away by surviving Galderkhaani?

He tugged on it several times, putting real muscle into it, but the contraptions were stuck fast. He shined his light all around them and fumbled between them and around to the back. Although his fingertips sensed protrusions from the wall, there were no vises or hooks. Apparently these could not be obtained as easily as the masks. Perhaps they'd been considered more valuable or, considering that the mosaic wasn't lit, less crucial.

Mikel spent a good ten minutes trying to figure out the attachment mechanism, wiggling the contraptions in every direction but coming up with nothing. Finally, with a grunt of frustration, he gave up. The ancient locks, whatever they were, had worked. He was starting to feel like a bit of an idiot, like an alien discovering New York City, and spending all its time fooling with a broom closet. He closed the panel and turned back to the tunnel.

So, he thought as he shone his head lamp down the corridor in one direction, then the other. *Which way?*

He looked up at the place where he'd entered and calculated that to head toward the continent he wanted to turn to his left.

He took two steps forward and was blown off his feet.

Snapped into survival mode, Mikel hunched into a fetal form as a rush of air rocketed him down the tunnel. The airstream was steady only in velocity, not in dynamics. With no warning it would suddenly twist viciously, then again and again. Several times it slammed him into the wall. He'd fall and then with no respite the wind would pick him up again and hurtle him onward. He wished he hadn't taken off his helmet but so far his arms were enough protection. Then he was slammed especially hard. His head lamp smashed and broke and the tunnel went instantly utterly dark.

A second later the airstream flipped him over and blasted him toward the ceiling, face-first. He kicked out to let his feet take the brunt of the impact and felt the jolt all the way up his spine.

Jesus Christ—

He needed a way out of this. He looked around for anything he could cling to.

Another flip, and then he noticed that he was primarily slamming into the wall on the left. To get back to center, he tried pulling his arms tightly to his sides, straightening his legs. The airstream responded with a push. He must have overshot slightly because he was whipped right out of the airstream directly into another one that slammed him into the opposite wall. Quickly he ducked his head back in the original direction, crossed what he sensed was the centerline, and slammed into the left wall again at an angle that would leave a bruise on his arm from elbow to shoulder.

He tried again directing himself toward the middle with a hell of a lot more caution. He was right, in the exact center of the tunnel the airstream smoothed out and lost some of its turbulence. He caught the sweet spot and stayed there, keeping his head bowed to shield his face. He was moving in the direction he wanted to go and there were no more collisions. For the first time he was able to draw a real breath, as opposed to panicked gasps.

The pneumatic airstream was propelling him at what felt like the speed of a car. Obviously this tunnel had been designed for humans inside contraptions of some kind. *The magic carpets?* But just in case there was some kind of accident, just in case air pressure became a threat, the designers had provided protection for the body. *The mask!* he thought suddenly, and almost laughed with the marvel of it. Mikel had felt his lungs firm up but now he realized that his eardrums must have been protected against increased air pressure too; an eardrum would rupture long before a lung collapsed. Perhaps even his bones and muscles had received a boost, which might explain why he hadn't fractured anything yet. The effects of the mask could have been giving his whole body extra resilience.

Magnificent technology, he thought, humbled, and it would fit in his pocket if he ever headed home. He suddenly felt overwhelmed with the realization that he was plugged into both history and legend. This airstream was Aeolus, the Greek keeper of the wind. Here it was—real, not myth. Undetected by the outside world, perhaps only just revived, and Mikel was in it.

Suddenly, he was weeping.

The tears came fast and puddled inside his goggles, steaming the insides—not that he could see anything anyway. It had finally hit him, after so many close calls. He probably would not make it home. He was underground, in the dark, in one of the most remote spots on Earth. Worse, he was the only person to know one of the secret wonders of the world *and he was going to die in it.*

Eventually his tears stopped and the profound sense of loneliness froze within him. He was plunging through a pneumatic system that was not designed for human bodies and he didn't see how he was going to come to a stop except catastrophically. Whatever resilience the mask had given him, it would not help him survive a full stop at a dead end.

Mikel had always thought that if he saw his life flashing before his eyes, it would be the result of an involuntary spasm, but now he felt that he was choosing to do it, seeing his crazy Basque grandmother, then school, university, grad school, Flora and the Group, the scientists—more than one—whom Mikel had stolen artifacts from. With most of his family either deceased or self-absorbed, he didn't think there was one person on Earth who would mourn him—except maybe Siem, but that would be more a function of feeling overwhelmed by tragedies. Even Flora. She had seemed distraught over the way Arni died and also by his absence—but mourning? No. Mikel couldn't imagine her grieving for him.

Suddenly, Mikel realized that there might be a way through this. The quartz-and-olivine panels he'd left behind: perhaps they were set in terminals. There might be a way to pinpoint the next one, if there was one.

He listened carefully to see if there was any change in the sound of the wind. His senses on high alert, he wondered how long he'd been suffering the now-painful howling. But then he heard it: a slightly hollow sound, deeper than the shrieking in the rest of the tunnel, nearly a full octave lower.

It came and went and then a minute later it came again, passing him faster than he could make a move. But now he knew what to listen for and when the next one came, he was ready.

Damn it, he missed. But he had the rhythm. Timing it out from memory, he anticipated when he would feel the next sound beside him and jackknifed toward it.

Whipping across the airstream into an opening on the side of the tunnel, his body dropped heavily to the ground as the air support disappeared, but it was not nearly as bad as a crash.

Collecting his wits and his breath, Mikel could not believe he was still alive and in one piece. He waited for the tingling and fear to stop shaking him, then he finally got to his knees and then to his feet. The new space welcomed him like Prospero's beach in a tempest, sheltering him from the hell of sound and wind.

Still in total darkness, he felt all around the space and realized it was quite small, with no entrance for lava to have spewed through, but it did have what he recognized as another quartz panel. Once again it popped open under his fingertips and just as he'd predicted, it was one of the "bobsleds." Almost praying, he fumbled around the back of the contraption, trying to free it. Nothing. It was as mysteriously secure as the others.

Many attempts and long minutes later, Mikel cursed and drove his fist into the rock. Feeling claustrophobic and trapped, he began to pry the mask off his face so he could get one damned breath of fresh air. Then, as soon as the mask was in his hands, the area flashed with an extraordinarily bright light. A millisecond later the light was gone. Purple and green afterimages flooded across his eyes. Mikel reached out to feel the niche again to see if he could locate the source of the flash. He was interrupted by a sharp knock on his knee. With a crisp sound like wicker snapping, one of the contraptions had dropped out of the niche and hit his leg, then toppled onto the floor. Mikel had the sudden impression that he'd just been photographed—and approved.

He picked up the sled, praying it hadn't cracked when it was released.

"Let's hope you know what to do."

With one hand on the stone wall to guide him, he stepped back into the tunnel but stopped short of the airstream. He restored the mask to his face, then carefully climbed into the surprisingly firm contraption placing his head in what he saw as a cobra-like hood. He suspected it would fill with wind when he stepped back into the airstream, to carry him along like a sail.

"God I hope I've got this right."

His heart slamming hard, he shuffled to where the sound told him the winds began. Then, like a sledder on a mountainside, he turned ninety degrees and dropped flat into the wind flow.

Incredibly, the slightly concave shape of the struts caused the wind to raise the little vehicle from the floor. There was some initial wobbling, which he corrected by positioning his body in the center. As disconcerting as it was to be moving at this speed in the dark, it wasn't half as bad as going without. The hood protected his ears, fed on the wind, and he was not uncomfortable. And because he was finally using the mechanism that must have been designed for the tunnel, he felt safe.

There was nothing for him to do except stay still, and because his last dose of REM was incomprehensibly long ago and far away, Mikel actually drifted to sleep. He dreamed of a hand stretched toward his bowed head, the fingers pointing at the nape of his neck . . .

He woke to a strange sensation. Still floating in the air, he was moving much more slowly. The sound of the air changed again as well, lower than before. It was as if he was being invited to stop.

"Yes," he answered. *"Yes!"*

Mikel angled his body toward the wall and the nose of the sled went with him, effectively pinwheeling a quarter turn so it was facing into what he presumed was another niche. His weight, held forward, caused it to lurch in a little farther and stop.

Smiling at the simple beauty of the system, Mikel gratefully stood and moved in the direction where he imagined the wall should be, but he doubled over something thigh-high and very hard. He landed on rippled and rocky stone. Crawling forward, his hands found an arched doorway in the wall that was, like the other, sealed shut by a long-solidified lava flow. Mikel pushed against the wall to stand and feeling his way along it, discovered another set of mosaic tiles under his hands, but these weren't glowing either. Exhausted by the thought of having to make one more intense decision, he impulsively pressed hard against the tiles.

With no warning, Mikel was suddenly looking into a pair of hazel eyes. White eyebrows sat close above them and a white beard displayed dozens of carefully made ringlets, swoops, and curls.

Mikel Jasso was looking at Pao, the hesitant, recalcitrant man from the stone and fire chamber. Only now the man was very, very different.

He was somewhat translucent, the images of the real world blurring slightly when he passed. The man was pale and gaunt and moved with strange, ethereal sweeps of his arms. He seemed to control objects around him without touching them.

This man was dead.

CHAPTER 13

Questions flooded Mikel's mind as he watched the spectral figure.

Years before, he had attended a séance at the Group's headquarters. It was an exercise to contact any surviving spirit of the ancients. Artifacts had been positioned around the table and Arni, the synesthete, had served as a very effective medium. Though the effort had failed in terms of opening a useful pathway, everyone felt a shift in the character of the room. There was a weight, a slight pressure of energy like shallow water. It was as if someone—or several someones—had been present who wasn't present before. Flora, ever the one for empirical proof, declared it a form of group hypnosis and that was that.

Mikel had not been convinced. For him, the sensation had remained in the room for days after. Now he knew the truth: she had been wrong. The previous "recording" offered up by the tiles had shown living people. This one showed a soul, a ghost, a poltergeist, whatever label one wanted to attach to it.

This man and his colleagues believed in souls, Mikel told himself. *They tried to bond them, to unify, to rise to some other plane.* Had they succeeded? Had this one intentionally remained behind?

Or is that the fate of a soul that did not bond? he wondered.

Argh! *To be so close yet unable to communicate with this man*, he thought. *To not have the chance to study the room personally—*

"Talk to me!" Mikel yelled.

The figure went about his wraithlike business. With a frustrated cry, Mikel drove the side of his fist into the tile. The image jumped ahead. Now there were two specters in the chamber: Pao and another, an aged woman.

"All right," Mikel said to the tile. "Why did you stop here?"

There didn't seem to be anything exceptional about the moment. *Had the projection jumped to this spot because there was some kind of bookmark*? Then, suddenly, Mikel realized something that sent a jolt through his belly. *Or—*

Is it real? Is this happening now?

His chest felt heavy under the weight of the thought even as his heart and mind raced.

He hit the tile again. The image did not change. *That could only mean that this was no longer an image.* Was he watching figures who were present *now*, behind the tiles. Were the stones relaying activity that was taking place behind them: the actions of spirits in the present day who had been here, he surmised, for untold millennia. He recognized one as Pao, the other was in shadows, barely visible.

As his eyes adjusted to the scene he saw more that confirmed his assessment. There were skeletons on the floor, close to one another. The bones had crumbled almost completely away, but Mikel could still make out the supraorbital ridge of a skull defining the hollow of an eye, and the arch of a pelvis. He felt the cold shock of realization. The skeletal remains belonged to these two souls.

Looking closer, he saw that the spirits were moving among scrolls and piles of stones with markings that appeared to shift and move, like animated drawings. Each time they did, Mikel noticed a barely perceptible flicker among the tiles before him: here and there a glow brightened slightly, as if they were acknowledging—or recording?—the change. That did, after all, appear to be their function.

The two spirits were speaking. Though Mikel was still trying to understand the mechanism by which living spirits were visible to him, the words they spoke were clear and comprehensible. Pao paused to look at a petroglyph.

"We cannot afford to spend more time," he said.

"We cannot afford to leave," said the other—a woman, bent and small, her voice low and grave. It took Mikel a moment to realize that this was Rensat, the woman who had seemed much closer to Vol in the last "vision."

This Pao, too, was much older than he'd been in the chamber. The beard was still lush but age had whitened it even more. His face was etched with deep lines and his voice cracked.

Suddenly Rensat moved from the shadows.

"I will not go without knowing what happened to Vol," she said. "And we still have work to do, a traitor to locate."

"And . . . a mysterious savior, perhaps," Pao said, more resigned than hopeful. He turned back to the stones moving again from one petroglyph to another.

But something else was different, something more than just the jump forward in time. The air around Mikel himself felt hollow, like the low-pressure system created by an approaching storm. Someone, some*thing*, was also present in his time, in the chamber. He wanted to look around but he did not want to take his eyes from the living history. The only experience Mikel could compare it to was the séance, the way the atmosphere in the room had shifted: it felt empty of life, even their own, yet full of something else.

Mikel pulled off his mask, took a deep breath, unzipped a pocket, and stowed the mask inside. He hesitated, preparing himself for the onrush of that feeling again before placing his hands on either side of the tiles. His fingers fidgeted, until he realized there was something for them to fidget with. The bank of tiles was loose. With a quick push and pull, the tiles came off as one whole section in his hands. It didn't feel accidental. The panel was designed to be removed, and there were tiles around the back as well.

He looked again at the projection of the room. The two people inside seemed suddenly uneasy.

"What was that?" Rensat asked.

"I don't know," Pao said. "But we must go. It is time."

Rensat shook her head and returned to her work. With a glance toward Mikel—and eyes that appeared to be searching, seeking—Pao sighed and then also resumed his studies.

What are you looking for . . . still, after all these eons? Mikel wondered.

He looked at the panel of tiles in his hands. They were pulsing and burning, not just with heat but with light. He had the sense that if he screamed at them, into them, the ghosts would hear. But Mikel was methodical. He was not there yet, not ready to act rashly . . . irrationally.

If any of this can be called rational, he thought.

Mikel set the tiles down and rooted his fingers into the empty slots where they had been fixed. The ghosts didn't change, reinforcing the idea that they were present in the moment. But by accident, fumbling around in the opening and perhaps activating another tile, he revealed a map. Ancient, it seemed, with unfamiliar contours. It appeared like a scrim between himself and the specters, and then was gone.

"Damn it—I *want* that!"

He jabbed his fingers in all directions, but nothing. And then he hit a sweet spot. Images flashed this way and that like minnows. Airships with nets strung between them, plumes of lava shooting into the sky, crops growing in clouds, seagoing vessels, faces, pyres, alabaster buildings, plans for buildings and then—the map was back. Mikel froze his fingers. Relaxing his hand slightly without so much as moving his fingertips, he glided the map into a prominent place. Swelling—seeming to *anticipate* what he wanted before he struggled to achieve it—the map filled his vision, layering across the tunnel and glowing blue. It was beautiful. Its key elements were ten black dots or points grouped in one area—settlements, towns, cities, hunting grounds . . . he had no idea which. There were also orange dots clustered around one region. He memorized the pattern. If he could figure out where he was, he could find the others.

Mikel took a moment to regard the image in its entirety, continental contours familiar in some spots, utterly unrecognizable in others. Still, there was no doubt what he was looking at.

Galderkhaan, he thought. After all these years, after *centuries*, the Group would have it.

Mikel Jasso did not have an ego, not in the same way Flora did, but there was pride of accomplishment: he would be the one to bring it home.

The emotion of the moment was overwhelming but there was no time to savor it. Not far from the orange spots was a fine, fine series of lines in red, blue, and black. He concentrated on the network and it expanded.

So you can *read my mind*, he thought incredulously. The mechanism didn't matter right now, but he couldn't help but wonder what else the tiles could do. And *how* they did it. Clearly, the infinite possibilities in the arrangement of the stones brought up different information—an impossibly complex but brilliantly compact data storage system.

In one spot on the map he recognized the path he had taken. It was black. He pinpointed his location generally and mentally marked the spidery legs of the tunnels. He assumed that blue meant water, red—magma? He wondered if those substances still flowed there.

Probably not; tens of thousands of years would have altered the pools or bodies of water from where they'd originated. Mikel let go of that spot on the wall and the map disappeared.

He carefully replaced the panel and positioned his hands in their previous place on the tiles. Pao and Rensat filled his vision as before, the room reappearing as if the tiles had gone transparent—or, more likely, were projecting data like the big TVs at sporting events, only at a far greater level of detail. He wondered if they were doing the same thing on the other side, feeding data to the Galderkhaani. The two were in slightly different positions; of course they were. The present day had unfolded while he studied the map.

Once more mentally present, Mikel was swept up in the shuddering feeling of unearthliness. The tiles also felt it, felt something, or maybe they were causing it: the glow intensified slightly.

What's going on? Mikel thought uneasily.

He looked into the ghostly room. Rensat was closing a door in the glass panel behind her, having just come from the massive chamber.

"I do not understand," she said. "You felt it, I felt it, yet the tiles tell me there is no one else out there."

Are they feeling it too? Mikel wondered. *Or are they somehow sensing me?*

"Is it possible?" Pao asked, a trace of hope in his voice. "After so much time, their eternal silence—is it *possible*?"

"I would like to think that devotion is rewarded," Rensat said with a bitter smile. "But why would the Candescents wait until now to reveal themselves? Now, when we are very nearly beaten."

"Perhaps that is the reason," Pao suggested. He raised his shoulders weakly. "Who can know the mind and will of the Candescents?"

Unlike Pao's, the woman's voice and expression seemed utterly without hope. "Everyone has been so elusive for so long. The traitor.

Our dear Vol. This witch or ascended soul or demonic Technologist—whatever she was who tore the rest apart at the end." She looked at Pao. "Maybe it *is* time to depart."

Pao looked around. "Our existence mattered, though, Rensat. We have failed to save Galderkhaan but we proved the *cazh*, finally. We remained bonded." His eyes sought hers lovingly. "That is not a small thing."

"I still feel as though I have failed." Rensat smiled thinly. "We are denied the higher planes. We are denied the fellowship and richness of others, of rising to the cosmic plane. *That* was the reason for the *cazh*. That was the reason you joined us that first time when we were much younger."

"I stayed because I loved you as I loved Vol," Pao said, gently correcting her.

Rensat hugged herself. "I am afraid to leave, Pao. I am afraid to face an eternity in this way."

"At least we are transcended, not merely ascended," Pao pointed out. "We are not in silent isolation."

Mikel recognized the words from the library. Ascendant . . . transcendent . . . Candescent. Was there a hierarchy, like angels? Was this the root of all faith? There was still so much he did not understand in just the few things they had said. A witch—what kind of aberration was that?

Without realizing it, Mikel's hands had moved, like they were resting on the planchette of a Ouija board. Suddenly another image, this one clearly a window into the past, swept across his field of view. Momentarily disoriented, then horrified, he was looking at a courtyard, hearing human screams. The floor of the courtyard was full of carvings—and stones. Olivine tiles. All around him people in yellow and white robes were engulfed in walls of fire. They were shrieking in anguish as they died a torturous death. Feeling sick, Mikel forced himself to keep looking, to see the volcano erupting in the distance.

A caldera filled with lava, he thought. *One of the orange spots on the map?*

As he let his mind absorb the spectacle of people burning, their souls clinging to their tortured, disintegrating bodies, their hands linked and their melting tongues trying hard to utter words, he experienced some of the fury of the volcano. But this was not just a window to a disaster. It showed more: bodies falling from ethereal shapes—*souls*? Some were only there for a moment before blinking out. Others rose away in pairs.

He looked desperately through the image for the Galderkhaani Pao and Rensat had been discussing: the witch, the demonized figure, the one who would not seem to belong. His eyes were drawn to a dim figure above the flames, above the city, hovering in the sky like a banshee of Irish lore. He tried to bring her into focus but lost the image when his fingers returned to their previous position.

Pao and Rensat returned, standing still and silent like clothes stored for the winter. Is this how they had spent part of their endless time as earthbound spirits? In some kind of contemplative stasis? Did time even have any meaning for them? Without periods of sleep to measure the hours, did the destruction of Galderkhaan seem no more than a few decades distant?

Mikel began to search through the images again, posing himself a scientific question: here on this side of Antarctica there were no volcanoes. The bedrock had long since been mapped. Yet if he was here watching history, there *had* been a volcano, at the very least the remnants of a caldera somewhere. Unless—

Absolute devastation, he answered himself. The mountain must have been leveled, then swallowed by the sea, then ice.

Rensat and Pao began to move again. They were still very silent. Suddenly, Mikel felt a very low, slow vibration pass through the room. The walls themselves were vibrating. The tiles were becoming almost blindingly luminous. The sound was deeper, much more internally loud than the erupting volcano had been. Amazingly, as Mikel's body wavered under its force, he watched Pao and Rensat tremble in exactly the same manner and motion. Mikel felt terror return, stronger than before.

"What was *that*?" he said to himself.

Rensat asked the same thing, a moment behind him.

"I don't know," Pao admitted.

Behind Mikel, the tunnel began to glow with a dull orange. He heard a distant cry from the direction in which he'd encountered Jina.

Something was coming. Something—tracking him or the other two? Was that what Rensat and Pao had felt, what she went in the other room to find?

Rensat looked in Mikel's direction. "There is another . . . no, several others," she said.

Pao studied his companion. "Rensat, is it possible that it is Enzo?"

"How?" Rensat asked. "She was lost, her mission unfinished. And the ascended cannot communicate with anyone, not in her plane, not in ours."

"What if she has found another voice?" Pao asked with rising enthusiasm. "What if she has found a body?"

"But how? I don't understand."

"You remember Sogera, his experiments with braziers," Pao said. "Enzo was there, I remember her clearly. She saw how the flaming sunbird continued to hiss as her flesh was consumed."

"But not her soul," the woman said. "Blessed Enzo, if it is so!"

Rensat began to share Pao's renewed—*fervor* was the word that came to Mikel's mind. It was as if they were born again, their eyes and expressions almost manic.

The rumbling remained constant, the glow grew brighter, and now the heat began to rise. Mikel began to feel like he imagined the poor figures in the vision had felt . . . only in slow motion. Helpless as the fire neared, with nowhere to turn, except to each other. He wondered if the tiles had somehow anticipated his future, showed him something he needed to know, to experience by proxy—death throes by fire—in order to escape his own possible fate.

Dear god, he thought. *To die without sharing what I've discovered—*

That mustn't be, it *would* not be. If it were true that the stones had some kind of access to his mind, they might also save him. He looked at the ghostly couple and placed his hands in the widely splayed position he had in the previous chamber.

Do something! he yelled in his mind.

But he wasn't sure what he wanted to do, except escape, and, obviously, the tiles could not teleport him free.

Looking into the room Mikel realized, suddenly, that the material Pao and Rensat had been studying was an instruction manual for the tiles. His eyes scanned them desperately for guidance. He saw one figure walking—and a wall opening.

Right, he thought. *The tiles can be removed.* He looked them over from bottom to top, side to side. *Which one is the key?*

Now a tile just to the right of his face began to glow brighter. Without hesitation he placed both hands on it, just as the figure in the drawing did. One hand above, one below, fingers spread. Nothing happened. He moved his fingers slightly. Then again. Then again.

Come on, Mikel!

All the while the heat grew against his back with a predatory ferocity: this wasn't a fireball spit up by the earth. Something was coming toward him and bringing with it a shrieking victim. Perhaps, as Rensat had said, it was Enzo—with her newfound and unwilling voice, Jina Park.

Another minute shift of his fingers and, almost at once, the tiles opened like the door to the cave of the forty thieves. He surged through like a bull, the tiles snapping shut behind him, locking him in and blocking the fury on the other side. The heat was gone.

Mikel came to a skidding halt, standing upright in a moldering room with dry powdered bones beneath his feet and the living tiles bright before him. The smell of something akin to gunpowder hung in the air like incense, tart and inexplicable.

And there was something else: he was not alone. Before him stood the two spirits of the dead Galderkhaani.

Spirits who were *seeing* him.

CHAPTER 14

It was dark in Caitlin's apartment but even darker inside her head. She refused to allow her fears to drag her into despair, which meant doing what she always did: fighting back. As much as she wanted to be alone, watching over her son, she knew she shouldn't be. Which was why she let Ben stay.

Caitlin kept Jacob home from school, something she didn't like to do, but after his experience the day before, she thought it prudent. The vice principal concurred. Ben called in sick.

Sitting cross-legged on the floor while Jacob read in his room, they had spent the morning and early afternoon reviewing everything they knew of Galderkhaan, trying to figure out the meaning of what Jacob had said: *"en dovi."*

"Those letter combinations don't appear in any of the language we've encountered so far," Ben said conclusively. "Which leaves us two possibilities. First: they aren't Galderkhaani. Jacob might have been speaking English. Or maybe phonetic French. That novel he's reading, by Jules Verne, is in both languages."

"What's the second possibility?" Caitlin asked.

"The second possibility," Ben said, "is that they are proper nouns. The names of places or people."

Caitlin considered that. "I wish I'd paid more attention to names when I was back there," she said. "Then I could be of some freaking *use* here."

"Hey, hey, hey," Ben cautioned. "Beating yourself up: not gonna help."

Caitlin nodded. "Maybe I should go back and steal a goddamn telephone directory and a dictionary."

"Not the worst idea I've heard," Ben told her. "I wonder if they had something other than scrolls and tablets to write on. Just because they were pre-everything, doesn't mean they were as relatively primitive as the ancient civilizations we know."

While they spoke, Ben had been passing a large, green glass orb back and forth between his hands nonstop. The piece was beautiful, with an almost spectral aura created by the way the lines caught the light and shone white within the green. An artisan acquaintance of Caitlin's had crafted it years before, using a kiln to bake the glass sphere and then submerging the orb in ice water.

Caitlin finally stopped him with a gentle hand.

"Sorry—making you nervous?" he asked.

"No, nothing like that," she said. "But you keep doing it, you may induce a trance."

He stopped at once but he didn't put the orb aside. They just stared at each other.

"Well, hell," Ben said after a moment.

"I know," Caitlin agreed. "When all else fails, do what's left."

Ben couldn't know how real Caitlin's experiences were but they both knew, in that moment, they weren't going to make any further progress unless he erred on the side of taking it very seriously. Though Ben couldn't deny that he'd walked the rim of some of those experiences, he had said repeatedly through the afternoon that he preferred to seek a more logical, analytical approach to the questions they had to answer.

"I don't know, Cai," he said.

"I do," she said. "When it's the only proactive option on the table, you take it."

Ben agreed that he would help to re-create an environment similar to what Caitlin had experienced before at the UN and see where it took her as long as she didn't use the *cazh*.

"But you keep your hands away from me," he said. "You can try any of the other techniques you know—hypnosis, energy direction, astrally projecting above the city—anything, but not that."

"Why? You afraid it might work and you'll be stuck with me for eternity?"

"You know I'd sign on for that," he said, correcting her. "But right now we're exploring, trying to help you and Jacob. That doesn't include buying a one-way ticket to Neverland. Isn't that exclusively what the *cazh* was designed for? Knock-knock-knocking on heaven's door?"

"We don't exactly know, do we?" she asked. "That's one of the things we're trying to find out."

"No, it isn't," he said. "We're trying to find out who may—*may*—have their hooks in Jacob and why. That's it for now. Are we on the same page?"

"Don't be dumb," she said.

"What do you mean?"

"Of course this is primarily about Jacob but if I see something interesting, I'm going to check it out!"

"No! Caitlin, I am not going to try to explain to a 911 dispatcher that my friend has fallen into the past and can't get up. If you can't agree to that, then get yourself another playmate."

Caitlin sighed hard. She could not help thinking that all the information about Galderkhaan was holistic: if she unraveled the riddle of their belief system she could understand everything about them and help Jacob at the same time.

But Caitlin put a hand on top of his. "All right. I mean it. You're absolutely right. The chant isn't appropriate for this situation. I have to get back to Galderkhaan and have a look around, that's all."

"Okay, then," Ben said, smiling.

Following her instructions, Ben held the orb before her. He moved it slowly, the light shifting in her eyes, in the back of her eyes, in her brain. Nearby sounds were magnified: his breath, her breath, the cat moving away.

And then she was back.

"Shit and shit," she said.

"What's happening? Or not?"

"I'm sorry," she said. "Something's holding me back."

He pushed his face toward her. "Don't let it. I'm here. You won't get lost there, I promise. Hey, remember? I've been down that road with you, Cai. I haven't lost a trance walker yet."

Caitlin smiled and nodded sweetly. Ben smiled back.

"Ready for takeoff?" he asked.

In response, she relaxed and stared into the orb. He began to move it again.

Almost at once, the tendrils of the glass turned from green to red. The red—

"Contrails," she said softly. "I see . . . fingers of color, like smoke."

Without stopping, Ben stretched his fingers to the dining room table and grabbed his phone. He began to record. He felt like the Infant of Prague, the orb resting in his cupped left hand, the phone upright in his right. He couldn't help but wonder if every archetype in the history of humankind repeated itself and was perhaps traceable to Galderkhaan.

And then a sudden iciness fell on the room, as though someone had turned an air conditioner on low. Ben felt the shift instantly and then watched Caitlin's hair begin to rise, as if reacting to static electricity. In the distance, Arfa bolted into the bathroom, to his litter box.

"There is ice . . . below," Caitlin said. "Acres . . . more acres . . . miles . . . peaceful."

She forced herself to look back up, back at the contrails.

"Red . . . above and . . . and behind," Caitlin went on. "Fire!" she said more urgently. "Flames . . . Enzo! No!"

Caitlin's eyes were still open, staring. They grew wider. Her breath came faster, harder. Her hands were reaching for something, holding something, pulling—ropes? She looked like a fisherman pulling his boat to its moorings.

"You've killed us! *Why!?*"

Caitlin began swatting at her face, as though she were surrounded by gnats. She winced with pain.

"The name!" she said. "I will tell you . . . tell you . . ."

And then Caitlin screamed in her mouth. It rose up her throat and stuck at the top, as though she were vomiting.

Ben discarded the orb and phone down and took her hands in his, holding them tight. Almost at once he released one hand as if it were electrified: Ben had forgotten his own admonition. He did not want to give any Galderkhaani access to the *cazh*.

Even holding one of her hands, anchoring Caitlin in the present, caused the cold to begin to dissipate.

"No, Dovit! Let me go!" the woman wept.

"Cai, it's Ben!" he said softly but insistently. "Cai, where are you?"

"Falling from the sky!" she said, gasping. "I told Enzo . . . why did she do it? *It will never work!*"

And then Caitlin was back, panting, leaning forward, collapsing into Ben's arms.

"I've got you," he said.

"I . . . thought I died!"

"It wasn't you," he told her.

"I know, but I felt it. I *felt* it!"

"Who was it?"

Caitlin shook her head firmly. "Her name was Azha. We were in the air, in an airship of some kind, and it was on fire."

"Who is 'we'?" Ben asked.

"A man and a woman—the woman was on fire, burning the ship with her own body. I couldn't stop her."

"It's over," Ben said. "And you got what you went back for: names. That's what Jacob was trying to say."

Caitlin pulled back. "Ben, is that woman here?"

"You mean talking through Jacob?"

"No, *now*. Did you see anything?"

"No, but I felt cold," he admitted. "Very, very cold. I saw your hair rise, like it did at the UN. And the cat ran away."

Caitlin continued to breathe heavily. She jerked her head around as if looking for something.

"What is it?"

"She's here. She is *here*."

"Caitlin, no—we're alone."

Caitlin got up, ran down the hall, putting her ear to Jacob's door. He was reading aloud. Captain Nemo was having a hard time of things with *his* ship but Jacob sounded fine. She turned and shuffled back unsteadily, falling into the nearest chair, and stared at the floor. After a moment, her eyes rose and found Ben.

"It was Maanik all over again," she said.

"No, it was not that. What you saw was an old vision of fire."

"I don't mean that," Caitlin said. "I don't mean they were souls trying to do a ritual. The woman I saw, the woman I was, is trying to communicate something now, through a child. *Why?* Why Jacob?"

Ben crawled toward her. He took up her hands again. "Maybe it's got nothing to do with a child, or with trauma as it did last time," he suggested. "Maybe they're doing it because they know you will listen."

Caitlin stared at Ben and nodded. "Okay. That may be true. But . . . listen to *what*?"

"I don't know," he said, picking up his phone.

"Did you at least get any new words?"

"Just the names. Which is pretty considerable, if you think about it. We can start building a who's who with Enzo and Dovit—"

No sooner had the names been uttered than the burst of cold returned with a plummeting shriek, a whistle that could have been the wind or a scream. It swept around them like an unbottled genie until they felt as if they were inside a column of ice.

"No," Caitlin yelled, scowling at a point between her and Ben. *"No!"*

The wind stopped and an instant later Jacob cried out. Caitlin bolted from the chair and ran to his room. Squatting by his bedside, she looked into his eyes to make sure he was present.

He was. His eyes were searching behind Caitlin, but they were not lost in an ancient place. They were darting through the room as though he were looking for a loose parakeet.

"What is it, hon?" she asked, touching his hair with one hand as she signed with the other. "Did you just call me?"

"I thought there was a snowman," he said.

"A snowman?" Caitlin said, forcing a smile. "Tell me about him."

His eyes stopped moving and narrowed in contemplation. "Maybe not a snowman," he said. "A snow woman. A pretty lady made of ice."

That was all Jacob said before lying back on the bed. Caitlin did not press for more. She placed the covers under his chin and then lay beside him. Ben, who had been observing from the doorway, smiled and left them alone.

Mother and son stayed that way for quite some time as late afternoon shaded to dusk.

Ben stood staring out the window, where the last of a brilliant red sunset was ebbing from the dark sky.

"What do we do next?" he asked after she finally emerged from the bedroom.

Caitlin shook her head. "I hate to say it, but I'm thinking the next move is up to a snow woman."

Ben made an unhappy face. "I don't feel good about leaving you here."

"You know, I'm okay with that. Despite all that's happened with

Jacob," Caitlin said. "This time I didn't get the feeling that . . . whoever I was wanted to hurt him, or me. Any of us."

Ben's mouth twisted slightly. "Let me ask you this—and I need an honest answer. Would you have come back if I hadn't brought you back?"

"I don't know, Ben."

"So what will you do if it happens again?"

"I don't know that either, Ben."

"Two 'Ben's," he said. "In Caitlin speak, that means 'Time to go.' "

"It is, but only because I'm really beat," she said. "I'm gonna make dinner for me and the lad and try not to think about any of this tonight."

Ben nodded in accord. That was easy to do when there were no other options.

She thanked him for his help and for taking the time off from work and kissed him good-bye on the cheek. He gave her a brief, part-sad, part-wry look of *That's it?* before she shooed him out the door. The click of the latch sounded uncommonly loud, like the door of a walk-in freezer.

Caitlin stood by the window and looked at the remaining crescent of sun, the same sun that had set over Galderkhaan.

She woke Jacob for dinner and together they made franks and beans; why was it that passed gas always lifted boys' spirits? When they finished, they channel surfed for a while until Jacob fell asleep with his head in her lap. Not without effort, Caitlin carried him to bed. She wondered how many more times she'd be able to do this. The kid was getting big. She wondered if he would be six-foot-five big like his father, or five foot six like her father.

A pointless mom-exercise, she thought, smiling at herself. But right now, pointless felt good.

The apartment was quiet. The whole city felt quiet. Caitlin looked at lamplights across the street, figures sitting down to meals, and thought about the people she and Ben had passed on their walk toward Paley Park. Everyone had seemed remarkably buoyant. It had been such a difference in tenor from the weeks when Kashmir had verged on nuclear war. Individual confidence had surged back. People's lives were brightening here despite the darkness in other parts of the world.

The observation gave Caitlin no comfort. The opposite, in fact. The last recession had driven home the fact that confidence too easily spawns rashness, then crashes, then despair. She felt like she was seeing the beginning of the next end already.

She sat on the couch and rubbed her temples, trying to relax. It wasn't coming. Of course not: there was unfinished business. Whether it was her own life or the life of a patient, she could never compartmentalize that easily.

Caitlin was almost grateful when her phone rang and though her screen gave only a number, she accepted the call.

"Yes?"

"Dr. O'Hara?" said a young woman's voice.

"Yes, who is this?"

"It's Maanik Pawar."

Nausea and fear filled her throat. Caitlin hunched and both hands involuntarily clutched the phone in panic. *It's starting again!* her mind screamed. She fought hard to sound natural.

"Maanik, hello! It's so nice to hear your voice. How are you doing?"

"Really well!"

Caitlin suddenly felt like crying. "Tell me!" she said.

"I've gained back all the weight I lost and you should see my arms. My papa arranged for a doctor to use this stem cell spray stuff. They said it was the fastest recovery they'd seen so far. My skin completely healed from the scratches in like a day. Well, they were more than just scratches, I guess."

"Gouges," Caitlin said very gently.

"Yes." Maanik sounded thoughtful, not upset.

"That's, well, incredible, Maanik. How are you sleeping? Are you having any strange dreams or even daydreams?"

Maanik laughed. "I've been daydreaming about becoming a bioengineer instead of a diplomat, does that count?"

Caitlin laughed. "Sorry, no. By the way, you know I spoke to your parents last week."

"They told me."

"They said you didn't seem to remember anything that had happened?"

"Yeah," Maanik said. "To be honest, I'm kind of relieved about that, Dr. O'Hara. Do *you* think my memory will return?"

"No," Caitlin said. "At least it hasn't for others who experienced trauma like that."

"Anyway, I wanted to call and thank you personally. I don't know what you did for me specifically but you saved my life. I don't think my parents were exaggerating when they said that. And I'm so grateful."

Caitlin couldn't say anything for a moment. She was wiping tears from her eyes.

"How are you?" Maanik asked, her voice full of concern. "You experienced these things with me, right?"

"Fine," Caitlin lied. "I absorb a little something from all my patients. I'm used to it. Lots of lead shielding."

"My father has that too," Maanik said. "I hope to be like you both."

"I do hope you'll keep in touch sometimes," Caitlin said, sad to let her go.

"Absolutely. Okay, I have to go now—"

"Quickly, Maanik," Caitlin said, "how is Jack London?"

"Oh." Maanik was silent for a long moment. "Well . . ."

Caitlin's stomach dropped through the floor. She remembered Maanik's mother threatening to put him down.

"He was a little crazy last week," Maanik continued.

Caitlin was about to ask what kind of crazy, but Maanik kept going.

"We decided to put him through obedience school again," the

young woman said. "He had his first class yesterday and he was a superstar, so we think that will do the trick."

"That's good," Caitlin exhaled.

"And now I have to go," Maanik said. "But thank you, Dr. O'Hara. Thank you so much."

They said good-bye and ended the call, and Caitlin sat there for a few minutes holding her phone like a warm mug of tea. The words had been comforting but the reconnection, even through the phone, had been unsettling. She was trying to understand why.

Unbidden, a thought occurred to her.

The cazh *got the Priests' minds out of the way. Without it, they were no better at focusing than the rest of us.*

And Maanik's phone call had gotten Caitlin's mind out of the way. Distraction, as she well knew, could be a useful psychological process, helpful for finding answers. Just stop thinking and it will come . . .

She and Ben had spent hours talking and thinking. Time to stop.

Caitlin put the phone down and uncurled herself on the couch, feet flat on the floor. She was going to begin with what she knew: the gesture she'd learned from Atash on his hospital deathbed. Caitlin crooked her right arm over her torso with her right fingers pointing toward her left shoulder. Then she angled her left hand to point away from her knees toward the floor, and immediately she felt something lift away from her left shoulder in a wave. The Galderkhaani gesture for "big water"—"ocean"—had worked. All of her intense emotions washed from her head down her spine and seemed to fly away from the base of her back. For the first time since she had helped Odilon, she felt in perfect balance.

She looked up and her eyes fell inexorably on her green globe. As if the orb felt her eyes upon it, the glass responded. The white web of lines inside elongated past the curve of the sphere into the air. It looked like the fin of a sailfish, glowing in light that wasn't really there, now that the living room had darkened into full night. It was so beautiful Caitlin wanted to infiltrate it, be part of it. The lines extended forth, growing through the room until they filled half of it, with some of their tips touching Caitlin's throat. This was different from before. There was no other person present, just . . . joy? She found herself singing in her mind. She and the orb were in tune with each other.

The music of the spheres, she thought. *The harmonics of the universe*. She didn't feel safe but she felt comforted, somehow. Not with a spirit but not alone.

Maybe you've been cazhed *with someone without knowing it!* she thought, not entirely in jest.

In Iran, Vahin had suggested that the psychiatrist's closeness to patients who had been traumatized essentially bonded her to them, and through them to past events—the trauma of Galderkhaan.

Caitlin returned her focus to the living room. In memory, not vision, she saw Vahin drinking jasmine tea across from his red-patterned wall in Iran—but inexplicably, an image of Madame Langlois followed with even more intensity. Cigar smoke wafted between her and Caitlin.

This is not of Vodou, the priestess had said toward the end of Caitlin's time in Jacmel.

And that, Caitlin thought now, *is why I need you here, someone here who understands. I need an anchor.*

Holding the madame's gaze through the smoke in her mind, Caitlin closed her eyes. Unbidden, she still felt the fingerlike span of light from the orb. Relenting, giving in to their touch, she gathered her deepest sense of self and slowly spun it forward, merging with the orb, while drawing on the energy of those she had met and bonded with over the last week—

And then the energy of another person was back, the newest bond, the dying woman falling from the clouds, fire all around. But in that fire was something else. Something green appeared in her mind's eye. Not a bottle green. Paler, more yellow in it, tessellated and glowing with its own light.

The object was oblong, a tile of some kind pulsing with incredible power, like a magnet whose arcs of energy were visible. It blazed through the dying woman, all but obliterated that image, and dominated Caitlin's mind with other images.

Beckoning. Somehow, the object was pulling her toward it.

Caitlin suddenly felt an enormous pressure on her eardrums followed by rapidly increasing pain. The pain was not *in* the vision: it was real. The green object, too, seemed to have substance, presence, *power*.

Break the connection, she told herself.

With a physical jerk that nearly sent her sprawling from the sofa, she found herself back in the living room. She was disoriented, frightened, and even more so when she realized she was looking at a woman—a woman with short black hair, the woman who had shoved her backpack in the door of Caitlin's subway train and then had wiped the air, flooding Caitlin's mind.

And here she was in Caitlin's apartment, down the hall from where Jacob lay sleeping. Caitlin pushed herself up from the couch. As she came to standing, the woman wiped the air before her, propelling Caitlin backward as if she'd been punched in the gut.

And then she was gone.

CHAPTER 15

Mikel's brain was a suddenly empty vessel.

The two souls from Galderkhaan gazed into the eyes of the living man who had invaded the ruins of their city.

Rensat spoke first with some disbelief. "You are alive."

"Yes," Mikel said. "So far." He added, "I think. How—how are we communicating?"

"The stones in the corridor," she said with pleasure. "You physically activated them. They have connected us."

Pao circled the intruder as if he were a specimen in a jar. Perhaps he was. "You have a stone of your own?"

Mikel followed where he was pointing. "That—that's a radio," he said. "I use it to communicate with fellow men but only on the surface."

"Why did you enter this room?" the Galderkhaani man asked.

"Something was out there," Mikel said. "A presence of some kind." He shook his head. "Forgive me, but—how am I understanding you? I do not speak Galderkhaani."

"The stones in this library have the wisdom of language," Pao said.

"But my language did not exist when you did, when they were . . . made," Mikel said.

"Then someone who spoke your tongue has ascended near this place," Pao told him. "What the living knew, the stones now know."

"How? By what mechanism?" Mikel asked.

Pao started to answer but a touch from Rensat stopped him.

"Your attire, the materials are—unfamiliar to us," Rensat said. "Where are you from?"

"The north," he answered. "Far from here, both in time and place."

"By your reckoning, how old are we?" she asked.

"Judging from the map I saw out there, the contours of your coastline are familiar yet they had not been defined by the end of the Ice Age. That would make it about thirty thousand years ago."

"An 'ice age,'" Pao said, shaking his head. "The Technologists were right about that, at least."

"Yes, and they should have stopped where they did," Rensat said.

"Please explain," Mikel implored. "There is so much I do not know. These Technologists—what were they trying to do?"

"In the beginning of their rise to power, they sought to tap heat from inside the earth, to melt the ice and protect our city," Rensat said. "That project was accomplished and it led to the development of a larger idea. To burn their way to Candescence."

"What you were discussing with the other man, Vol, at the ritual," Mikel said.

Pao's eyes showed surprise. "You saw that too?"

Mikel nodded.

"Have you seen Vol elsewhere?" Pao said, pressing him.

Mikel shook his head.

Pao and Rensat exchanged glances. A flicker of hope had risen and quickly perished.

"You've mentioned the Candescents several times," Mikel said. "Who were they?"

"Who *are* they," Rensat said, gently correcting him.

"I'm sorry," Mikel said sincerely. That was clumsy. He had to be careful.

"They are unimaginably ancient beings who inhabit the cosmic plane," Rensat explained.

"So you *believe*," Pao added. "We do not know."

"The tiles," she said confidently.

"That is *one* explanation for the power of the stones," Pao said. "Some of us agree with the Technologists that the tiles are simply minerals that vibrate in alignment with the planetary poles, that by some unknown mechanism they store and release everything they encounter along those lines: the energy of human thought, of animal memory, of all that has ever been witnessed or conceived."

Mikel thought of Flora's vectors. He was with the Technologists on this one.

"Some of us do not believe in miraculous physical 'mechanisms' that have defied understanding," Rensat said. "The stones could not exist without intelligent creation."

Mikel had heard this very same argument many times in many contexts; it would not be resolved here and now.

He had the sudden urge to drop it on the conference table before the Group, let them finger through it like an unassembled jigsaw puzzle.

Pao interrupted his thought process. "You said something was out there."

Mikel nodded. "Fire. The . . . the ghost of a woman who died recently, on the ice. Burned to death."

"You saw this—this 'ghost,' the ascended one?" Pao asked.

"No, she said her name," Mikel answered. "I knew of her."

"Did she say anything else?" Rensat asked.

"Yes," Mikel told her. "She said, 'Release me, please.'" He studied the two. "What was holding her?"

The spirits did not answer. But he remembered something they had been discussing earlier.

"Is it your 'blessed Enzo'?" Mikel asked. "Is Enzo in the flame?"

"It is to be hoped," Rensat said.

Pao regarded her sternly. "Enough!"

They stood mutely, stubbornly. That line of questioning was closed but Mikel had a great many other things he wanted to ask.

"Tell me about the Source," he said.

"The Source is everywhere in Galderkhaan," Pao told him. "Tunnels of magma connecting pool to pool."

The orange spots on the map, Mikel realized. "The winds I rode to get here," he said. "Those tunnels were conduits for lava?"

"Yes," Pao said. "The entrances to the tunnels were placed where the winds were fierce and could be channeled underground, used to drive the sails of the digging apparatus."

"They were expanded in secret, like so much of what the Technologists did," Rensat added. "It is why the Source was so much stronger than any of us knew. No one realized the pools were already linked."

Pao approached Mikel. "It is one of the reasons we have remained here," he said. "We seek the identity of the one who turned the Source on. Do you know anything of that?"

"No," Mikel said. "And—why should that matter now?"

The two souls fell silent. Their selective cooperation was starting to frustrate him. They were like Flora, always holding secret cards.

"Pao, Rensat—I don't know much, but I've learned enough to know that there are inordinately dangerous forces here. I need to understand much more in order to protect my people."

"How are they in jeopardy?" Pao asked, suddenly.

"I found a stone," Mikel said. "It was drawn from the sea near here. It had the same olivine insets as these many others, and like them, it would vibrate, unpredictably. It gave me . . . visions. One of my associates was studying it. We think it killed him. It melted his brain."

"Describe this stone in detail, please," Rensat said.

"I just told you it melted a man's brain," Mikel said with rising irritation. "Does that even matter?"

"I am sorry he died," Rensat said. "So many have, you know."

Mikel did not appreciate the mild rebuke.

"The stone," Pao said. "Tell me about it."

Mikel did not have the patience to argue. He closed his eyes, visualized the design, and described it in detail.

Pao nodded, nodded again. "You found a stone from the *motu-varkas*—the tallest and most powerful tower, farthest out at sea. One point of the grand triangle."

"That ring of tiles was the oldest and strongest in all of Galderkhaan," Rensat said. "It contained a great concentration of energy." Her tone grew somber. "That ring was crafted by Aargan, the chief Technologist, the one who made the whole construct come together."

Pao added, "I have long suspected that she was the one who activated the Source, just to prove she could control it with the ring of *motu-varkas*."

Rensat took a moment to consider her next words. "The Technologists used to call us, the Priests, a 'cult of suicide,' yet they were the ones who ravaged Galderkhaan. The Priests believed—we *proved*—that bodies are simply a vehicle to the ultimate goal of soul bonding to reach the higher planes."

"You proved the existence of these other planes—how?" Mikel asked dubiously.

"In the *cazh* rituals we performed, stopping short of physical death, we had visions of the transpersonal plane, even the cosmic plane," she said.

Pao approached Mikel. There was something new in his expression: impatience.

"There is another one we seek," he said. "We have been searching for her as long as we have been down here."

"Who is she?" Mikel asked.

In response, Pao plunged his hands at the tiles. The tiles hummed, formed an image of a woman's face. It was indistinct, distant, but obviously in pain or stress. Given the flames that glowed below it, it appeared to be part of the same recording Mikel had seen earlier, of the destruction of Galderkhaan.

"You must tell me," Pao said. "In your searches, you have encountered no one like this woman?"

Mikel looked at the face. Nothing registered. "Why is she so important?"

"Concentrate," Pao said with obvious frustration.

Curious himself, and becoming inured to the spirits' occasionally brusque manner, Mikel ran through the catalog of faces from his decade with the Group. He wished he had a laptop or tablet with the Group's facial recognition software. He really wanted to help these two, who were truly lost souls.

Suddenly, he recalled that just over a week ago, when he'd been on board the ship on the Scotia Sea, right before seeing the airship burst from the iceberg, Flora had been sending notifications about the stone melting her deep freezers. She'd also mentioned a woman in a video in Haiti. Mikel had been too busy to chase will-o'-the-wisps. He remembered streaming the video at some point, with a lousy Internet connection. Though it had been a pinpoint of thought, now it was bright and clear—and important.

"That's her," Pao said, and turned from Mikel.

Oddly, horribly, Mikel felt like a drained glass. Had Pao been inside his mind? Or had the tiles done that? Without realizing it, during this brief interlude, Mikel had leaned against the wall. He could feel the power of the stones vibrating through his shoulder.

Mikel broke the connection by pushing off with his back. He looked at the two spirits, their expressions suddenly triumphant.

"You have seen her! She is of your time!" Pao said. He turned briefly to Rensat. "We cannot leave. We cannot give up now."

She nodded in firm agreement.

"You must find her," Pao said to Mikel. "You must bring her to us."

"Why?" Mikel asked, surprised by the timidity of his own voice.

"What good can that possibly do you? You can't change the past." Then, with a shudder that started in his knees, he added, "Can you?"

"You saw!" Rensat said with a cruel twist to her mouth, as if he had been complicit in something. "It has already been done."

"When?"

"At the end," Pao said. "Someone was present who did not belong."

"You mean, this woman? From my own time?"

"So it appears," Pao said. "A few of us managed to bond before she appeared in the sky and prevented the great final *cazh*."

Mikel did not share the jubilation of the two Galderkhaani. He felt very, very sick. "You want me to bring her here to change the past," Mikel said with awful clarity.

"To stop an annihilation!" Pao yelled.

Mikel cried out with shock as his eyesight was ripped away from him and turned toward the previous vision. He was back in the courtyard with the screaming, dying horrors rising above their burning bodies. It was like a Doré etching of hell from Dante's *Inferno* come to ghastly life, with shrieks and flames mingled and rising through a canopy of black, cloudy death. He heard the souls of the dead shrieking with agony as they blindly passed other ascended souls in the sky—all of them lost, untranscended, alone, drifting aimlessly above the churning smoke.

Mikel regained his equilibrium somewhat and continued to watch the image. Then he saw the ultimate, final destruction of Galderkhaan. He saw a momentous pulse of fiery energy fueled by pool after pool of magma shooting from the direction of the sea. It rushed into the pavement below their feet and above, immolating the survivors, driving the mass of souls apart.

Above the dying city, he saw the image of the woman hovering and then the image vanished so swiftly that Mikel felt psychological whiplash that left him spinning. Pao was standing very still, his hands hanging at his sides, his eyes on the bones on the floor. Mikel didn't think he'd ever seen anyone look so sad. Rensat took a step closer to him but could only hover, could not touch him.

"The *cazh* was working, damn her blood!" Rensat said. "We might have taken thousands of souls to the transpersonal plane instead of leaving them stranded, strewn about in horrible isolation, unable ever to rise."

"Why?" Mikel asked. "Why would someone from *my* time do that?"

"I don't know," Pao admitted.

"And I ask again: finding her now," Mikel said, "what good will that do?"

It was Rensat who answered. "We seek two," she reminded him. "This woman . . . and whoever activated the Source. Finding *that* genocidal maniac, we will use her to stop him."

The implications were immediate and deep and they staggered Mikel. He couldn't even respond. Pao and Rensat intended to rewrite all of history by preventing the destruction of Galderkhaan.

Desperate, impossible questions flooded Mikel's brain. If they succeeded, if Galderkhaan were saved, would the whole course of history change? Would he suddenly cease to exist, since his own lineage would be altered through tens of thousands of years? Or did his existence prove that they had failed, since history had not been changed?

Mikel stood there shaking his head. "You will save—tens of thousands, maybe hundreds of thousands at the cost of billions?" he asked, stumbling through his own thoughts.

"What would you do to save your home?" Pao asked.

"To prevent its loss, I'd do a great deal!" Mikel agreed. "But I wouldn't go back centuries to do it!"

"You are not *cazhed* in permanent, eternal stasis," Pao said. "So few Galderkhaani were able to reach the transpersonal plane, even being stuck here with a loved one . . . it can be desolate."

"So you restore Galderkhaan," Mikel said, "put the Source on hold, work out your issues with the Technologists, create a playground for your souls . . . and six billion people still die! No, far more than that—all of the people who lived for the last thirty thousand years!"

"Your thinking is flawed," Pao said hotly, for the first time. "Ninety-seven thousand Galderkhaani would get to live and the result would be billions of Galderkhaani *born* in succeeding generations! Advanced, enlightened beings!"

"We have been blessed by the Candescents, we honor the Candescents, and we will be *with* the Candescents," Rensat said. "That is our destiny and that is our mission."

Mikel felt his gut knot and his mind blaze. If he could have struck these two, he would have. Their scheme defined religious fanaticism: no matter what the cost, they and their acolytes had to have their way. Even if they were right, even if some cosmic glory and eternal survival awaited the hundreds or thousands of Priests and Priestly followers who remained ascended but alone, not joined and transcended in some mythical higher plane, that did not justify imposing their will on countless civilizations that followed.

He had to get out of there. He needed counsel, not just Flora but this other woman . . . the one they sought. How had she gone to the past, and why, and what information could she add to this numbing mix?

The good news, for Mikel, was that Pao and Rensat had spent a long time looking for two people and had failed to find them both. He, at least, had a clue from the video about how to find one of them.

There was other good news. He didn't have to stay there and listen to them anymore. He was pretty sure these beings could not hold him.

He hoped.

Pao had turned to Rensat while Mikel processed what he had heard. There was tenderness between the two, and Mikel reminded himself that even the world's most notorious tyrants had families they loved. He did not feel compassion for this man, but a kind of terror he had never known. Mikel understood a love of home; of course he understood that. But theirs was gone because of its own failings. Other homes had taken its place, homes that they had no right to obliterate.

Mikel used Pao's distraction as an opportunity to pull out the skin mask. He slapped it to his face and visualized the tunnel map he had seen. He couldn't go backward, to where the tunnel had been aflame. There was only one other exit, the large chamber with the glass panel door through which Rensat had entered. If Mikel read the map right, it opened into another series of tunnels.

Not that it mattered, really. It was the only option he had.

Boring through the startled specters, he launched himself forward and threw open the glass panel.

CHAPTER 16

We must do something."

Adrienne Dowman turned to look at Flora, who had spoken almost inaudibly. She was staring through the window panel at the relic as if it had mesmerized her. After two full days, the stone was still floating, still stable.

"So," Adrienne said. "You're one of those."

"One of what?" Flora said, not turning her head.

"One of those people who has a single success and takes that as a mandate to do anything you want."

Now Flora deigned to look at her. She had avoided her new associate as much as possible, spending the day trying to find out where the hell Mikel was and looking for any scraps of new data about anomalies in the South Pole. So far, both endeavors had been unsuccessful. She was feeling uncommonly frustrated and didn't feel like listening to a subordinate.

"I thought we had the conversation about my being uninterested in your opinions," Flora said.

Adrienne smiled an annoying half smile. "The way I look at it, Dr. Davies, you do not have a choice but to listen."

"Not?" Flora suggested.

"I don't see that as an option," Adrienne replied. "You've said it before: the rest of my career is going to be spent right here, working for you. You can't let me off my chain until you go public with your results about these objects, and you know next to nothing about them. So that's pretty far in the future. The equation, then, is: 'you need me' plus 'I wish to be heard' equals 'you will listen.' "

Flora stared at Adrienne for a moment longer, not quite believing what she was hearing, then looked back at the stone. "And *you* will find that I'm capable of very selective hearing."

"We'll see," Adrienne said. "Let's start with this. You've solved *a* problem with that stone. I suggest—I *urge* you not to turn off the system and start messing with it again or you may have to solve others before you're ready."

"We have no choice," Flora said. "You've been taking readings since it's been in stasis and learned very little—"

"Oh, I haven't learned very little," Adrienne replied. "So far, I've learned nothing. This object is like an electron. Stop it and it's just another particle. You only learn when it's active, in motion."

"Then what choice do I have but to shut off the—what did you call it?"

"The node," Adrienne replied. "That's the location in the array of sound waves capable of sustaining the levitation."

"Yes. All right, Adrienne. Give me an option."

"Patience," Adrienne replied. She cocked her head toward the stone. "I've had to tiptoe around this relic, literally. Every garbage truck, every bus that passed by on the street had me on edge. Vibrations of any kind affect sound."

"I understand that," Flora said. "But I don't think *you* understand what we have."

Adrienne opened her mouth to speak but thought better of it.

"The stability of a singularity that suddenly, inexplicably reaches out and expands, that creates massive inflation," Flora said. "What does that describe?"

Adrienne replied immediately. "The Big Bang."

"Quite so," Flora said. She gazed at the artifact. "This is the beginning of the universe in a bottle. And it is artificial, though constructed of naturally occurring minerals, and possibly made by intelligent hands. That's significant."

"Dr. Davies, it's an ancient stone in a node," Adrienne said, correcting her.

Flora chose that moment to selectively not hear.

"And you said 'intelligent,' not 'human,'" Adrienne pointed out as she replayed the statement in her head. "What did you mean by *that*?"

Again, Flora ignored her. Instead, she asked, "What would happen to me if I walked in there? It's just ultrasound, right? The same that's used on pregnant women?"

"And that we use to break up kidney stones. Or, perhaps, Group directors."

"So it could be destructive."

"Yes," Adrienne sighed. "I'll just say I hope you won't do that. It would be a seriously flawed decision."

Flora smiled.

Adrienne was not warmed by the smile. "You're not going to listen."

"All those vehicles that passed by, the trucks and buses—they did not cause an imbalance, did they?" Flora asked.

Adrienne's mouth tightened. "Dr. Davies, you were smart enough to hire me and now I'm asking you to be smart enough to stay out of the lab until I figure out a safe, sane next step."

"When will that be?"

"Next Friday, four-oh-one p.m."

Flora ignored Adrienne's unwelcome quip. "Worst case—what happens if I go in?"

"All right, here's the truth," Adrienne said. "Let's ignore the question of stability. It's ultrasound on steroids in there. What that means is, if you don't stay inside too long and if you're protecting your eardrums, any other effects on you should be minimal. Your body heat will probably rise."

"How long is too long?"

"When you start feeling like you have a fever, that's too long."

"Seconds? Minutes?"

"Maybe two minutes," Adrienne said. "I just don't know. And I repeat, I do not want to find out."

Flora had faith in the iron constitution that came with her Welsh heritage. She wanted to test that envelope. "Anything else?"

"There's a minimal risk of cavitation, bubbles forming in your blood, tissues, or organs."

"The practical effects of which are?"

"Your blood vessels could rupture."

Flora gazed at the stone. "How minimal is minimal?"

Adrienne rubbed her eyebrows. "Almost nonexistent if you don't linger once the other symptoms set in."

"Good." Flora swung away from the window and strode down the hall.

"Get me out of here," Adrienne said under her breath, her eyes betraying fear as she watched the relic hovering, quiet and still and ominous.

Flora came back gloved and holding a tray with eight objects, all about the same size and shape as the artifact. Adrienne could see at a glance that none were made of the same type of stone. She guessed ancient clay, wood, and copper right off the bat. One looked like it might be alabaster, and another looked sheathed in a beige leather with an odd sheen. Flora balanced the tray carefully in one hand, thrust a pair of surgical gloves at Adrienne, and tweaked her headphones more securely over her ears. Then she opened the door to the chamber.

"Come on," she ordered.

"Thank you, no," Adrienne snapped.

"You're not going to be inside," Flora returned. "You're going to stand in the doorway and hand me these."

Adrienne stood still for a moment, then pulled on the gloves with an insolent look. She received the tray dubiously. "Do any of these have a history of acting up?"

"No, they've never misbehaved," Flora said as she eyed the room, the boundaries of which were set by the black panels on the walls, floor, and ceiling.

Adrienne reached into the pocket of her lab coat and thumbed on a recorder. She announced the time. Flora stood still and shook out her hands. After taking a long breath, she slowly stepped into the frame of inaudible sound waves—

And felt nothing. Flora did a head-to-toe check. Heart rate: unchanged. Breathing: normal. Vision and hearing: neither deprived nor hallucinating. She grinned and approached the artifact.

"Dr. Davies, can you hear me all right?"

"I can."

"If you start to feel that the world is going swimmy in any way, or if you suddenly feel like you're sort of distanced from everything, like it takes extra effort for your hand to reach an object, that's a warning sign."

"I'm always distanced from everything. It's called objectivity."

"Is that a joke?"

"Yes. Hand me one of the artifacts."

Adrienne surveyed the objects. She selected the alabaster one and leaned forward into the room to convey it to Flora's outstretched hand. Once Flora had received it, Adrienne quickly backed out into the doorway.

Flora regarded the carvings on this stone and compared them to the triangle on the relic. She had memorized the patterns long ago, knew that there was no obvious sequence among them.

"At the risk of stating the obvious," Adrienne said, "do not move the main stone in any way."

"Okay. It stays on its back. So. What's the pattern? The creators of these were not children playing with dominoes."

"Unlike you."

Flora did not bother responding to that. She continued where she'd left off. "I'm going to align the faces first." And with that, Flora carefully slid the alabaster artifact into the space above the main stone, as close as possible without their touching.

"What does it feel like?" Adrienne asked.

Flora was glad her companion's first priority was still science. "I feel a slight repulsion between the objects." Quickly, she flipped the alabaster so that its carvings faced the ceiling instead of the main stone. A very gentle feeling of suction resulted and she let go of the alabaster. She heard Adrienne gasp. Immediately the stone settled in, floating in the air a bare millimeter above the other.

"The node's not big enough to hold all of these up," Adrienne said.

"Next," Flora ordered.

Adrienne regarded the tray. Carefully, she picked up the wooden artifact. Its center had begun to petrify but its edges had the fragility of very, very old organic matter. Adrienne held up the object carefully, then leaned in to hand it to Flora.

"This is about an ounce, roughly one-third the weight of the first stone passed into the chamber," Adrienne said into the recorder. "We should have taken accurate measurements."

"It's twenty-six point four grams," Flora said.

Adrienne's mouth clapped shut as Flora slid the wooden artifact above the alabaster one. Again, with a slight suction the object began to levitate, not touching the one below it.

Both women remained silent as, one by one, Adrienne passed the items from the tray. She didn't speak again until there was only one artifact remaining.

"This is impossible," Adrienne said.

"Isn't it, though?" Flora asked with an edge of delight. Her ears were pounding slightly and she felt warm but not enough to be concerned.

"Dr. Davies, I don't think you realize—they don't all fit in the node. The artifacts are helping each other. You're sure they're not magnetic?"

"Wood? Fabric?" Flora said.

"They could still be affected by any magnetic fields in the stones."

"No." Flora slid the last artifact onto the top of the stack. "They are not magnetic. The other objects are not being impacted by paramagnetism or diamagnetism. We did those tests." Then she just stood there and looked at them.

"I just want to remind you that you've been in there for well over two minutes. How do you feel?" Adrienne asked.

"Wonderful, actually," Flora replied. "It's . . . clean here. Pure. I don't know how else to describe it."

Adrienne's eyes shifted from the objects to the Group's director. It was the first time she'd seen her smile like this. "Dr. Davies, why are you obsessed with these?"

"A scholar's interest in the inexplicable."

"No," Adrienne said. "A scholar would be publishing articles about these in journals, and asking every scientist and researcher she could contact for help with studying them."

Flora ignored her.

"You're keeping secrets," Adrienne said.

Again, she made no reply.

"Who or what are you protecting?" Adrienne asked. "What did you cover up a death for?"

Flora turned ever so slightly and glanced back. "What death?"

"My predecessor," Adrienne said. "I asked around, I heard about Arni Haugan."

Flora smiled mirthlessly. "You appear to be a better detective than you are a scientist."

"Not fair and not true," Adrienne said.

Flora turned her back on the younger woman.

"Any idea what really happened to Haugan?" Adrienne asked.

"The artifact," Flora said grudgingly. "But we don't know how. We have no idea what he was doing with it at the time."

"Doesn't that bother you?"

"Not enough," Flora admitted. "This is a lab and it was a workplace accident. They happen."

Adrienne frowned but she decided not to pursue the issue now. She didn't like Flora but she couldn't afford to conflate that with the truth of what Flora had just said.

Flora surprised her then. "Besides, Haugan is not gone. Not really. Not if some theories are correct."

Adrienne took a step forward. "Doctor, I think the ultrasound may be affecting you—"

"Be quiet. Here's something you don't know," the woman went on. "The civilization that created these artifacts proved that there is life after death. More than proved it, in fact. We think they systematized their access to it."

Adrienne stared at her. "Myth."

"Fact."

"What are you going off of?"

"Partial translations. Very partial. Drawings. A gut feeling and dreams."

"Dreams?" Adrienne's voice was soaked in doubt and frustration.

"*Shared* dreams," Flora stressed. "As we gathered these artifacts together, my associate Mikel and I began to have the same dreams."

"Elaborate, if you don't mind," Adrienne said.

Flora did not respond. She felt fine, still, but she was puzzled and transfixed by the miracle of what she was seeing in the chamber. Cautiously, she reached into the node and removed the top artifact. When nothing changed, she slid it, carvings faceup, beneath the main stone.

Instantly they felt the room heat up. Within three seconds sweat was beading on their foreheads.

"Whatever you just did, undo it!" Adrienne pleaded.

Flora didn't hear her. She was suddenly having difficulty breathing. The heat was as powerful as a sauna set on high. Her head felt heavy and she put a hand on the back of her neck.

"Dr. Davies!" Adrienne shouted. "Grab the artifacts and get out!"

Flora heard a hum and saw that the main stone was vibrating. She reached a weakened hand forward and carefully removed the top artifact from the stack.

"Doctor!" Adrienne screamed. "Don't be gentle about it!"

Flora took two at once but she was trembling at the knees now. She placed the objects in the crook of her arm. Then she realized she was not the only thing shaking, so was the floor. Suddenly, all the stones began to wobble madly. The bottom one dropped from the stack and hit the floor. Flora reached down as fast as she could manage and saw that the black floor panel was bubbling. She pulled the artifact from the chaos.

Adrienne yelled something incoherent and started to move into the chamber, but she found that her feet wouldn't lift properly. The concrete floor was liquefying and creeping toward the doorway, as if trying to escape the room. With effort she could lift her boots free from the slow sludge but it took a lot of muscle.

She looked up to scream at Flora again and saw the entire stack of artifacts collapse and fall to the floor. The main stone almost leaped from the pile and Flora was able to snatch it midflight as the other artifacts hit the bubbling, oozing black panel. She grabbed at the scattered stones and managed to retrieve them all, albeit dripping black liquid. Then she tried to turn and run but the floor gripped the edges of her shoes as it flowed.

Adrienne took a giant, heaving backward step from the doorway. She almost fell over but shoved the edge of the tray at the wall to gain equilibrium. She was horrified to feel the wall soften beneath its edge and jerked the tray away as soon as she felt balanced. Then she yanked her other leg out of the doorway too.

"Throw them to me!" she told Flora.

Flora, still lunging slowly forward, threw the first artifact, then the next, and the next. It was so hot she wanted to vomit. She felt tears in her eyes as she saw fragments fly from the wooden artifact as Adrienne caught it. Only the petrified center was left now as the rest of it melted into the custard concrete floor.

Flora held the last artifact, the main stone, the Serpent, which was vibrating so hard she could feel the waves through her arms down to her feet. Her vision clouded, suffused with red, and she thought she smelled sulfur. Vaguely she could hear Adrienne screaming at her. She took another weak step forward and with all her willpower, she let go of the Serpent in Adrienne's direction.

The stone tumbled through the air and Adrienne dove forward and snatched it from the liquid concrete. Then the girl disappeared from the doorway. Flora heard the sound of running and suddenly realized she was hearing again. Her mind was clearing. The heat was lifting. She was gaining more control of her limbs. She lurched from the room and the floor seemed steady beneath her so she stopped, resting against a wall. She looked back at the chamber. The black panels had melted halfway down the walls. Long drips trailed from the panels on the ceiling. But the melting had stopped. The floor was still. The panels were no longer bubbling.

"Damn it!" she heard from down the hall. "We need another room!"

Adrienne was heading back down the hall in Flora's direction, yelling. "I'll get the rest of the panels. That deep freezer will give us fifteen minutes, max!"

CHAPTER 17

"But he'll *die*!" Siem der Graaf shouted.

The taller man blocked Eric Trout's path to the spiral stairway. They were standing nearly nose to nose in the "jam tart," the large red module that served as Halley VI's social hub. Eric's mustache hung in two tendrils past his chin, and days of sharp frustration had burned his typically jovial expression to a frazzle.

"Der Graaf," Trout huffed, "this is essentially the only situation where the title 'base commander' actually means something. Step aside."

The younger man opened his mouth to speak but just shook his head.

Trout's chin sank into the collar of his heavy turtleneck. "Der Graaf, we're following orders strictly on this. We start the move off the ice shelf in thirty minutes."

Trout raised a thick-fingered hand and gently pushed Siem to the side, then hurried down the stairs.

"But surely you don't need everyone for the move," Siem argued, following on his heels. "You will have excess personnel, in fact. Or do you plan to have them sitting around inside the modules as you tow them?"

"Anyone without a specific job will be in the trucks and bulldozers, heading to the new location."

"Fine. Then give me two men for just *that* amount of time, before you need them to start hanging pictures back on the walls."

Trout fired back a severely disapproving look.

"Two men and Ski-Doos to save a life!" Siem said, pressing the commander.

Trout turned to face him in the empty dining area.

"You cannot have them," Trout said finally. "We have to turn off everything for the move except the hydraulics. No electronics. Communications will be off. It's unconscionable to send out one man, let alone three, on a dangerous rescue mission with zero radio contact. I simply cannot, der Graaf. I will not."

"Then you're killing him."

"He did this to himself, without orders," Trout replied. His expression softened. "Has it not occurred to you he might want that?"

"What, to die?"

"No," Trout said. "Not to endanger anyone *else*! You said he sent you back—"

"I don't think he fully understood the danger," Siem replied. "No," he went on. "I think he just made the greatest discovery of his life and he wasn't thinking clearly. He would want to live to see it brought to daylight."

"Der Graaf, I've spent five winters and summers on the ice, watching people's minds bend in the twenty-four-hour darkness or light. If there's one thing I've learned, it's not to ascribe logic to someone behaving illogically. That's how to get more people killed!"

"He was as sane as any of us," Siem snapped.

"Really? You mentioned that he ran out of ice screws so he slid the rest of the way down the crevasse."

"It was not very far."

"Far enough that he couldn't climb it?"

"Yes—"

"Thereby leaving himself without a way back up. He knew this, did he not?"

"He did, which is why I hammered in the screws he'll need."

"Did he ask you to do that?"

Siem was silent.

"Der Graaf. Did Mikel Jasso *ask* you if you had extra ice screws?"

After a long moment Siem answered, "No."

"Then he was mad. Or a reckless fool. I don't know which, and sadly, I cannot afford to care."

"So, then, we let a mad, reckless fool die in a crevasse, because it is dangerous and inconvenient to rescue him *and* recover his scientific find—which, I may add, is one reason we are out here. To expand human knowledge."

"Damn you. You're not even a scientist! You're maintenance!"

"That, sir, is not an argument."

Trout waved away the rebuke. "Anyway, you know me better. We have to get the station onto grounded ice, ice that isn't inexplicably melting, ice that isn't subject to unpredictable seismic occurrences as our Norwegian friends have cautioned us. Now, you are wasting my—"

"We can do both," Siem said. "We can. We must."

"No."

With a brusque sweeping movement, Trout made sure Siem left the module ahead of him. He also assigned the young man to assist Ivor and Dr. Bundy on all tasks, so that he couldn't steal a Ski-Doo and try to rescue Mikel by himself.

Outside, tempers were hair-trigger and the clipped conversations were tense. It was more than just the pressure of setting up to tow the jam tart and its seven blue sisters, one by one, across almost forty miles of ice. Every person on the team felt that the outside world was filled with odd shadows that did not seem to align with the position of the sun. Over and over the workers' eyes snapped toward things that weren't there. No one ever took safety and security for granted here. But no one had ever feared their surroundings quite like this, either.

The weather was cooperating at least: almost no wind, and not cold enough to comment on it.

Eric Trout did the rounds, checking in by radio with each person to make sure they were a go. Then, from inside one module, he started flicking switches. First their radios died. Then the modules. Everyone felt instantly forlorn and abandoned; even Ivor, who had been singing a Scottish drinking song, stopped.

Trout clambered down and signaled to the engineer in charge of the first blue research center to be towed.

Siem, who had been working with Dr. Bundy securing the laboratory, stopped suddenly.

"Do you feel that?" he muttered to the scientist.

"What?"

"In your stomach," Siem said. "Pressure. Waves of pressure."

Bundy hesitated, then replied, "A little. It's just nerves."

"Just nerves . . . doing what?" Siem asked earnestly.

Bundy looked at him strangely and didn't reply.

Several men worked with shovels around the ski tip of one strut of the blue unit until it began rising. Siem joined them, trying to give himself something to focus on besides his uneasiness. When the leg had completely retracted, they began to pack snow a meter deep beneath it. Repeating this process with the other three supports would create a new, sturdy foundation for the structure to rise on its hydraulics, allowing for its hitch frame to be attached. Then the team would attach it to a bulldozer and a truck for its long trip across the ice.

As they worked on the snow beneath each leg, Siem noticed that his discomfort increased when the jacking stopped and the team was working in silence. He also noticed that he wasn't the only one feeling it. Several of the people paused to adjust their waistbands or rest their hands on their ribs.

Even Bundy noticed and glanced around, his goggled eyes coming to rest in Siem's direction.

Suddenly Ivor griped, "What in the great white hell is goin' on? I feel like I'm at a bloody rock show!"

With little wind to scatter sound, his words rang clearly over the work site. There was a chorus of agreement.

"That's exactly it," someone said. "I feel like I have a big sound speaker on my stomach."

"Not a speaker," Ivor said. "A subwoofer."

"Yes," Siem said. There seemed to be a very low-pitched, sub-audible frequency, something none of them had ever experienced.

The team was silent a moment, looking toward the horizon. But their world was still empty save for the modules and vehicles . . . and shadows that looked out of sync.

Everyone jumped when the last hydraulic leg started jacking up.

"That's all we need," muttered Bundy. "Mass hysteria."

"What about the PALAOA recording?" Siem asked. "Could that be the problem?"

The Perennial Acoustic Observatory in the Antarctic Ocean was a German effort located northeast of the Troll station, under the ice and underwater. A year or so ago they had picked up a remarkably loud, very deep buzz that sounded like a droning airplane engine. "A bit like the world's largest didgeridoo," as one of the Australians had described it. And the Germans had confirmed that there were no ships anywhere within a thousand miles of the receiver, so to date the source was another of Antarctica's multitude of mysteries.

"We'd actually hear it if that were it," said Bundy.

"And we're not underwater anyway," Ivor said, wandering over.

"Maybe we'd better call the Norweg—" Trout started, then looked back at the dark power module. "Oh. Damn."

"You think it could be seismic?" Siem asked.

Trout shook his head. "If it was an earthquake, we wouldn't feel it in our guts but nowhere bloody else."

The hydraulic leg stopped when it had fully retracted. The silence was as empty as the vista surrounding them. Everyone set their shovels to the snow. Because the air was still and crystal particles of ice did not stir, no one saw a blank space of air pucker about a hundred feet from the module. Slowly, the void sucked itself into the invisible shape of a circle. Then it blew itself out.

The team didn't see it but they felt it in their bellies. Nearly everyone cursed and swung their hands to grip their torsos, dropping their shovels.

The air puckered again in a different spot, in the shadow of a module, collapsing on itself like a vertical sinkhole. The shadow shrank, then expanded, so this time half the team saw it and cried out. A moment later the air snapped back to normal. Amid the shouting, Bundy, the nearest, ran to the spot and stood in it, waving his arms around.

"I don't feel a damn thing!" he called.

Then there was a horribly recognizable sound—metal, wrenching. They spun and watched as the facing wall of the nearest blue module pinched inward, as though grabbed from the inside. It continued to implode with a crunching noise until it formed the shape of a circle. Then the metal flew outward with a metallic shriek. The surrounding joints held, the wall did not detach, but it warped as it expanded, leaving it bulbous and grotesque.

Almost instantly, the air behind Siem sucked back, his shoulders with it. Trout grabbed his sleeve and pulled hard. Siem opened his mouth but couldn't scream. Trout jerked him free just as the air blew convex, knocking Siem to his knees, then facedown. In shock, he quickly raised his head and shook the snow from his face as Trout bent protectively over him.

There was another metallic squeal. This time it was a leg of the module they'd been working on. As the air pulled back, the leg bent with it, and suddenly there was a flash of light like sustained lightning, brilliant and unyielding. As the first painful shock of the magnesium-white flare subsided, the glow seemed to possess a shape.

"Do you see that?!" Ivor shouted.

"Yes!" everyone called out.

They were staring at the mostly featureless mask of a human face. As it continued to form it began to burn. Strangely, the high, all-consuming fires did not throw off any heat.

What appeared to be a mouth opened wide.

"Ul . . . !" it cried in a voice that sounded like a monstrous Antarctic gale.

Almost at once another metal leg bent the other way. Unsteady now, the huge module began to list to one side. The team shouted and ran from under it. Fingers struggling beneath his thick gloves, Trout dragged the still-prone Siem by the shoulders, as the big blue beast leaned until its side crashed to the snow.

The team was openly scared now, looking in all directions for the next anomaly, unconsciously clumping together for protection. Trout urged Siem back on his feet.

There was another suck of air about seven or eight feet above them—and the face beneath the fire took on greater substance, now with more rough detail: its mouth open, eyes wide.

"Ul . . .vor . . .ul . . .vor!"

Two men fell to their knees, clutching their sides.

"What is it?" Trout said in a trembling voice as he retreated from the group.

"This is insane!" Bundy shouted back, looking from Trout to the circle.

"I see . . . eyes . . . the mouth!" Siem whispered.

Bundy didn't answer. He was looking up at the face of fire, its dark eyes scanning the group as though they were searching. The manifestation seemed to be struggling, repeatedly trying to stabilize and failing.

"Ulvor!" it cried again. *"Ulvor o Glogharas!"* This time it was clearly a human-sounding voice, intensely magnified, the words echoing across the ice like a sonic boom.

The face gained sharpness, clarity, even as the flames licked at it. The eyes were pearls of black amid the bronzed silhouette.

Parts of a body became visible now too. There was a bare shoulder and hands that were engulfed in tongues of flame moving in slow, sinuous gestures.

The air was pulsing more violently now. A full figure formed, all of it ablaze, hovering in the air, looking, looking . . .

"Vol!" it screamed. *"Enzo pato Vol!"*

And then the air exploded and the figure was gone.

The researchers remained where they were, stunned into silence. All except Siem who sought and found Trout.

"Can you explain that?" Siem demanded.

"Localized aurora . . . St. Elmo's fire. There *is* a sane explanation."

"Well I know someone who might be able to," he said. "I am going to get Mikel Jasso."

PART THREE

CHAPTER 18

Caitlin was done with caution.

She'd been careful after the incidents with Jacob. She'd been tentative but complicit about communing with Galderkhaan. She'd been taking advice from well-meaning but cautious, cerebral people who barely understood what she had experienced, who did not grasp what she felt she was capable of.

That time was over. It was time to treat these deep mysteries like she had treated the rest of her life before Maanik had entered it: with action.

Caitlin let Jacob sleep. She arranged him under his covers, and, without hesitation, stalked to her living room, grabbed her keys, and left her apartment, locking Jacob in. She pushed the door to the stairwell so hard it crashed against the wall. She'd take the bad-mother guilt if he drummed and she didn't answer. What she had to attempt would only take a few minutes and either fail . . . or succeed. She could risk that. The presence of strange persons in spirit was bad enough. But this new intruder had somehow appeared in the flesh. Running up the steps two at a time, she jabbed a key at the final door and burst onto the roof of her building.

Planks were laid for a deck but the furniture had been pulled aside and tarped against the early onset of cold. It wasn't quite a 360-degree view; a building loomed to block the north, another impeded half the view of the Hudson River. But to the east and south, it was all streetlights, the dark silhouettes of water towers, a few luridly colored LED spires.

Caitlin raised her arms as if to embrace the skies and all the time that had passed under them. Her soul felt primal, stripped of civilization and inhibition, ready to journey.

She couldn't use the *cazh*. For one thing there was just one of her. From everything she had seen in Galderkhaan, the ritual required at least two or more. For another, she could not risk leaving here, spiritually. If Jacob did more than drum, if he woke and she wasn't there or god forbid went into crisis . . . well, she had to be there.

Finally, and perhaps most frightening to her, Caitlin could not risk *wanting* to leave. She remembered how ecstatic she'd been in the UN that night as the mass of souls took her up with them. It was like the addicts she had treated: To a one, they knew what they were doing was unhealthy. But they liked the way it felt.

With purpose bordering on fanaticism, she planted her feet toward the southeast and looked across the city. The bay wasn't visible but she knew where it was. She oriented toward "big water" just as the Galderkhaani had done so many millions of years ago, and extended her arms toward it. The connection was immediate. It was similar to what she had felt in the train coming back from the session with Odilon—total expansion of self in every direction. But now that she wasn't resisting, it was exponentially more intense and more pervasive. The Eastern mystics professed it and people made it a joke: "Make me one with everything." But that's exactly what it was.

This is real. I'm not imagining it.

Very slightly, she pointed the first two fingers of her right hand. The result was almost visible, it was so potent. A white—*veil* was the only word that came to mind—stretched from her body and began to coagulate, to writhe like smoke, moving, seeking through the city, probing and elongating. Caitlin felt her heart galloping as the serpent moved south and east, rising and hovering below the clouds and then suddenly striking down toward the earth. It stopped cold on Chinatown. There was the woman from the subway. Caitlin could feel her as if she were standing right next to her. She turned toward Caitlin in shock.

Come back here, Caitlin thought at her sharply. *Now.*

Her own voice was loud in her head and, apparently, outside of it; Caitlin heard several dogs barking before she dropped her hands and the conduit snapped shut. Arfa must have been freaking below her.

Her breathing and heartbeat became regular as she came back to where she was. She was proud that she had *done* it. And she *had* done it. Now all she had to do was go downstairs and wait.

Jacob continued to sleep peacefully. Arfa was nowhere to be seen. When she tired of waiting, she paced into the living room and, by force of habit, turned on the TV. The local station had breaking news about animal insanity across Manhattan. Now that Caitlin was paying attention, she realized that the dogs she'd heard barking hadn't yet stopped.

Central Park Zoo got the most attention. Cell phone video showed monkeys that wouldn't stop howling. The sea lions were screaming too, and some of the birds kept flying into the sides of their cages. On the phone, the keeper for the zoo's rain forest habitat reported that the animals had grouped together, regardless of species, with their bellies flat on the ground and as much foliage for camouflage as they could find.

"The boa constrictor is apparently taking a nap," the anchor reported. The video showed the reptile coiled in a corner, wrapped around itself seemingly at rest.

Caitlin thought back to the profound experience with the snake in Haiti.

"What are you doing?" Caitlin asked aloud, pondering the snake. "Observing? Waiting? Ignoring?"

Perhaps all or none of the above. Caitlin thought about other snakes that had fascinated her throughout her life, from the serpentine shape of her "spirit" headed toward Chinatown, to the snakes of Medusa and the Garden of Eden, to Cleopatra and the caduceus—the symbol of the medical profession. Her world.

"Why you?" she wondered, watching the big snake on TV. "Maybe the scientists are right," she mused. It was all there in an airplane magazine article she read a year or so ago. Researchers believed that superstring structures bound all matter on a subatomic and supercosmic level. Perhaps they got the name wrong. It could be the strings were snakes.

The news report concluded with a late-breaking update that emergency room visits were up dramatically with victims of bites, mainly from dogs, cats, rodents, and what were being described as "kamikaze pigeons."

Caitlin bolted from her seat and went searching for Arfa. She found him in her bedroom closet, having forced his way under the door. He was cowering and emitting the tiniest of mews. He hunched even more as she ventured closer. Unlike the other animals, he did not attack.

"I understand," Caitlin said with a soft smile. "I'm kind of radioactive to you. Attacking will hurt you more than me."

She returned to the living room, shut off the TV, and began to pace just as the intercom buzzed. Caitlin hurried to it. "Yes?"

"I am here," said an unfamiliar voice. Her accent was odd enough that Caitlin couldn't place it.

"Come up," she said.

"There is one condition," the woman said before Caitlin could hit the buzzer to release the door.

"What is it?" Caitlin asked.

"Do not access Galderkhaan while I am there. For both our sakes."

"Fine," Caitlin said grimly. "You answer my questions, I won't push the boundaries."

"And I won't cause you harm," the woman answered coldly.

Caitlin hesitated, then buzzed the woman in. Standing outside the door of her apartment, Caitlin watched as the woman approached. In person, she was much smaller than she loomed in Caitlin's memory. And here, outside the rocking subway car, she moved with a grace that seemed utterly without effort. She did not meet Caitlin's gaze and seemed to flinch almost imperceptivly as she moved past Caitlin inside.

The woman remained with her back toward her host.

"I'm a damn good psychiatrist," Caitlin announced as she shut the door. "If you lie to me, there is a very good chance I'll know it."

"I trained with wild hawks and horses in Mongolia," the woman said. "You don't intimidate me."

"Nor you, me," Caitlin assured her. For a moment she just stared at the woman's back, waiting for something to happen.

"It obviously took some kind of knowledge to show up in my living room like you did before."

"Yes, some kind of knowledge," the woman replied, looking around the apartment. "That is something we possess."

"We?" Caitlin said. "Who?"

The woman turned and looked at her for the first time. "Descendants of the Priests of Galderkhaan."

Caitlin wasn't surprised or alarmed, yet she still felt a profound chill. It's one thing to believe something in spirit, in theory. It's another to look upon the very embodiment of those ideas.

The woman turned away and stared especially hard at the hallway that led to the bedrooms. Caitlin moved between the woman and the hall.

"What did you do to my son?" Caitlin demanded.

"I did nothing," she insisted.

"I don't believe you," Caitlin spat.

"Dr. O'Hara, consider your words before you use them, or you will continue to grope."

"Don't lecture me, please," Caitlin retorted. "I asked you here to get answers."

The woman regarded Caitlin before answering. "I didn't access his mind. Location is accomplished via the entire spirit. I read yours in the subway, easily. To me, you glow like a beacon."

"If you didn't do anything to my son, who did?"

"An ascended soul, or souls," the woman said. "Only the dead can do such a thing."

Caitlin fought the sudden urge to drop into a chair.

"Does that mean—" she started, breathed, and then started again. "Does that mean Jacob is beginning to undergo the same process as the teenagers I've encountered?" Caitlin's mind did not go to the two young women she'd helped but to the one she'd failed to save, the Iranian boy, Atash.

"Think," the woman said. "You will not always have a guide."

"As if you're actually guiding me now?" Caitlin said.

"You must learn to see with different eyes, reason with a different mind," the woman said. "That is as important as data."

"No. It isn't," Caitlin replied. She had done enough thinking, with Ben, on her own, on the run. She did not want to *think*, she wanted to be *told*. But clearly answers were going to come on this woman's terms.

Resigned, Caitlin exhaled and attempted to "think" aloud. "The . . . the 'ascended,' the dead, can reach anyone alive."

The woman's eyes opened slightly with encouragement.

Who had reached souls in the modern day? Caitlin asked herself. "Not just the dead," she said. "The *bonded* dead. The souls who performed the ritual."

Caitlin paused and looked to the woman for confirmation, received none, but at least she wasn't told to "think." So she was apparently on the right path.

"I freed Maanik and Gaelle," Caitlin went on. "If that link could be broken, so can this."

"Perhaps."

"Perhaps?" Caitlin cried.

The woman's look told her to think harder.

"Okay. All right." She thought of the earlier cases. "I see. To free them, I had to go back. I had to break the *cazh* of those who were attacking them. You're saying this is a *cazh*?"

"I believe so, from some ancient moment of death," the woman said, at least giving her that much.

"But we don't know *who*." It wasn't a question Caitlin had uttered. It was a desperate statement of fact. She regarded the woman. "What's your name?"

"Yokane," the woman replied.

"How long have you been watching me . . . Yokane?"

"Since you first visited Galderkhaan," she said. "You and the young girl created quite a ripple."

"You felt it—where? How?"

"I am not prepared to tell you that, yet," Yokane said. "May I see your boy?"

Caitlin winced inside at the overfamiliarity. "To do what?"

"Observe," she replied. "Only that. It may help answer your questions."

Caitlin wasn't happy with the idea but she understood that it was probably necessary.

"Briefly," Caitlin warned, making it clear that she would remain on the edge of active defense. "Lead the way," she added. "I'm sure you know where he is."

Yokane looked around. "I must leave something outside of his room," she said.

The woman pulled a small package from inside her coat, wrapped in a beige material. Caitlin was instantly on alert, as any New Yorker would be, but realized that if the woman had wanted to harm her she'd have done so already.

Yokane walked to the dining room table but still, she hesitated to put down the package. "I haven't parted with this in twenty years," she said as she unwrapped a small, rectangular stone with embedded green crystals. Caitlin started.

"I saw that—in a vision!"

"When?"

"Today, earlier," she said.

"This one in particular?" Yokane asked, holding it nearer.

Caitlin could sense that it was vibrating silently in the woman's hands. She didn't recognize the pattern but the general use of crescents she knew very well.

"No, not that one," Caitlin replied. "The design was different. What is it?"

Yokane regarded her precious item. "It's from the Source of Galderkhaan," she announced. "The *kavar*. A preferred design of the Technologists."

"I thought you said you were with the Priests," Caitlin said.

"I am," Yokane replied. "This was entrusted to my family by the Obsidian Priest."

Caitlin waited but the woman did not continue. Pressing would only meet with resistance but she suspected, as with her patients, that this woman wanted to say more.

"The stone," Yokane went on, "has been passed down through my ancestors for millennia. The oral tradition has lost many details, but there is active danger in this object and others like it."

"How many are there?"

"That I do not know," she admitted. "But if it is active, others are active."

"When you say 'active,' what exactly do you mean?"

Yokane fixed her eyes on Caitlin. "It is screaming."

"You don't mean that *literally*—?"

"I do," Yokane said.

She had to mean it was vibrating, like a magnet trying to reach another magnet. Caitlin let the specific wording pass.

"Why? Why now?" Caitlin asked.

"For reasons that have forced me from concealment," Yokane said. "Before they became obsessed with the transpersonal plane and beyond, the Technologists helped us achieve greatness. They linked a network of stones, a series of mosaics, to the Source. Powered by the planet itself—the magma layer that would one day become the Source—the stones were a record, if you will, access to the achievements and intellect of our race."

"So . . . a living library?"

Yokane said with deep respect, "A means of unwinding time would be closer to it."

Caitlin was barely hanging on to the concept. She tried to dumb it down for herself. "You're saying that through that stone you can see the past?"

"Not through *one*, no." Yokane smiled sadly. "It is a lost *shavula*. Separated from the flock, all it can do is attempt to link to the others. It is not just the stone but the pattern of stones and access to the Source that give it vitality."

"In and of itself, then, it has no intelligence."

"No," Yokane said. "But it has access to so much. So very much. Finding that access has been our goal for millennia."

"A database of Galderkhaani minds," Caitlin said, awed, as the idea took hold.

Yokane cradled the stone and then laid it gently upon the table with an almost ritualistic reverence. It reminded Caitlin of the respectful quiet of a Japanese tea ceremony. The woman then turned from the stone as though wrenching herself from her beloved and paced to the hall. Caitlin followed quickly, maternal instincts on guard. But when Yokane stopped outside Jacob's door and looked for Caitlin's permission before entering, her fears subsided somewhat. Given a nod, the woman collected herself with a deep breath and silently let herself into Jacob's room. The two women stood just within the doorway.

Once again, the eerie sound of a nonexistent wind was accompanying Jacob's deep sleep breathing. But Caitlin barely had time to register it before Yokane shocked her by laughing. The woman's face and hands were raised up to the ceiling—as Caitlin had done, instinctively, on the roof.

Yokane's smile was broad and bright, her fingers spread widely, trembling not with dread but with a kind of euphoria. After a moment, the woman turned to exit without even looking at Caitlin. She only said, "I thought they all perished."

"Who?"

"Those at the final *cazh*," Yokane replied.

Yokane brushed past Caitlin on her way to the hallway. When Caitlin caught up to her and stopped her, Yokane was restoring the wrapped stone to her inner pocket.

"What did you see?"

"What your son saw," Yokane replied. "A Galderkhaani woman."

Caitlin waited for more. It didn't come.

"See, this is the value of having a conversation," Caitlin said. "I give *you* access to information, you give *me* your interpretation."

"There is no more," Yokane said, apologetic for the first time. "Not yet."

Caitlin regarded her suspiciously. "But you *expect* more."

"I do," Yokane replied.

Caitlin was beginning to catch on.

"You didn't visit me on the subway, in my living room, then come back because you were worried about Jacob," Caitlin said. "Hell, you were MIA during the whole thing with Maanik—even though you were aware of it."

"That is true."

Now Caitlin was angry. The only thing that stopped her from running into the living room and threatening to toss the mosaic tile out the window was that the woman could probably drop her with a twitch of her index finger.

Caitlin forced herself to calm. "Then why are you here, if not to help me and my son?"

"A serious situation has arisen elsewhere. I had to make sure you and Jacob were not the cause. He is just receiving, not generating or channeling. Neither are you."

Caitlin stiffened. "And if he had been?"

The woman was silent.

"You *would* have hurt him," Caitlin said.

"No," Yokane said. "I would have interceded, as you did with your patients. But it wasn't necessary."

"Necessary for *what*?"

"To save this city, for a start. And then the world." Yokane pointed to the living room windows. "You are aware of the animals in peril out there? The stones, thousands of them just like mine, are coming to life."

"How do you know this?"

"The stone," she replied. "It has not stopped screaming since a few weeks ago."

"You mean, it isn't like that all the time?"

Yokane shook her head.

"Why now?" Caitlin asked.

"Galderkhaan is being freed from the ice."

"You're saying that climate change has found *another* way to destroy civilization?"

"You are perilously flip," Yokane said, moving in on her. "I am not the only one who knows of the stones and their power. With Galderkhaan comes the Source. And there are those who would seek to use it."

"How?"

"If I knew that, I could stop them," Yokane said.

Caitlin backed off. She was silent, overwhelmed. She knew she could not fully trust this stranger, but she had always feared that the recent events had been larger, more encompassing, than the assault of souls on the living. From the madness in Kashmir to the rats in Washington Square Park, global discordance, unease, panic were afoot.

"So what now?" Caitlin asked. "Are we done here?"

"Here, yes," Yokane said and turned her eyes toward Jacob's room. "Whoever is in contact with your son has more to tell us."

"And you know *that* how?"

"There are no self-inflicted wounds. This is not a forced *cazh*, a strong soul preying on the weak. I believe she is trying to communicate, not trying to ascend."

"Communicate what?" Caitlin asked.

"I do not know," the woman admitted. "But we must find out."

"Then I repeat: what now?" Caitlin asked.

"I have established a connection with your son on my own," she said. "What he sees and hears, I will see and hear."

"Goddamn it!" Caitlin yelled suddenly. "You could at least have asked!"

The smaller woman looked up. "To help you protect this world? Would you have refused? Should we waste *more* time with debate?"

Caitlin moved away in disgust. She didn't like being outmaneuvered and out-thought.

"You must not interfere," Yokane said.

"You can't ask that."

"I don't ask it, I insist," Yokane replied. "Are you really prepared to feel around and across the planes of existence *blindly*, with your son?" she asked. "There are more powerful, elemental forces and greater minds at work than yours *or* mine. There is no room for trial and error like you had with your two clients."

Caitlin could not find a reply.

Yokane settled into a more relaxed tone of voice. "Now that I know there is another presence near Jacob, I will make sure they are never alone." Yokane's dark eyes bore into Caitlin's and once again, Caitlin believed her.

"So you'll be a guardian," Caitlin said. "You won't 'inhabit' Jacob."

Yokane nodded once. "I am not a vandal."

There was no irritation or condescension in her tone. Caitlin relaxed a little more. Yokane turned and Caitlin followed her back toward the living room. There, showing the same reverence as before, the woman wrapped and pocketed her stone.

"In return for my help," Yokane said, "you will do something for me, since we have limited time and I cannot pursue two goals at once."

"There is another stone," Caitlin said.

For the first time, Yokane seemed surprised.

"You've had that one for a while, and the animals have only been acting up for a couple of weeks," Caitlin said. "Something else had to be the cause."

"The stone has a companion," Yokane acknowledged. "It is located in a mansion on Fifth Avenue and Ninth Street, home of the Global Explorers' Club. It is comprised of people who know about Galderkhaan."

"Know . . . what?" Caitlin asked.

"That is what you must find out," Yokane told her. "Specifically, why have these artifacts suddenly become more active? Why is an ascended soul trying to contact Jacob?"

"Why can't you go?"

"I have been too long around this stone," she replied, patting her coat. "I vibrate with it; it *knows* me. If I were to get close to the other stone it would cause more havoc. Already, the two are forming lines of connection with their companions in the South Pole. Together, their impact would be exponential."

Caitlin understood, then, just how powerful the Galderkhaani mosaics had to be. Yokane wasn't subtle, but it was possible she wasn't exaggerating, either. "What do I have to do?" Caitlin asked.

"Speak to the people in the mansion, determine if *they* are somehow using the other stones . . . or the Source. They will not want to talk to you," she muttered as she walked to the front door. "You must make them."

Realizing that Caitlin hadn't followed her, she motioned urgently.

"I mean now," Yokane said. "You must go now."

"I'm not waking Jacob and bringing him to that place," Caitlin said. "And no, you cannot babysit."

Yokane brushed the air with her hand. "The Galderkhaani woman will not allow Jacob to be harmed." She smiled a little for the first time. "Not physically."

"Where was she when Jacob had a freakin' seizure?"

"No doubt she caused that establishing contact," Yokane said. "As you know, it is not a pleasant process nor a predictable science. If it helps, I am sure she watched over him when you went to the roof."

"That was the roof; but you're talking about sending me miles downtown," Caitlin said. "The only way I'll leave is to have someone stay with him. Sit there while I make a call."

Yokane sat. So she *could* be reasonable.

But when Caitlin picked up her phone, she wasn't sure who to ask. She was afraid to try to explain this to her parents, and besides, they lived too far away for "right now." Ben? She was afraid of explaining it to him too, especially with his recent commendable but inconvenient protectiveness. What about Barbara or Anita? It would certainly open their eyes to see a descendant of the civilization they didn't really believe had existed.

Christ. She didn't want to call anyone.

But she remembered with horror her vision, Jacob's terror, and called Ben with one hand while using the other to search through the kitchen for jasmine tea.

CHAPTER 19

A quarter hour later, assured that Benjamin Moss was on his way, Yokane departed. Then she walked to the nearest intersection and vomited into a trash can. She held the edge of the bin for a moment, her eyes closed, waiting to see if anything else was going to come up.

"Are you all right?" a man asked as he stepped from a taxi.

"Thank you, yes." Yokane smiled. "Bad seafood, I think."

"Would you like my cab?"

"No, thank you," she said. "The air will help."

The man turned and hurried on his way. Yokane pushed herself from the bin and stood more steadily than she had a right to.

This had happened frequently over the past few days—both food and images coming up. It began when her *kavar* suddenly and surprisingly linked to another power source, another stone, crafting something more potent. It had happened about two weeks ago on a street north of Washington Square Park, when she was walking home from one of her frequent late-night strolls. She had regained consciousness in the stairwell of the Group's mansion. It was the claws that had woken her up, and the writhing, and the piercing squeaks of hundreds of rats on top of her, claws and tails scraping across her face, catching in her hair, burying her from sight. She'd frozen in a fetal position, in abject horror as the rats scrabbled in their mad panic.

It was over an hour before the rodents finally relaxed and wandered off, the ones that were still alive. Yokane, shaking, had stood among the lumpen piles of death and staggered away. No matter how many showers she took, eye rinses, teeth brushings, she didn't feel clean for days afterward.

Now, having involuntarily relived the experience again in her open state, her stomach had rebuked her. She walked west toward the Hudson River, then south. She hoped that the view of the water, the river emptying into the bay, would steady her. It did, somewhat. But not nearly enough.

The situation was dangerous, more dangerous than she had let on to the psychiatrist. Someone was trying very hard to get through—someone who had *cazhed* with another. A woman and a man, both of them pushing toward any soul that could hear them.

They had found Caitlin O'Hara but Caitlin O'Hara refused to listen. So they sought her son.

Why? Yokane wondered. It had to have something to do with the two *kavars* being active. The timing was too proximate.

Yokane continued to walk. Whatever the cost, she could not give up. She wished she could go in Caitlin's stead but that was not possible. She had gone back to the mansion one more time, only to feel the young scientist die. She was too afraid to go back again, so there was only the other path available to her.

Is she varrem? Yokane asked again and again as she walked. That was a crucial question. *Is she ours?* She seemed to be a person of strong spirit, but that did not mean she was descended from the Priests. Though the lineage had been carefully tracked, the chaos of the last day left potential loopholes. Galderkhaani may have slipped through, those who had put flight ahead of *cazh*.

Yokane had nursed a hope that Caitlin was *varrem*. But even there, she was torn. The doctor had fought to prevent Maanik from bonding with a desperate soul from Galderkhaan. And then there was the rainy, genocidal night when Caitlin had rent the sky with her force, and suddenly Yokane had felt soul after soul, her entire Priestly family, simply wink out of existence.

That sudden, overwhelming loneliness had paralyzed her for days. The Han woman renting a room in Chinatown to her had thought she was ill and kept trying to ply her with herbal teas. Yokane had only starved and wept and hated Caitlin.

When she regained rational thought Yokane knew that hatred was pointless and irrelevant. She knew she had to watch this woman, learn as much as she could about her. See what light and perspective the woman could provide on the hazy vision she herself had been experiencing.

Now she knew.

Yokane walked on through the lamp-lit night, her hands held at the center of her torso. She pointed the first two fingers of her left hand down, the first two of her right hand up.

Awareness flooded her inner and outer senses. The very spaces between the buildings of the city became as tangible as the buildings themselves. The millions of breathing bodies were knots of density across her field of sensation. Her emptied spirit filled with energy—

She stopped on a corner and leaned against a lamppost. But the energy was being drained.

"No . . . not *again*!"

Yokane was suddenly wrenched away, pulled back across fathoms of time and space, to a huge chamber with a domed ceiling, open to the sky. She had been here several times over the last few months but returned now with greater force and sharper awareness. She could not inform Caitlin O'Hara but it was the two souls central to the vision that filled her with dread.

In the heart of the chamber amid water and fire, a dozen people in robes had gathered. A woman at the very center was performing movements and gestures that Yokane recognized from her training. As the woman moved, the others followed her exactly, and Yokane could feel immense pulses of energy rushing in torrents from their hands, through the air, through the walls, and away. The movements were slow but the intention behind them was pure fire, controlled ferocity and rage and conviction. Yokane felt a strange blend of horror and elation, a flood of anger and triumph rising within her, until the door to the chamber slammed open and a voice shouted in Galderkhaani, "Rensat! Gather everyone, quickly!"

It came from a short, elderly man with wildly curling white hair, hurrying as fast as he could across the chamber. The woman at the center never faltered in her movements but spoke simultaneously.

"What is wrong?" the woman asked.

"Out there"—he pointed in the direction from which he'd come—"there are rumors that the Source is active!"

The woman stiffened. "It must be stopped," she said.

"We cannot access it!" the man said.

"Then we must find those who *operate* it and stop them!"

"You will kill them?"

"If necessary, as Enzo's sister tried to do."

The man stood there, uncertain how to proceed. Suddenly his nose crinkled.

"The air!" the woman said, insisting. "Smell the air!"

The man inhaled as if he were already dismissing the notion, but the result caused confusion. "Sulfur," he replied. "It's true—"

The ground-shattering sound of an explosion rocked through the room. It came from outside. The Priests lost their sequence in the movements. Rensat looked up in panic. Visible through the latticed ceiling was smoke, huge, throttling clouds of smoke. The man rushed to the stairs by the wall and lurched up them. He approached the nearest window and looked out, looked east.

"Oh gods," he breathed. "The *khaan* . . ."

The woman beseeched everyone to join hands with another, as many others as they could, and recite the *cazh*.

"Come to me, Pao!" Rensat cried. "Quickly, while there is time for us!"

"Oh gods!" Pao screamed as he grasped her outstretched fingers.

Then there was fire and torrent and Yokane's body fell sideways, sliding down the lamppost. She breathed heavily, losing the little energy she had gathered.

"Oh gods," she murmured, repeating Pao's last words.

She pushed herself from the streetlight and began to walk. Walking had helped before and it worked now. Soon her head was clear again and the vision of Galderkhaan held only the weight of a memory and the message that had demanded tonight's action.

She had not wanted to open herself to Caitlin, but she knew she needed help immediately. She knew that working through the boy would force Caitlin's hand.

Yokane continued to walk but she remained closed to the city and the past. She wanted to avoid Fifth Avenue and Washington Square, continuing over to the East Side and down toward her closet-sized room.

She had told Caitlin to contact her—by phone—after her visit to the Group's headquarters. When that was done, when Yokane had rested, she would know better what had to be done in the past to protect the future.

Mustering her strength, the woman continued to walk. The night had been more exhausting than she had anticipated, and after a few minutes more she decided she had walked enough. It was time to rest. She hadn't seen many cabs pass by so she hurried for the subway and took the D train to the West Village.

The respite was what she needed—though the buzzing in her pocket as the train passed below the Group's mansion was noticeable not just to herself but to those nearest her. Most of the passengers probably assumed it was her cell phone, but their annoyed looks put

Yokane on guard: she couldn't afford a confrontation, especially if there was a police officer on board. She wished it were a pet *thyodularasi* whose smooth flesh she could stroke and calm, and it would calm her . . . at least, that was the legend. She had only seen the animal's bones, held in secret and treasured by the generations who had come before her. She left the subway at Lafayette Street—well below the Group's mansion.

Between her worried thoughts; her increasingly sad, wistful reflections; and the stone buzzing in her pocket, Yokane had very little attention to spare for her surroundings. She walked through Little Italy, then continued east. She only half-turned when approaching footsteps seemed uncommonly close.

Three fingers jabbed into the angle of her jaw and neck and Yokane's body dropped. Her last thought was of Caitlin and the Group's headquarters, and the silent scream her body was no longer able to make—

Casey Skett caught her so quickly that to a young woman walking on the other side of the street, she seemed only to wobble. With one arm Casey lifted Yokane just enough so that her feet would not drag on the pavement and walked her to the open passenger door of his Department of Sanitation van. He checked and no pedestrians were looking to see what had happened. He lifted Yokane into the seat, taking care to make it look friendly and romantic in case anyone was gazing from a nearby window. With the female belted into the passenger seat, he shut the door and moved around to get behind the wheel. He drove into the Group's underground parking spot, parked, unfastened Yokane, and dragged her into the back of the van. There, he pulled the object from her pocket but did not pause to inspect the still-vibrating artifact. He'd known since Arni died what this descendant of the bloody Priestly suicide cult had been carrying. He put the stone in his own pocket, removed a leash hanging from the wall of the van, and strangled Yokane with it until her feet stopped their spasms.

Then he drove straight to the animal hospital to utilize their incinerator.

He would decide later if and when he would tell Flora about any of it . . . including his ties to the people she sought.

The Technologists of Galderkhaan.

CHAPTER 20

There was a sharp chill in the air and an intermittent wind coming from Washington Square Park. Fallen leaves crackled as they skidded along the dimly lit sidewalk and scratched the sides of parked cars.

Caitlin was oblivious to all of it. Standing on the front steps of the Group's mansion, she was prepared to try the word "Galderkhaan" as her admittance password. Since it was around ten o'clock at night she couldn't pretend to be a tourist or a neighborhood outreach representative from the Church of the Ascension across the street—though the name was apt enough.

But excuses weren't needed. The young woman who opened the door wearing green sparkly eyeshadow seemed a bit surprised at the sight of her, then immediately asked Caitlin to come in without another word. Flora had hired Erika as an assistant for many reasons, but the fact that she verged on having an eidetic memory was especially helpful. Erika did not say aloud that she remembered the visitor from a video she'd seen of a gathering in Jacmel, Haiti.

She showed Caitlin into Flora's office. It was filled with a mishmash of antique furniture that showed a preference for Art Deco and long brown-and-blue velvet drapes that covered the windows.

Erika found Flora coming up the stairs from the basement and warned her who had arrived.

"She's *here*?" Flora exclaimed. It was all the Group leader said in response. The words had the weight of continental drift, an acknowledgment that large things were in motion.

Donning a smile, she entered her office.

"I am Flora Davies."

"Caitlin O'Hara," her guest replied. "A mutual friend sent me in your direction. Yokane?"

"Oh, yes," Flora said.

"You know her?" Caitlin asked.

"I know of her," Flora replied. In fact she had never heard the name but she certainly wasn't going to give the woman a reason to walk away. She didn't say anything else, simply gazed at Caitlin.

"I'm a psychiatrist," Caitlin continued.

The comment invited a response, but Flora offered none. The silence stretched out.

After years of talking with teenagers, Catlin recognized the recalcitrance tango—similar to the slow dance she had done with Odilon across the Ping-Pong table. Flora Davies's demeanor was notably polite and polished, and Caitlin had no idea how long she would maintain her silence. It was likely that she had been presenting this pleasant facade for decades. So Caitlin just stared around the room at the antiquities, maps, and books. If Yokane were right about Davies's having a Galderkhaani artifact somewhere in this mansion, then hiding everything would be much more natural for her than confiding. Caitlin might have to say something inspirational, irresistible, to break through that wall.

Yet Caitlin wasn't sure what she could or should say. Mentioning Yokane had elicited little response and no flicker of familiarity, no smile of liking or flash of dislike. She was betting Davies had never heard of her. And an archaeology group that hadn't publicized one of the greatest finds in the history of the field was probably not to be trusted. It went against academic tradition. You find something big, you announce it, *then* you go to radio silence while you study it and prepare to publish. That way, if someone else finds one, you still get bragging or naming rights.

Besides, Caitlin didn't want to share her knowledge of Galderkhaan without getting something in return. Flora might take the information, thank Caitlin with practiced politeness, and kick her out the door. Caitlin needed information and her silence was the only bait she had.

There's only one difference between us, Caitlin thought as her eyes scanned the heavy desk. Flora had obviously been here a while. She had time. Caitlin did not. Her experience with Galderkhaani told her that if there were one ancient soul attached to Jacob, there could be others not far off.

She was suddenly, sorely tempted to surprise Flora by taking a shortcut through an energy exchange, but Yokane's trepidation about "accessing" while in the proximity of a Galderkhaan artifact seemed wise to heed. Forming such a conduit was also one of Caitlin's hidden assets that she would not reveal until she had some sense of common purpose with this woman.

Or until you've got nothing else to work with.

Flora made a careful opening move, a bland statement of the obvious:

"What does a psychiatrist want with our Explorers' Group?" Flora asked. "Yokane must have thought there was a good reason to send you."

"I've been doing some exploring of my own," Caitlin said mildly.

"Where?"

Caitlin decided to take this to the next level. "Everywhere. Through patients. They've had visions."

"You used hypnosis?"

"Something along those lines," Caitlin said mildly. "May I ask—what do *you* explore?"

"The rather more mundane physical world," Flora replied apologetically. "Would you care to see?"

"I would," Caitlin replied, trying to hide her surprise that Flora had offered.

Flora began the speech she reserved for senators and university presidents. The speech was accompanied by a tour through two floors of the mansion.

"Definitely not a museum," Caitlin observed as she stepped—vaulted, in fact—over a leaning pile of spears obscuring a doorway.

Flora laughed politely and fluttered her hand at the jumble of objects in the room, which was actually slightly more organized than the others.

"This is a storage area for our explorers," Flora said. "We offer categorization, authentication, and appraisal services. Many people like to donate old rocks and stones and such for tax benefits."

"An old-school approach to collecting?" Caitlin said.

"Like medieval nobility," Flora admitted. "Getting material is the thing, and discussing the rarities with each other over drinks."

"But not with anyone else."

"This is an old, very private sandbox, Dr. O'Hara," Flora remarked. "Most of the donors and some of the archaeologists we fund have an inflated sense of the worth of their finds."

Or deflated, Caitlin thought.

The mansion was a very convenient spot at which to purposely devalue and conceal goods. The eccentric non-filing system had a cultivated sloppiness to it that screamed "underfunding"—an excuse to raise donations or grants that went to other work. The real work, whatever that was. Caitlin had no doubt that Davies also functioned as a fence for unwanted items whenever the opportunity arose. The woman might even trade something of enormously high value to a collector or museum for something she particularly wanted.

Caitlin noticed that there were more weapons among the artifacts than any other functional item, yet nothing of Galderkhaan . . . until in a cramped, claustrophobic hallway they passed a closed door that gave Caitlin the faintest sense of vertigo. She experienced it for no more than half a pace, thankfully, so she covered it just as Flora glanced back at her.

"Mind your head," Flora said, patting a low beam as they passed into another Crock-Pot of a room.

"You know what this place needs?" Caitlin said lightly. "A dog. An Irish wolfhound, negotiating Polynesian oars and the like. To complete the picture."

Flora laughed. "I've thought about it," she said. She hadn't.

"Crazy what happened with the animals today," Caitlin tossed out.

"Oh, I'm sure they'll trace it back to some sort of emission," Flora delivered smoothly. "Remember that maple syrup smell all over Manhattan in the mid-2000s? Turned out to be a fenugreek factory in Jersey. With all the communication waves that are floating around now"—she whirled her hand above her head—"who knows what kinds of bandwidth are affecting our brains." She added as she returned them to her office, "Have you experienced anything like that? Disorientation?"

The question was quite unexpected.

"No. Why do you ask?"

"All this talk of hypnosis—and you seemed to stumble back there," Flora said, taking her own seat and gesturing for Caitlin to do the same.

"Did I?" Caitlin replied weakly.

"A little." She smiled thinly. "Was there anything specific this Yokeen said I could help you with?"

"Yokane."

"Yes, of course. What did I say?"

Caitlin didn't answer, nor did Flora wait for a response. It was a transparent but necessary game the woman was playing. Caitlin sat but decided that in the next five minutes she was going to get the hell out of this building. Davies had intentionally mispronounced Yokane's name, lied about knowing her, and everything else she'd said was just too facile, too controlled. Caitlin had nothing to show for her investment of a half hour.

Damn it. Moving pawns on a board wasn't going to cut it. Yokane had been clear that there was a spirit affecting Jacob, so whatever was happening here, whatever its consequences, was just a second priority for Caitlin.

"I'm sorry," Caitlin began. "I think there's been some kind of mistake."

"What do you mean, Doctor?"

"I mean, I don't know why I'm here."

Flora smiled. "Well, you *are* here," she said. "Do you have any idea *why* your friend might have suggested you come?" Her eyes were still, like little cameras, her expression showing curiosity but not concern.

"I'm not certain," Caitlin confessed. "Look, I'm—could I use your restroom actually?"

"Of course." Flora did not stand up. "Back in the low hallway, second door on your left."

Caitlin rose carefully to make sure she didn't pass out.

After the psychiatrist had exited, Erika heard the tiny squeak of the door that drove her crazy every time Flora entered the basement. She poked her head into Flora's office and, seeing her there, warned her where their guest had gone. Flora nodded. Once Erika had returned to her desk, Flora wrapped her hand around a heavy glass paperweight, placed it in her trouser pocket, and quietly followed Caitlin to the basement steps.

At the top of the narrow concrete stairs, Caitlin's slight vertigo returned but quickly passed. But the fear beneath it stayed.

There's no safe way out of this, she told herself. *You've got to get as much information as you can.*

She quickly but quietly descended the stairs and, at the bottom, caught a glimpse of a long corridor full of deep freezers. Her mind flooded with images so suddenly that she lost her balance and had to flop down on the last step. The flashing, strobing visions jumped from a young woman in a lab coat lugging several black panels down the hall, to Flora carrying a tray of objects going the other way, to a skinny man pacing down the hall, sticking his head through each doorway before he turned and walked up the steps through Caitlin. And then it made a giant leap—to a great airship, clouds, burning clouds, burning passengers—

Caitlin put her face in her hands but they couldn't block out the images that kept coming, of Flora and a man who looked Spanish or Italian arguing on the steps; a tall blond man in a white shirt walking away while unbuttoning a lab coat—

Unwinding . . . time unwinding.

Something down here was spooling her through the recent history of the hallway. How was that possible and how could she stop it?

Unseen by Caitlin, who was blinded by time, Adrienne Dowman appeared at the end of the corridor. "Dr. Davies!" she cried.

At moment later, Flora paced down the stairs toward the unheeding guest, her right hand gripping the paperweight in her pocket. Adrienne was already there, leaning slightly over the woman but not reaching down to help. She caught Flora's eye.

"Who is she?" Adrienne asked.

"Not now," Flora said, indicating Caitlin with a nod. "What happened? Why did you call me?"

"It lit up."

Flora stepped past Caitlin. "Dr. O'Hara," she said over her shoulder, "it's best if you sit quietly for a moment. Do not follow—"

But Caitlin grabbed her ankle. "That doesn't work for me," she said.

Flora turned and spent a moment she did not have. "What are you talking about?"

"You have a mosaic tile in this building," Caitlin said through her teeth. "It's not very happy to be here."

She saw triumph in Flora's eyes. Caitlin had cracked first. Flora believed this was her game now.

"Stay here," Flora said.

"You don't know what you're doing," Caitlin replied, letting go of the woman's ankle.

"On the contrary. We have control of it," Flora said evenly.

Caitlin decided not to mention the other tile, the masses of them in the South Pole. That, and the details about Yokane, was information she would trade if necessary.

Shooing Adrienne ahead, Flora turned and strode toward the room the younger woman had exited. Caitlin tried to stand but wavered immediately and had to sit back down. The reverse flow of events had dimmed but not stopped. She tried making the "cut off" gesture she had used on the subway but it didn't work. She was weaker in this mansion than anywhere else. She huddled into herself, feeling enhanced and powerless at the same time.

Flora, on the other hand, was fueled by purpose. She entered the chamber as if it were a shrine and cautiously approached the Serpent. Its former resting place, the room with the ruined floor, was locked away from sight with a mat rolled up outside the base of its door to disguise the damage to the cement. Here, in the new chamber, Adrienne had restored the acoustic levitation and once more the symbols on the stone were faceup. As Adrienne had indicated, the symbols were indeed glowing an ivory white. The luminescence wasn't very strong and nearly disappeared by the time it hit the black soundboard looming above it. The light was leisurely flickering through the symbols in some kind of sequence and the stone was still vibrating faintly.

"Any indication that it's going to flip again, or alter its position in the node in any way?" Flora asked.

"None," Adrienne said, "and no changes to the environment."

They both involuntarily glanced at the floor: it was smooth and normal.

"Video?" Flora asked.

Adrienne pointed at a camera she'd set up on a tripod in a corner, behind a wall of bulletproof glass in case of an explosion.

"Get yourself a chair," Flora said, gazing adoringly at the object. "I don't want you to take your eyes off this thing."

"Not in here," Adrienne started. "We can hook the camera into—"

"Sit in the doorway then, Adrienne." Flora snapped as she walked away. "I won't have data slipping through the pixels."

As she arrived at the stairs, without asking, Flora reached down, put a hand under Caitlin's elbow, and hauled her to her feet. She walked the psychiatrist down the hall to the room she still thought of as Arni's lab and plopped her on a stool.

Caitlin looked up. Her visual feed immediately reset itself to the present time. She was able to focus on Flora's eyes now.

Flora noticed her gaze. "I recognized you," she said.

"From where?"

"I saw you in a video and I wondered if you were just a Vodou voyeur." Flora smiled with a mean twist to her mouth. "Yet here you are with all sorts of knowledge. Tell me what you know."

"About what?" Caitlin asked. She was not being coy.

"Start with Galderkhaan. What have you to do with it?"

It was still strange to hear someone other than Ben say that word. Beaten mentally, psychologically, and now physically, Caitlin opened up—selectively. First she explained her history with the Galderkhaani Priests who had failed in their *cazh*, taking care not to mention the names or locations of the teenagers who had been affected. Flora pressed for details but did not fight her when Caitlin resisted.

Caitlin talked about the dead souls' possession of the living, admitted it had happened but said she didn't understand how or to what extent. She skipped her travels back in time but mentioned that she'd had help translating some of the Galderkhaani language.

"Who helped?" Flora demanded. "And what did you find?"

"Not now," Caitlin said, thinking the deciphered words could be an additional bargaining chip in the future.

Suddenly, Caitlin gasped. She felt something hit her, a connection, hard but fleeting. She saw Yokane's face, heard her cry out, felt the stone she had carried, saw a final glimpse of a skinny man moving her dead body—all of it directed into her brain with spearlike precision. Though the impression was fleeting, the damage was not. Caitlin's mind remained open and here, in this room, she saw the skinny man once again, bundling the corpse of a tall, blond man into a bag, then a Mediterranean man looking on while Flora probed the dead man's skull.

Flora arched her eyebrows. "What is it, Dr. O'Hara?"

"The dead man in this room. Others."

"What others?"

Caitlin ignored her. She sat there, still, as though she'd seen Medusa. The hit from Yokane's stone had connected her to the tile that had been in this room. Caitlin felt terrified and out of control, yet at the same time she had never experienced such energy coursing through her. It was as if she had become Arfa, Jack London, all the unsettled animals in New York. But she *had* to keep it contained.

Flora saw her inward look. "Talk to me," she ordered.

"It's radioactive, the stone you have, with the carvings of crescents in a triangle."

Flora's body jerked as if she'd lost balance on the stool. "How do you know about the carvings?"

"I'm looking at the stone. No, *into* it. It . . . it's showing me the history of this room."

For the first time, Flora seemed unnerved. Caitlin's eyes snapped back to her. "Your dead man studied it and it was radioactive."

"Nonsense," Flora sputtered. "We checked it for radioactivity."

"That Geiger counter was ticking hard right before it killed him," Caitlin said evenly. Finally she felt she was back on an equal level with Davies.

Flora grabbed Caitlin's forearm. "Before *what* killed him? The stone?"

"I don't know if it was intentional or just a consequence. But it did."

Flora's phone went off and she cursed. She wrenched it out of her pocket as if she were going to throw it across the room but out of habit checked the screen.

"I must take this," she said, then stood, turned her back on Caitlin, and walked into the hall.

CHAPTER 21

Pao and Rensat shrieked after Mikel as he raced away from them. He was surprised that they did not pursue him. Perhaps they were bound to the room by some mechanism he did not understand.

The wind in the tunnel will not be much help to spirits, he thought.

Their echoing cries were a combination of pent-up rage and hopeless frustration.

Mikel tore through the huge room, but not blindly. It was lit with the fires of hell.

It was the opening to one of the pits that serviced the Source—a hot-tub-sized vent that had apparently been designed to release the steam pressure lest it rupture the pipes. There were small openings above that must have led through the tunnel to the surface to give the steam some way out; perhaps they had originally been used to melt the oncoming ice, to keep the glaciers at bay. There were also tiles along one wall: Mikel could only surmise that Rensat had been in here earlier looking for clues to the identity of whoever turned the damned thing on. Or trying to find Enzo or who knew what else.

The chamber was a well of unfathomable energy, power so compact and deep it seemed to have mass. That pressure was softened somewhat by the life-sustaining mask; even so, his body was vibrating, oscillating at a cellular level from the energies that surrounded him.

And that was just the beginning, he realized. The force traveling through the Source would be unimaginable. Not just the part that was manifest here, but throughout the world: for all he knew, the Galderkhaani had probed deep, sent their tiles or some other construct far into the crust, the mantle, perhaps beyond.

Mikel had only those few seconds of total awareness to himself. Then he saw, in his mind, Rensat touching the tiles on her side of the room—activating a sequence of some kind. And then Pao was there, with her, also in his mind.

There was no reason to pursue me, Mikel realized. *The tiles are projecting their thoughts along an arc, to other tiles throughout the ruins.* It was the same way that pure energy had gotten into the minds of animals caught along lines between New York and Antarctica.

As Mikel feared, Pao was not about to let him leave without an agreement to help.

"I will not permit it!" he heard.

The immaterial Galderkhaani attacked the only way they could—by forcing Mikel's mind to open itself to images stored in the ancient library and to Pao's own warnings.

He cannot harm me, Mikel thought . . . *hoped*. If it were possible, Pao would have done so already. But he had not reckoned on the ingenuity of the Galderkhaani. The safeguards were clearly designed to cause intruders to make their own mistakes, make them unable to distinguish between the real and the unreal.

The first visual assault were the fangs of a leopard seal. As the enormous head of the animal lunged at him. Mikel felt the horror though not the pain or disfigurement of the animal biting at his throat. His heart beat hard and fast despite the structure imposed by the mask's skin. Every instinct he had screamed at him to turn back, to seek Pao's room with a promise to submit, behave.

But he had never listened to his saner angels and refused to do so now. Mikel ground his teeth together.

It's not real! he thought hard.

Mikel stepped uncertainly forward, head bowed against the pressure being released by the vent—a cyclonic wind that was dissipated, he now noticed, into a series of funnels above. There had to be a doorway of some kind to the tunnel and the airstream beyond, he thought, so he continued into the maelstrom. The leopard seal retreated; Mikel could see it swimming in a long-vanished well, a pool, a short distance away, staring at him. It did not attack again, not physically. It lurked. Mikel's will had rolled the vision back.

Better than having my brain melt, he thought.

"*You will not get away!*" he heard Pao shriek after him.

I will . . . Mikel thought.

"*Your efforts will fail!*"

They must not . . .

"*I will join with your soul and trap you among the bones of Galderkhaan for all time!*"

You are not real! Mikel screamed inside.

"*Listen to your words,*" Pao sneered. "*They are uttered in a dead tongue that you have never learned. This is very real!*"

And then, through the stones, Pao's entire mind dissolved into Mikel's brain like salt in water. Pieces of living Galderkhaan poured in—towers and villas, airships with nets strung between them, the odors of the sea and jasmine, the laughter and tears and chatter of citizens.

Mikel wrenched his brain into focus. *The stones*, he thought, *I have to get away from them.*

But then there was something else. Something whispering and beguiling under it all like the serpent in Eden or the Sirens.

"*Seek that which I seek,*" Pao commanded. "*Be what I am. The joys of all-knowing await.*"

But Pao misjudged his subject. Mikel was not so far enamored of their eternal power as he was of the power to be gained of its knowledge in his real world. Fighting the temptation was seductive but easy. What would life or ascension or whatever awaited be like if he had to endure the guilt of its deadly course of action?

Galderkhaan is already gone, he told himself. *You are fighting to save everything and everyone you know!*

Mikel's desire to resist created a slight but tangible split that gave him a foothold in his own identity. In that moment he both felt and understood the spirit's driving obsession: to find the woman Mikel knew from the video taken in Haiti, the one person they believed could actually go back and prevent what Pao was calling the *ulvor*—traitor—from destroying Galderkhaan. That singular desire was lodged in his brain, in Galderkhaani, now that he was away from the stones in the library.

As Mikel continued to make his way into the tunnel, its walls lit with phosphors, he was forced to live through images and episodes of Pao's life, the life of his body. It felt as if Pao were trying to meld their lives somehow, draw Mikel's soul into the past through emotional and physical experiences, shove it aside and insert his own soul in the young man's body.

The images were disjointed and out of chronological sequence. He saw and felt Pao's joy at holding a newborn daughter. He felt the anguish and ecstasy of his flaming death clutching Rensat. He sang to Vol in jubilation just after he finished writing the first chant of the *cazh*. Pao made love with ferocity. There were glimpses of many lovers, many places, many emotions. As a small boy, he pressed his hands against the great *hortatur* skin of a grounded balloon and marveled at the technology of Galderkhaan.

Then he stood on the side of a mountain, Pao as a much older man, weeping at the loss of Vol when Pao decided to join the Technologists. Then he was with more women, many more, and saw other lives that were too dim to discern clearly. Mikel sensed profound energy slither through his body as the earliest Priests began to decipher the gestures and movements derived from Candescent *grymat*—blood writing. He saw gory designs on the wall, bloodshed, violence . . .

Through Pao's eyes, from a place of concealment, Mikel watched Priests commit suicide as experiments, use their blood as paint. He cried out his feeling of tragedy and betrayal when two huge gangs of Priests and Technologists both ripped to fragments the banner that was supposed to hold the city together. Back on the mountainside, he felt the urge to raise his arms to the banished red-haired woman in her airship, and suppressed it. He felt guilt for half-believing her but never defending her. He had implored her for a name, to tell him who was planning a grievous assault on Galderkhaan, but she had refused to participate in the insanity. She only wished to get away. Pao had spoken to her sister, Enzo. She left too.

Then the dial of his life whipped madly once more. As a much younger man, Pao felt one glorious moment of ascension, just short of transcending, when the Priests first realized it might be possible to become Candescent. He felt the weight of a dead daughter in his arms, fatally burned in an accident with the Technologists' fire, an event that began the irreparable rift. Over and over and over, he felt Pao's heart shatter as his friends, his city, died one way and another in the fire and liquid rock. He relived the spirits' attempting to bond in dying Galderkhaan, their shrieking agony as flame ate them, flame commanded by her, by the woman in the void . . .

And yet strongest of all, Mikel felt Pao's yearning for Vol. He felt Vol disappear from Pao's life and then from the periphery of his life. He felt the loss of that connection after Pao ascended. Though Vol was also dead, the ascended could not communicate without having transcended as Pao and Rensat had done.

There was much more, out of order, out of joint, often moving so fast as to be incomprehensible. As Mikel fought to hold on to who he himself was, other memories fought back, threatened his physical and mental balance. The leopard seal was back in his mind. Mikel was becoming squeezed by images, sensations, emotions, *terror* . . . he was a very narrow entity in the middle. He tried with all his might to resist—

Back! he ordered himself. *Come back! Stay in the physical!*

Slowly, one at a time, Mikel picked up his feet and prayed that when he set each down, it would find the floor. He wasn't sure how long he had been walking through the cavernous tunnel toward the airstream but he knew he was much nearer to the point of its generation. And his shaking skin, organs, and bones warned him that, the mask notwithstanding, this attempt could surely be fatal.

Through it all, Pao was still present. Pao was reaching in and stretching out, trying to thin and control what little of Mikel remained.

The tiles, activated by Pao, added to his woes. Fresh images flooded in, of elegantly appointed row houses in a Scandinavian city, then a staggering fjord—a chasm of lesser gods.

Then a sudden leap to vast grasslands and people hunting with hawks. They looked Asiatic, perhaps Mongolian. These were things *he* knew. Mikel's own knowledge was now part of the ancient database.

Next, Mikel's personal memories were front and center. He was back in Antarctica, scanning the American bases, the planes landing for the summer season, the large supply ships toiling slowly toward the continent. Pao was now merging with Mikel's memories, making them one.

Christ, is this what the stones did to Arni? Mikel thought fearfully.

He felt the increasing pressure on his ears, on his skull, vibrating through sinew and blood and bone.

And then a jolt, a shock, a mental kick that Mikel had not anticipated. The Galderkhaani hooked into the thought of Flora, and suddenly Mikel's vision filled with the Group's mansion on Fifth Avenue. It gave him a flash of confidence, an anchor. But the location quickly became unpegged in time. Mikel swung from Arni's first interview there and his synesthetic reaction to Flora's office, to a lab where Flora was comparing the first two artifacts Mikel had obtained, to Flora's new assistant opening packages to reveal black soundboards.

Mikel rejected the image, fought back to the fast-narrowing window that was himself in the present. As he proceeded he heard the sound and feel of the air change and hoped that this was the start of the airstream. He could not afford to hesitate, to think. He had to find the way out.

The force of the wind grew stronger and he knew he was close. Then the rippling haze of the heat from the vent began to flow beside him, then behind him. He was closer. Then the howling of the wind returned, faintly at first, and he saw an opening ahead. There was no door and he realized that this room was inside a cave like the one where he'd found the sled. The Technologists had been ambitious but practical: they used existing geology wherever it was feasible. The wind tunnel would provide the added benefit of a primitive form of ventilation, providing a cooling aspect to the room.

Mikel wrapped his arms protectively around his head, and with a guttural cry jumped forward into the stream. The air lifted him as before and smashed him into the wall. Mikel shrieked in pain—his right wrist was surely broken. He took several more hard knocks to his shoulder and arms but not hard enough to break them, or him. And then he was in the sweet spot—rolling over and over helplessly but managing to stay in the center, without a sled. According to what he recalled of the map he was flying away from the city toward the sea. His broken wrist was numb but as long as he remained relaxed he could keep from spinning out of control.

But he was not out of Pao's reach entirely. The tiles were still all around him. The clarity of the images faded even as the pace of Pao's search increased, frenetic with determination.

Get out of my head! Mikel screamed inside, but to no avail.

Pao knew he could not count on Mikel but he was probing, desperate. Mikel saw Fifth Avenue, his own apartment. He saw places he had been in Manhattan that he had forgotten.

And then Mikel felt his own mind unsqueeze and return. Countless hours after it had all begun, it all swiftly faded. Every feed from Pao simply dribbled away. Distance must have become a deciding factor.

Mikel's first complete thought without Pao there to interfere—or help—was an immediate, very practical concern: he had no idea how to locate his entry point to the tunnel—the entry point on which his life depended. If he missed it, was there another route to the surface? Even if there were, he would be too far from the base to survive.

Mikel mentally manipulated his way along the network he had seen on the map. After many long minutes of re-creating them carefully, Mikel detected something ahead that he had seen before: a mosaic where the tiles were silent. Their darkness practically shouted to him from the expanse of wall, where gleaming tiles were as regular as subway stops. Perhaps this one was missing pieces, the circuits broken. All he knew was that they were unique among the mosaics he had seen since descending the dormant lava tube and it was the only hope he had.

But how to get out of the airstream? Mikel shifted his body and was immediately thrust up to the ceiling, lost his breath, but then rolled to his right and dropped. And suddenly, he was at the base of the broken tower, skidding forward painfully. He let his body do all the work, turned his will over to muscle memory, and surrendered control to his body and to the mask.

A minute later he felt for the panel. He found it and stopped moving.

There was no time to do a status assessment. His head was like a bag of cement powder, opaque and thick and lacking the porosity even for thought. He hobbled as fast as he could on his sprained ankles up the twisted, overturned spiral stairway, hauling himself up with his left arm, his right arm stabbing him with pain.

There was just one word in his head:

Safe.

He pulled himself from the tower and collapsed on the surface of the lava tube. With trembling fingers he pulled the mask from his skin so he could breathe the air firsthand.

Safe.

And suddenly, he was looking into the eyes of Siem der Graaf.

"My god," Siem said, crawling between two pink flares toward Mikel's stricken, ravaged face.

"You're still here!"

"Something happened. Something we could not explain. They agreed to let me come back—"

Mikel fumbled for his belt. "I must . . . call New York," he gasped, pressing the mask into Siem's hand. "My . . . I have to tell her."

"Wait until we are out of here," Siem implored.

"No time!" Mikel said. His arm shaking, he retrieved the radio and called Flora. Though he was nearer to the surface, the static was thick, communication difficult.

"Where are you?" Flora answered abruptly.

"I'm near a tunnel under the ice—I *found* it!" he blurted. "I found Galderkhaan!"

"Oh my good lord," Flora said.

"*Listen*. I have been with two Galderkhaani souls—you must find that woman . . . the one in the Haiti video."

"Caitlin O'Hara?"

"I don't know her name, just . . ."

"She is here with me now," Flora said.

"Protect her from the souls!" he said as interference broke up their communication. "Damn it!" He tried to fuss with the buttons, but it was no use.

"Please, let me get you out of here," Siem said.

Mikel was panting, looking around.

Siem put the mask into a pocket and reached for Mikel's right arm. Mikel groaned in pain. Siem tried the left arm, gave his support to the man, and the two of them staggered toward the crevasse on their knees. "The base move is delayed so our radios are back on. You've been through hell it looks like—I'll have them lower a harness."

"Quickly!" Mikel urged. "If he finds her, if he finds the *ulvor*—"

"What did you just say?" Siem asked, his eyes suddenly fearful.

Mikel reacted to Siem's look. "Why? What's happened?"

Siem held Mikel's hand to keep him from grabbing at his face. "Mikel," he said sharply, needing to get through to him. "I heard that word before. We all did. And others. They were something like '*Enzo, pato, Vol.*' "

"*How* did you hear that?" Mikel demanded. "Siem, *where*?"

"Something happened earlier—a vision, fire, a voice!"

"What kind of fire?"

"It was like something alive . . . a face."

"The flame that was pursuing me," Mikel said, more to himself than to Siem. "It had to be, it could *only* be. A soul afire, locked in that state by the tiles—like Pao and Rensat. But that soul was only ascended, unable to communicate with them."

"Mikel, *what are you saying*?"

Mikel ignored him. *Enzo. Pato. Vol.* He didn't know what *pato* meant, but he inferred, almost at once, what Pao and Rensat must never have suspected of their beloved friend Vol: that it was *he* who initiated the Source. Yet it made sense that he would have wanted to sabotage it, or turn it on to show that it wouldn't work. How horribly surprised he must have been.

"All right," Mikel went on, "someone, some soul, possesses this information. But Pao doesn't have that information, and even if he did he couldn't get back to stop him. He doesn't know—"

There was a punch inside Mikel's skull. His mouth swung slack as he stared into Siem's eyes. All in a rush, Pao was fully back in his mind. There was a cry of unutterable anguish as Pao realized the truth about his lover and friend.

Suddenly Mikel knew that he had been used, that Pao had pulled a ruse, only pretending to fade out with distance. The power of the tiles, controlled by Rensat, had allowed Pao to remain with him. And Mikel also realized with horror that now Pao had both names: Vol, from Siem . . . and Caitlin O'Hara, from Flora, from his own gullible stupidity.

"I gave it *all* to him!" Mikel cried. *I told him that it was a radio . . . to communicate with. And he knew I would use it for just that! All he had to do was wait a little longer.*

Now Pao departed, for real. Mikel's vision cleared though his head swam. His mind was his own again.

But in exchange for that freedom, he may unwittingly have given Pao the world.

And then, held tight in Siem's arms, he passed out.

• • •

Mikel clawed to wakefulness.

He was in a truck, lumping across the Antarctic terrain. Crushed between Bundy, who was driving, and Siem, who was half-leaning against the passenger-side door, Mikel was still in the harness that had been used to haul him up; the retreat from wherever to wherever had obviously been hasty.

"Thank you," Mikel said, his mouth dry.

Siem looked over at him. "You're welcome."

"I—I know you won't understand, but what I said before—we have to warn the Group. Warn the woman."

"We will," Siem said. "Hold on . . . let me get you some water." He reached into the mesh pocket hanging low on the door, by his feet.

"Not important," he said. "She's in terrible danger. I must call. Stop so I can get out and find a damn signal!"

"Wait until we reach—"

"Damn it, I *must* get it," they heard Mikel moan. "Please."

"We can't stop the truck!" Siem told him.

"Why not?"

"Some scientist you are, you bloody dope!" Bundy said. "This fast on the ice—the momentum will crash the module into us, so just . . ."

"Dear god, what's wrong with you *both*?" Mikel said. "You have no idea what's happening here!"

Mikel struggled to reach across Siem and grab the door handle.

"What are you doing?" Siem cried, grabbing his wrist.

But Mikel had enough of a head start to get his gloved fingers around it and tug up. The door opened and with a momentary sense of weightlessness, he and Siem flew into space, hit the ground, and the truck and its module swerved dangerously as Bundy tried to brake, but collision was inevitable.

When it came, the module hit the truck hard, sending it forward with a jolt, the two coming to a stop at jagged angles in front of the two former occupants.

"You've killed us!" Siem roared. "If that truck is damaged—"

"It won't matter," Mikel said, painfully climbing to his knees and reaching under the harness to where his radio was belted to his waist. His face frozen, lips numb, he tried to steady his trembling fingers to punch in the Group's radio-phone link.

Before he could do so, he felt the ground heave. Ahead, miles away, he saw flame shoot through the ice, a burning pillar that was as incongruous as it was biblical. Raising himself on one aching hand, Mikel watched as it reached for the sky like the straight, superhot issue of a burning oil well.

Beside him, Siem also watched as he raised his bloodied face from the ice. He was dazed but his eyes found the fire and stayed.

"Now . . . what?"

Behind them, Bundy had left the cab and run over. He crouched behind them, watching as the fire spread into a familiar shape.

"It's the same thing we saw before," Bundy said as a face appeared within it.

"No," Mikel said.

"How do *you* know?" the man asked—and then his question was answered.

The fire suddenly spread like a fan, dissipating as it expanded.

"What is it?" Bundy asked.

"That, I believe," Mikel said weakly, "is what a soul looks like when it is sent back to hell."

"But it's going—up!" Siem said in a rasping voice.

"Hell is where you make it," Mikel replied.

Bundy put his overwhelming disgust for Mikel into one powerful, "What the *hell* are *you* talking about, you lunatic?"

"Salvation," Mikel replied quietly. "At least, I hope that's what it is. I'm going to try to find out."

Bundy snorted. "Good for all of us. *You* may have wrecked our module."

Ignoring the pain and the risk of frostbite, Mikel resumed his dialing. "I am very, very sorry," he said. "I am calling some people who will buy you a new one."

CHAPTER 22

Flora stalked back into the room, stowing her phone in her pocket.

"No more shallow pickings," the woman said. "I need to know everything you know, Dr. O'Hara."

Caitlin looked at the woman sideways. "Who was that?"

"Someone who informed me, Dr. O'Hara, that you are far, far more connected to Galderkhaan than you're letting on. Possibly more than you know."

"Oh, I know how connected I am," Caitlin admitted, looking up at her and feeling rage for the first time since coming here. "And that makes me powerful in ways I don't think *you* understand. It's time you talked to me, Madame Director. Respectfully, and now."

"Or else?"

"How about a simple, mundane fact, for starters," Caitlin said. "Your employee's body was not removed by any authority approaching the word 'proper' and I guarantee there's surveillance video."

"You're being irrational now."

"You bet," Caitlin said. "Talk to me, Flora."

Flora weighed the request but briefly. "That call was from my colleague in Antarctica."

"Antarctica," Caitlin breathed. "I see. So you're fairly well connected too."

"Our reach is global," Flora replied. "He's just as worried as you are, so I strongly suggest we start treating each other as resources and not as enemies. He knows who you are."

"He does? How?"

"He also saw the video from Haiti," Flora admitted. "He is concerned for your well-being."

"That's refreshing," Caitlin said.

"He's a good, good man," Flora admitted. "We are not voyeurs or spies or blackmailers, I assure you."

"All right," Caitlin said, not sure she believed any of that. "Who is this associate?"

"His name is Mikel. Why?"

"Mediterranean?"

"Basque," Flora said.

Caitlin touched her head. "I've seen him. Here, in this room. Why is he concerned?"

Flora paused, marginally impressed. "He found a tunnel and ruins and spoke with the dead of Galderkhaan. You'll never guess what they're looking for."

Caitlin took her at her word and didn't try.

"They are looking for you, Dr. Caitlin O'Hara. They are very specifically looking for you. Mikel told me to protect you."

Caitlin shrunk in horror, not just at the news that she was being targeted by some ancient force, but the fact that they got Jacob in the bargain. She had to make it stop, to separate them both from whatever the Galderkhaani wanted.

"You look unwell," Flora said with the slimmest hint of compassion. "Perhaps we should continue this in my office?"

Caitlin forced herself to stand. "No. I have to go."

Everything else be damned, Caitlin had to make sure he was okay, serve herself up if necessary.

"That's not a good idea," Flora said.

"This is not a discussion," Caitlin said, literally pushing past her.

"You should not face this alone!" Flora said, grabbing her.

Caitlin wrested her arm free and pinned Flora with a glare. "Forgive me, but I believe that I am safer watching my own back. Please don't try to stop me."

Caitlin's fury propelled her to the top of the basement stairs where she stopped in her tracks from sudden indecision.

Goddamn it, she thought.

She had an increasing, hideous sense that whatever she did next, someone would suffer. The lodestone of her life had always been helping and protecting the innocent, and obviously, right now she needed to get to Jacob. But she could not forget that last time dogs howling, the news reports of suffering animals, and similar events had heralded the crises of Maanik, Gaelle, Atash, and who knew how many other young people.

This is different, of course, Caitlin reminded herself. *It's worse.*

If Yokane was correct, something was coming loose in the South Pole—something big and old and ferocious. And there was every reason to believe she was right, especially since Flora's man Mikel had corroborated enough of her story.

Caitlin was increasingly convinced that something bigger was happening than what even Yokane had known, and that Azha and Dovit were trying to tell her what it was. This was part of what was impacting the stones and was not likely to stop of its own accord. Whether she wanted to or not, she had to intervene—or, at least, try to find out what was happening.

Caitlin turned to go down the stairs but Flora Davies was standing just behind her.

"I thought you might reconsider," Flora said with a self-satisfied smile.

"You've got it wrong," Caitlin said. "There's something I have to do."

"You promised to share."

"There isn't time."

"*Make* time," Flora said, blocking her way.

Without thought, Caitlin pointed the two forefingers of her right hand directly at Davies's neck. The connection was immediate. She saw the woman's irises widen and, again on instinct, Caitlin moved her hand to the right in the "shut down" gesture. The conduit closed and Flora staggered and slumped against the wall. Caitlin leaned close and checked that the woman was breathing normally; she was.

"Dr. Davies!" Caitlin said, and snapped her fingers. Flora's eyes tracked over to them. Then she looked up at Caitlin. It was enough to satisfy Caitlin that she hadn't harmed the woman. "That's how connected I am to Galderkhaan," Caitlin said. "From now on, you will not interfere with me."

Caitlin resumed her descent and on reaching the hallway, turned toward the room at the far end. The younger woman was perched on a stool just outside its doorway. As Caitlin came closer the stone shot visions of the past through her brain. Adrienne rose to her feet as Caitlin approached with wobbling steps.

But Flora, still slumped at the bottom of the stairs, gestured to Adrienne to let the woman go. So Adrienne remained on her feet but did not prevent Caitlin from looking into the room at the glowing, levitating stone.

The power of the artifact hit Caitlin so hard she quickly repeated the "shut down" gesture. It didn't cancel out the overwhelming presence of the stone, but it did take the edge off. The present shimmered like a mirage, showing the stone only vibrating, without the sequence of lights.

Caitlin speared Adrienne with a look. "What's holding it up, magnets?"

"Acoustic waves."

"Is it safe to go in?"

"That depends on what you're going to do and how long you'll be in there."

Caitlin started to take a step into the room. Adrienne put a hand on her arm.

"I don't recommend it," she said. Her grip wasn't a restraint but a gesture of concern.

Caitlin thanked her with a nod and stayed in the doorway. And suddenly, the past vision came to a rest. Before the stone was brought here the room apparently had been used for storage. Nothing was moving in it anymore.

Caitlin inhaled what felt like her first full breath since she'd entered the mansion. Then, before she could pay attention to her lingering fears, she did what she always did: put one proverbial foot in front of the other.

She had to challenge, expand, and master the new abilities she possessed. She had to obtain a bigger, clearer picture of everything that was happening.

Caitlin saw nothing in the room to hook into visually so she took a different approach: she used sense memory, the sound of Jacob's fingers drumming on the wall that separated their rooms at home. First she remembered just the small sound—then she remembered the awful, pounding amplification of it that she'd heard in that terrible opaque nowhere space—

And then, she was there, pinioned in the massive whiteness as before, with just a faint blur of turquoise behind the ice. Caitlin tried to scream to relieve the terror but her face felt partly paralyzed.

With extraordinary effort, Caitlin spoke to Adrienne, not knowing whether she was communicating out loud or only mentally. Her lips misshaped the words: "Did . . . anything . . . happen . . . when I approached the room?"

"The stone just went dark," Adrienne said with what sounded like awe.

Inwardly Caitlin smiled. Had she made that happen? If so, *how*?

Thinking back, she realized what it had to be. Until now, Caitlin had been regarding this stone as a problem, a danger. She had been giving it the wary, scheming respect due a menacing stranger. But this stone—or at least *a* stone, perhaps Yokane's piece, maybe the two of them together, *some* damn segment of the Source in some combination—was *not* a stranger to her. Standing in the United Nations conference room, floating in the sky above dying Galderkhaan, Caitlin had reached into the energy generated by an artifact like this and flung it at the ancient city.

She looked at the semidormant stone before her.

You can connect to it, she told herself. *You can work with it. The vibrations, the energy, something about it synced with you.*

She had quieted it somewhat. But she still didn't know how, still didn't understand the mechanism. Of more immediate concern: she didn't know how long the truce would last. *Would the stone somehow reach back to the rest of the Source in the present day, get more power, and come back more vigorous than before?*

"Dr. O'Hara?" Adrienne asked. "Can you give me data—?"

"Quiet, *please*."

Caitlin had to learn more. This was a standoff. She had made a fist without realizing it and flexed her fingers. And then she was jolted by an unexpected connection.

The superlatives, she thought with a burst of emotion. *The hand gestures.* Weeping inside, she suddenly grasped the profound intent of the physical arm, hand, and finger movements used in the Galderkhaani language. They weren't merely accents. They were a subliminal, subsonic, energy-based form of expression that added untold depth to the words.

Come back, she admonished herself. *Concentrate on the ice from the vision with Ben . . . something neutral—*

It came back to her, instantly and easily. Reaching to and through the whiteness, she found only tiny sparks of energy. It quieted the stone entirely.

I am the conduit that connected the stone with its home, she realized. The energy of the Source was not restricted by place *or* time. Her own energy was a link between then and now, just as it had been at the United Nations when she linked between the ancient *cazh* and the victimized kids in her own time.

That's why the acoustic levitation worked to contain the stone, she realized. Sound was energy too. The stone was stilled by a powerful cushion of it, its vibrations calmed.

Now she had to work on amping the stone up or down, to see the degree to which she could bond with it and control it. As Yokane had done to her, as Caitlin had just done to Flora Davies, so she must do to the stone. If there was another assault like the one that impacted the animals, she might be able to contain it. If ancient souls were using the tiles to reach children, including Jacob, she might be able to break that connection as well.

But which way? She considered pointing up at first, which was what the Technologists had intended. But some instinct made her slowly, barely, point down instead, reaching through her fingertips and far beyond them, searching for the way to connect.

There.

Her hand seemed to come alive—with an internal humming, a buzzing, a vibration that she automatically compared to the trembling of the stone in its acoustic aerie. The buzzing intensified until she felt the pounding in her palm. She directed her fingertips toward the stone.

Suddenly, the pounding in her hand was drawn powerfully toward and then onto the stone. Fearful, Caitlin almost pulled her hand away to cut the energetic bond.

But that would mean starting over. This had to be done. She calmed her knee-jerk reaction. The goal was engagement. She had to learn to use the mental-physical throttle. She began to twist the energy, turning it like a spoon in coffee, and slowly she began to sense something responding from the stone. The stone was expressing something *inside* her. The feeling was pure joy—similar to what she and Ben had experienced, drifting up and out into the cosmos, themselves, and each other. The core of this artifact was no core at all, but an opening. She hovered there, uncertain—

A new image flashed onto her visual field. There was no longer ice, just eyes—hazel eyes, eyes that crinkled in recognition and then in triumph, eyes in an old face with a white beard. Caitlin didn't wait around to see what the triumph was for. Her instinct told her to get out before this other presence could take control. With one movement she spiraled the pounding energy into the stone and pulled herself out of the sound stream.

The eyes were jerked away from her, leaving only the room with the levitating stone. She put her hands on her knees, dropped her head, and just breathed for a few moments. When she looked up again, she saw that the stone was still not lit, was not even buzzing. She wondered whether Yokane's stone had stopped buzzing too.

Peripherally, she saw that Flora had joined Adrienne. Both were staring at her.

"Please," Flora said. "Talk to me."

"Not now."

"But what should we *do*?" Flora said, pressing her.

"Be quiet." Then she added, "Please." To Adrienne she said, "Don't touch me and definitely do not touch it." She indicated the stone.

Caitlin sensed Flora's struggle, Adrienne's compliance, but then quickly forgot them both as she stood upright and ground her left heel into the floor for a strong sense of balance. With the stone in repose, she could attempt to take care of her other priority, although the Source and its dead inhabitant could not be underestimated.

Her main concern was how Jacob was affected by her connection with the stone, with ascended souls, with the past. Without leaving this place, without surrendering these connections, she had to know what was happening at home.

Caitlin reached out as she had when seeking Yokane from the roof. With the ensuing wave of energy she reached toward her home and found it almost immediately, not by sight but by feel. The visual feed wasn't there but she could sense that no one was in the living room and heard water running in the kitchen. She extended herself like fingers, searching for something she had a good chance of sensing—and yes, Ben had left his phone on the living room table. It had the same aura of life as hers, his clinging presence, an emotional hook that she could grab on to.

Once more she had the sensation of swinging herself toward the destination—grabbing for it across space, but hopefully not across time. Then the visual came in, as clearly as if she were standing in the room. The sound of water turned off and to her surprise Caitlin's friend Anita Carter walked out of the kitchen into the dining room.

"Anita?"

The psychiatrist turned, looked around. "Caitlin?"

"Yes."

Anita went to the front door, looked out the peephole. No one was there. She looked around for a phone.

"What are you doing there?" Caitlin asked.

"Me? What are *you*—where is that coming from? Laptop? You Skyping?"

"That's not important now. Why are you there?"

"I called, couldn't reach you, came over. Ben said you were gone. I figured I'd stay."

"Why?"

"Ben was with Jacob," Anita said. "He was talking in his sleep. Doves, ashes, flying—"

"Dovit? Azha?"

"I'm not sure," Anita said. She was still looking around as if suddenly Caitlin would reveal her hiding place. "Caitlin, seriously—what is *this*? Where are you calling from?"

"I'll tell you later, I promise," Caitlin said. "Is he all right, Jacob?"

"Yes, he's fast asleep and snoring."

"Can you stay, Anita?"

"Of course, but . . ."

"Tell Ben, Global Explorers' Club, Fifth Avenue and Ninth Street, now—no, never mind. I'll tell him."

"All right, fine. Caitlin—"

That was all Caitlin heard. She sought and found Jacob asleep and snoring in his room. He seemed calm. She felt only one other presence near him and it was Ben. A surge of mortal need rolled through her. More than anything else she wanted to hear Ben's voice, hug him, but she couldn't indulge right now. Still, she wanted him with her for support. He was the only one she trusted.

And then, like a dying fireplace, the apartment vanished, lost all its warmth.

Caitlin dropped her hands. She took a moment to feel her gratitude to Anita for going with a hunch that something was wrong and being clairaudient and fearless enough to hear her. Then, as Caitlin fully returned to her body, she pulled out her cell phone. While speaking to Flora she simultaneously texted Ben the address followed by the same information she was announcing.

"A man's coming," Caitlin said. "The man who translated what I know of the Galderkhaani language. He's going to watch over the stone while I'm otherwise occupied."

"I do not allow—" Flora started.

"In return," Caitlin continued, "he will share what he knows about the language. It's a fair bargain. Some trust, some distrust, in the end win-win."

She hit "send" and stowed the cell phone.

Flora approached. Caitlin pinned her in place with a look.

"Doctor," Flora began very carefully, "you *must* tell me how you—"

"When I'm ready. I'm not even close to being done here."

Flora braced herself defiantly, then shrank as quickly.

Suddenly Caitlin was vaulted from the room. It was similar to what she'd experienced in Haiti, when an unseen force had whipped her around like a dog on a leash.

For a moment she was simply in darkness. Then a face appeared. Not Yokane. Not hazel eyes. A woman with flaming red hair.

I am Azha, she said without moving her lips.

The woman was speaking Galderkhaani but Caitlin understood more words than Ben had already translated. "I am—" Caitlin began to respond.

I know, the woman said with quiet authority.

Fear cascaded through Caitlin's entire being, but before she could grapple with it, she was jerked away again.

Then she was somewhere—a place that was blue upon blue upon blue, and moving. She opened her mouth to speak and tasted salt. She was in the ocean, beneath it, but she was still breathing. Or perhaps she was beyond the need for breath.

She was suddenly afraid of something new—not of drowning but being stranded here and unable to get back to Jacob.

Azha? she called.

Not far away, the red-haired woman floated facedown in the sea. It was just a small section of water, an opening that had apparently been punched through the ice by whatever wreckage was around her and by the flames that still licked at it.

Caitlin felt sympathy and horror all at once. Whatever tragedy had befallen this woman, she had to prevent Jacob from experiencing her agony . . . her death.

You're the soul who's been haunting my child, Caitlin said to the woman. *What do you need from me?*

We must stop my sister, Enzo, she replied. *She seeks to help her mentor.*

Who is her mentor?

A Priest named Rensat, Azha informed her. *But Rensat cannot communicate with Enzo. They are not bonded through* cazh.

So they're trying to contact her—to do what?

Rensat is ascended, with a Priest named Pao. With the help of Enzo, Rensat seeks to undo the destruction of Galderkhaan.

How is that even possible, winding back time? Caitlin asked. Even as she said it, she knew the answer. She had changed the past before, when she'd gone back to Galderkhaan to protect Maanik. *They will compel me to go back.*

Yes. To stop a Galderkhaani named Vol from activating the Source. Just before my airship crashed, I revealed the treachery of Vol to Enzo, Azha said. *I told her of his plan to activate the Source prematurely. When she died, Enzo was trying to* cazh *by fire, to possess someone living in Galderkhaan, to pass this information to others. She failed.*

I have seen others try to do that, Caitlin said.

Enzo is trying, still, to communicate that information.

Enzo was attempting to do what the dying of Galderkhaan had done with Maanik, Gaelle, and Atash: to enter their bodies and bond with their souls. After millennia of trying, Caitlin couldn't begin to imagine how mad this Enzo must have been.

What am I supposed to do?

You must stop them. Pao seeks your intervention to restore Galderkhaan, but Rensat wishes to do that . . . and then destroy it.

Destroy it again? After *they save it?*

Yes. I have watched her when she is alone, seen her collecting ancient names, assembling an army. I believe she wishes to build the Priest class to unprecedented numbers and then in one stroke she and Enzo and their myriad followers will cause mass death—as many souls as it takes to reach the cosmic plane. There, they will become Candescent. But at a price.

Azha didn't have to spell it out. Caitlin could do the math: ancient Galderkhaan would die and the course of history would shift. It had become apparent through Ben's research that survivors of Galderkhaan had spread throughout the world. But if there were no survivors—or very few—the world Caitlin knew would be vastly changed. It was genocide of an existing race, and preemptive genocide of billions of others who would never be born.

You must not be taken, Azha said. *Yet they must be stopped.*

What can you *do to help?* Caitlin asked.

Like Rensat and Pao, I and Dovit are ascended but without power. This that I have conveyed is all I can do. You must succeed on your own.

And with that she was gone.

Caitlin swore loudly. She was not certain if any of that was really imminent or truly possible. The one thing she did know: Azha had access to Jacob. Yokane had gotten to him. Now that the other Galderkhaani knew who she was, they could probably find him as well—if not through agents like Yokane, then through his dreams.

She had to end this now.

CHAPTER 23

Caitlin left the mansion with barely a word to Ben.

"Caitlin?" He turned after her.

"Later, okay?" she said as she hurried down the steps. "Everything you need to know is in the text," she told him over her shoulder.

"All right," Ben said. "Be safe."

Ben had seen this side of Caitlin enough to trust that "need to know" was sufficient right now. Caitlin on the other hand felt far less prepared than when she faced the previous Galderkhaan crisis. And there was so much more at stake. If only Yokane were there to help.

Caitlin had an unknown span of time before Davies's stone regained awareness. That could work for her or against her: she might be able to use its powers, or it might try to take her over to connect with other stones. She had to use her time prudently.

First, she had to find a *place* to use time prudently.

Turning down Fifth Avenue, she walked at a fast pace partly to focus herself. Three souls, two of them bonded. Together, they had an agenda. The agenda had a focal point: Antarctica. Specifically, a place with active mosaics. If she could find that in her mind, she could use it the way she had used the courtyard tiles when she disrupted the *cazh* in ancient Galderkhaan.

That effort was going to require a powerful access point. Orienting toward the ocean had worked for a small bit of outreach like locating Yokane. But this?

For a much larger move through space and time Caitlin needed a big boost, something akin to what the trauma-soaked United Nations had provided the last time she accessed Galderkhaan. Preferably nearby since time mattered and preferably powerful. She was dealing with professional Priests. Priests who were also apparently resourceful psychopaths.

Briefly, she considered going downtown to the memorial park that was now stamped upon the former World Trade Center site, but something deep within her recoiled at the thought. Caitlin realized that if she relived any moment from that day and the weeks following, tapped the living terror of so many souls, she might run too hard in the opposite direction. She could take off so high and far into the transpersonal plane that she wouldn't come back, not even for Jacob.

Unconsciously she had been walking south and now she was facing the mercifully rat-free arch of Washington Square Park.

She looked to the east, where the Brown Building, the site of the Triangle Shirtwaist Factory fire, still stood. A hundred and forty-six people had died there in 1911, having burned, suffocated, or jumped to their deaths. She was drawn toward it, across the park, open to the horrible energy . . . then stopped.

There was also power below her feet.

Of course. Washington Square Park itself had been built upon a former potter's field. Tens of thousands of bodies, mostly dead from yellow fever, still lay below its diagonal paths and shrouding trees.

There was pain here, the agony of the forgotten dead. It clung like smoke. And there was running water here as well, not just in the central fountain but also Minetta Brook, which flowed through a series of culverts beneath the park and regularly flooded the basement of

NYU's law school library. Though it wasn't big water, she had a fond association with the brook: it was the subject of one of the first little stories Ben had told her the day he spilled coffee in her lap and they became friends.

"'Minetta,'" he'd explained, "is a corruption of a Lenape word, 'Manetta,' which means 'dangerous spirit' or"—Caitlin shuddered suddenly, remembering the other meaning—"'snake water.'"

She looked around, suddenly frightened by the place . . . and by the task, which wasn't clearly defined. She was going to power up with the ascended souls of this place, hope that the boost was strong enough, *and* hopefully ride that wave to a vague destination.

This is not very wise, she told herself. But as her father often lamented, there was no one else in the batter's box.

Was there anything else she hadn't considered? The lateness of the hour was a concern; the last thing she needed was to be interrupted by a well-meaning police officer. Caitlin would have to remain standing upright and hope that the gestures she used would just look like Tai Chi to an outsider.

She chose the southeast corner, which seemed less populated than other sections of the park. A thicket of trees, a small patch of evergreens, and a blessedly burned-out park lamp provided some measure of privacy. Caitlin squeezed between the trees and oriented herself toward the unseen harbor. There weren't many cars traveling around the park, especially at night, which was good because the headlights would be a distraction even through the tree branches. Caitlin had decided that while she was concealed she needed to layer images, if she could, to keep an eye on the park. Yokane's unexplained death demanded extra precaution.

She raised her hands. Before they were halfway elevated, a soul was there—but not outside her as Azha had been. He was within her. The figure was bearded, his flesh lined with age, but the eyes and mouth were vital . . . sinister.

Ny! she told him. *No!*

He did not reply. Perhaps he did not understand.

"You don't have permission to be inside my head!" she said aloud.

I do not require it, he replied. In English.

You speak my language.

There is no need to use very much of it, he replied. *I am Pao. You destroyed a great* cazh. *You will atone by helping me.*

You will get out of my head and stand before me, she replied.

A second image materialized, that of a woman. Rensat. Caitlin wanted to surprise the Galderkhaani woman, acknowledge her by name, but that would inform the woman that she was prepared at least a little.

Rensat spoke next. *I see a sleeping boy and I see a woman not far from him*, she said. *You will obey.*

I see two dead Galderkhaani who can do no physical damage to anyone, Caitlin replied, finding courage in indignation.

The boy dreams of flight, of our great airships, the woman said. *I can burn his mind.*

Caitlin felt her resistance drain with her courage. The thought of her sweet little man having his inquisitive, creative mind assaulted was as great a violation as she could conceive. She knew she would not allow his innocence to be brutalized that way. She had one secret, just one, but it was not time to bring it out.

Caitlin forced herself to put fear aside and concentrate as she never had in her life, bringing to bear what she had experienced in Galderkhaan, on the subway, with Odilon, in her visions, and most recently with the stone. She needed that Galderkhaani artifact.

Caitlin extended a hand to the north, to the Group's headquarters . . . to the slumbering stone. She was going to try to harness its energy and blast these souls out of their immaterial existence.

In an instant, the power she felt was stronger than ever before. She had plugged into *two* stones, Caitlin realized too late . . . the one belonging to the Group and the one belonging to Yokane. They were *together*, somehow, in the same place. There was no time to consider how or why they were together: it was all Caitlin could do to manage the power flowing into her left arm. She needed to balance that and extended her right arm—

A burst seemed to explode through Caitlin's hand, her arm, her body. The trail of energy continued inward and slammed into Caitlin's soul. She began to shake so hard she was sure she would collapse—but there was no body to fall. She was suddenly outside of it, pulled free by stones somewhere else in the world . . . or time, she couldn't be sure. Her right hand rose as the power continued to course through her, seeking the other tiles in the south. It found them, nearly wrenching Caitlin's immaterial arms from their sockets; the stress pulled at her soul, causing it to cry out.

For one instant, Caitlin saw Ben's face.

Ben saw her too and his expression flashed a look of madness.

"Cai!" he cried.

Then his face disappeared, lost in the electric conflagration that followed. Caitlin saw walls of olivine tiles flare to blinding life, burning out her vision but only for a moment—

They were hovering in a well wider and deeper than any she had ever seen; it was almost the size of a small lake. Caitlin's arms were in a different position now. They were extended up, toward a ring of tiles that lined the high roof of the well. The tiles glowed lime green and pulsed in time with her heartbeat. She felt their energy coursing through her arms, throbbing in her chest. She no longer felt the stones at the Group mansion; it was as if they didn't exist.

The psychiatrist in Caitlin saw this as the archetypical well in which so many hypnotherapy patients said they were trapped. But Caitlin's increasing understanding of Galderkhaan told her something different: this was part of the Source. The well was the inside of one of the great columns she had seen when she stopped the *cazh*. She surmised that they were in the past, inside the hollow column, almost certainly before the Source was activated. They seemed to be vents for the magma that flowed underground, throughout the ancient state.

Pao and Rensat stood across from her, near but at what she judged to be a respectful distance. It was almost as if they were in awe of her . . . or of her power. At least, they didn't charge her. She understood, then, that they hadn't pulled her here: she had brought them. She and the powerful arc she had created between the stones in New York . . . and here.

"The tower of the *motu-varkas*," Pao said. "The most powerful tiles . . . and we are in time. It is not yet destroyed." His features took on an angry, hawkish cast. "You will stop the bloody Galderkhaani traitor who killed us all!"

Without turning from them, Caitlin saw a sea of seething red ooze below, flames dancing across its surface, rock walls flickering from red to brown shadow to red again. All along the granite, reaching up to the tiles, were carved figures that moved and danced as the light changed. She understood, in a moment of epiphany, that these figures, like the carvings on the stones she had seen in New York, were not just representations of the arm and hand motions during the *cazh*; they were the entire ceremony but without the verbal component. The Technologists meant for the Source to do the heavy lifting; all the Galderkhaani had to do was gather around.

You bloody idiots, she thought angrily. The Priests and the Technologists believed the same damn thing, used the same basic idea of bonding. Only the Priests did it through what amounted to prayer and the Technologists' method was, in effect, automated and impersonal.

But it is the same!

Smoke rose in hundreds of hellish plumes, twining like vines and reaching up into whiteness beyond the glowing stones. Caitlin wasn't sure what to do next. She continued to watch her opponents, waiting for them to attack.

Instead, they were very still. "We are here," Rensat said in triumph.

Caitlin understood, then, that she had done exactly what Pao and Rensat wanted. She had used the power of the stones to go back, just as she had done by tapping into them at the UN.

"You will save us," Rensat continued. "You must." The Galderkhaani specter moved a hand. The smoke moved sinuously and began to form a face.

Jacob's face. His sleeping face.

It quickly gained clarity, texture, personality. Caitlin felt pain in her soul. Even if she could throw all the energy in her body at these two, Rensat still had a grip on her boy.

Another face formed, this one brought forth by Pao. It was a middle-aged man, his features rugged but tired looking, almost drawn.

"You will find Vol," Rensat said. "You will stop him from activating this column."

"If I do that," Caitlin said, "my son will die. My world will no longer exist."

"You will cease to exist with it," Pao assured her. "There will be no sorrow."

The casual, almost dismissive quality of his voice caused Caitlin to tremble. She had intended to continue trying to reason with them, to reveal what Azha had told her—but anger possessed her.

Caitlin swept her arms up, bringing heat from the magma to tear through the image Pao had created. The smoke flew apart and almost at once Caitlin brought her arms back down. The tester of smoke swept down, hot and thick, and the souls of the two Galderkhaani were caught in it. The draft pulled them down, dull shapes of light that were thrust into the boiling mud—

But only for a moment. The lava bulged and surged as the burning liquid filled the souls of Pao and Rensat, like molds, creating distorted demons in red with fiery eyes and gaping mouths. Then, very slowly, the lava fell away and the radiant spirits glowed even more brightly as they returned to their previous positions . . . hovering, drifting closer.

Rensat came nearer and shrieked at Caitlin, a cry of pain that had been building for millennia. The scream knocked Caitlin back, drove her into the stone. She did not feel the concussion but she could not move from the inside of the column.

"You will do this!" Rensat cried. "You will do this or you will never leave here!"

Caitlin was no longer thinking. She cut off her vision, allowed her mind to go free, blank, and was suddenly floating outside the column, hovering in the night, a strange world below her. But there was no time to get her bearings. Pao and Rensat came out almost immediately, charged through the column, the constituent stones glowing orange from the heat that came with them. Caitlin raised her arms again and cried out her own suppressed rage—not as ancient but no less feral . . . and protective.

"*You will not have him!*" she roared, pushing the heat back at her attackers. She closed her eyes again and powered herself through the ether, until she was once more inside the column, the two devilish souls beside her.

Pao tried to grab Caitlin. His mouth was rabid, fingers clawing helplessly.

He has to know it's useless, Caitlin thought.

But it wasn't useless: it was a distraction, Caitlin realized.

As Pao lashed out, Rensat rose, working to draw the flames with her, directing them to the hovering cloud of smoke where there were still vestiges of the face of a small boy . . . all the while uttering words that were becoming too familiar.

Aytah fera-cazh grymat—

That will be the instrument of death! Caitlin realized. They would burn Jacob by the *cazh*. He would not be bonded to them . . . he would simply die, his soul ascended and alone.

Caitlin screamed, flung one arm up, and threw the woman up through the smoke. With the other arm, Caitlin quieted the rising flames.

"You cannot do this forever!" Pao said as he repeated the same process Rensat had begun.

Caitlin released Rensat and turned on Pao.

"You will not get my son," Caitlin vowed. Yet even as she spoke, Caitlin knew that her grip on the past was growing tenuous, that she had to finish this now if she were to save Jacob. If she left, he would be defenseless.

She had to use the only weapon that remained, one that would require conviction—strength of a very different sort than she had been using. As a psychiatrist, she could not be sure how this would play out. It could backfire, join Pao more closely to Rensat. But there was no other play.

Caitlin turned to Rensat. "You cannot have my boy any more than you can have Pao," Caitlin charged. This was the time to hit her, not with energy—but with truth. "Does he know your plan to betray him?"

Caitlin felt Rensat shudder. She also saw Pao's expression change slightly, subtly.

Pao did not turn to his companion but asked, "What is she talking about?"

Rensat did not answer him; she could not. No words could possibly submerge the rage that was building inside of her. In that moment, Caitlin reached up with her right hand, beyond the tiles, beyond the cone, sending her fingers outward as she had done when they were still in the park, stretching, seeking a familiar sensation—

"Rensat, *what* is this woman saying?" Pao demanded.

"It is a lie to protect her son!" Rensat replied.

"There is no reason to lie when the truth will stop you," Caitlin assured him. "Pao, hear me. Rensat is working with an acolyte named Enzo. They have their *own* plan."

Pao was dismissive. "This is a lie."

"It is not," Caitlin said. "Rensat knows the truth. Enzo's spirit survives. It has been trying to communicate with you!"

"That is not possible," Pao said. "The ascended have no voice."

"She has *cazhed* with one in my time to transcend, to try and reach you," Caitlin said, challenging him. "As soon as you save Galderkhaan, Rensat and Enzo intend to destroy it."

"Another lie!" Rensat shrieked, and hurled a ball of heat so intense that Caitlin felt herself nearly torn apart. Screaming from the effort, Caitlin gathered every ounce of energy left in her and focused on her son, on saving him, and allowed the burn to pass through her.

As soon as it passed, before Rensat could try again, she said, "Pao, if I were to save Galderkhaan, Rensat will gather as many souls as she could, get them to speak the *cazh*, and *burn* them all, perhaps tens of thousands of souls! She will kill them, either willingly or unwillingly, so they can all rise to the cosmic plane!"

The specificity of her allegation caused Pao to hesitate. He turned to Rensat.

"Is this so?" he asked, in shock, deep hurt, but also belief. He knew Rensat's passion for her faith.

"There is *no reason* to exist *without Candescence*!" Rensat cried.

"But . . . Galderkhaan would still end, it would die with its citizens. That is not the goal we have worked toward."

Pao seemed utterly lost but Rensat's gaze was pure in its hate. Caitlin hoped that Rensat would continue to hate, for just a few moments longer. As long as she was directing rage at Caitlin, she could not turn it on Jacob. Caitlin's fingers continued to roam—

And then she found it. A section of mosaics above her, the heart of the construction, a sequence of stones that carried her like a living bolt of lightning from tile to tile, from mosaic to mosaic, from chamber to chamber throughout Galderkhaan. The charge that raced through Caitlin was greater than the one she had experienced at the United Nations or in the park. Unlike the ruins in modern Antarctica, this network of olivine stones was complete in ancient Galderkhaan. Complete and powered by forces that were like nothing on this planet.

There were visions, images, whiteness so pure it hurt, pain so deep it defied description, glory so great it could not be fathomed—all of that in a moment, a moment that Caitlin could not sustain.

Harvesting power greater than her mind or body could bear, Caitlin released it with a primal, nuclear flash. But it was not a destructive force, it was a cleansing wave, like the proverbial power of prayer raised exponentially. It wiped away the anomalies in time, rid the universe of those who did not belong there. Pao and Rensat contorted into something that resembled the drawing of a young child, stiff and ungainly and out of proportion. Then something else rose from below—a flaming face, bubbling up and rising through the center of the column, a soul being ripped from its fiery shell.

Enzo, Caitlin realized.

Dimly, through the omnipotent power of the tiles, Caitlin heard the echoing screams of two transcending souls being torn from the earth. The cries grew fainter by the moment, leaving a void that quickly filled with the heat and unrest of the magma. And then she felt the souls of Pao and Rensat vanish, just as she had felt the souls of the dying of Galderkhaan vanish. As soon as they were gone she saw the flaming remains of Enzo shoot skyward, dragging another face with it, a woman, not Galderkhaani but one whom she did not recognize. The woman fell away, dissipated, as the lost soul of Enzo continued to rise, to ascend to the lowest of the realms.

All of this effort, the eternity of flame, of waiting, and she did not even transcend. The tragedy was profound and weighed on Caitlin despite all they had done.

But when Caitlin tried to go she found that she herself could not break free.

The power she had plugged into was holding her. Caitlin had released it but it had not released her. Without knowing how much time she had—it could have been a moment or it could have been eternity—Caitlin fought hard to see Jacob in the smoke. And then she saw him for a flashing instant before his face vanished.

"I love you!" she cried.

And then the tower itself was gone, along with all sight, hearing, and touch and every other sensation . . .

• • •

In Flora's basement, moments after the tile fought its acoustic confinement and came fiercely to life, Ben's eyes rolled blank and his legs failed. Though he was still breathing, he slumped down the wall into a heap on the floor. Flora and Adrienne stared at him. Adrienne rose from her stool.

"No!" Flora snapped. "That wasn't a faint. It was like an epileptic seizure, without the tremors."

"So shouldn't we—"

"We're not touching a damned thing," Flora said, watching his ears and nose for a sign of liquefied brain.

Adrienne sat back down. The eyes of both women turned back to the tile. It remained in suspension but it was like a green sun, outwardly quiescent.

"Almost like it's alive," Flora said.

"It's a stone," Adrienne told her.

"It is a stone with secrets," Flora said, correcting her. "Secrets I believe Dr. Caitlin O'Hara has just begun to unlock."

As she spoke, Ben came to. He looked around, momentarily confused.

"What happened?" he asked.

"You appeared to have a seizure of some kind," Flora told him. "Can I get you anything?"

"How long have I been out?"

"A little more than a minute, I'd say."

Ben struggled to stand. "Caitlin's doing that," he said, referring to the stone.

"Very likely," Flora said.

"She shouldn't be."

"Also true."

On unsteady feet, he made his way as quickly as he could from the room. He tried calling Caitlin as he left but all he got was voice mail. He searched for a text. Nothing new had come through.

With sickness rising in his throat, he limped into a night that suddenly seemed very much darker than before.

CHAPTER 24

In Washington Square Park, the water of the central fountain exploded in flame.

The few people who were in the park saw it and screamed. A second later they were pulling out their phones.

Minutes later, two fire trucks shrieked down Fifth Avenue and firefighters poured through the arch, running toward the fountain. Spraying water on the twenty-foot-high flames proved its inadequacy. They switched to using fire-retardant foam and that had some effect. One captain shouted into his radio, ordering as much foam as the firehouses in that quadrant of Manhattan possessed. Several firefighters ran toward the NYU buildings to collect fire extinguishers.

No one saw a figure in the southeast corner with her arms outstretched, as though she were worshipping the moon.

No one saw that figure topple to the ground.

And no one saw Minetta Brook begin to burn in its culvert underground.

Lying beneath the trees, Caitlin could only glimpse a sky that was the wrong shade of orange, coming from her right. She climbed to her hands and knees, then knelt upright, noticing that her clothes were smoking but not on fire. She craned her neck out from the thicket and saw flashing lights from fire trucks, then the fire shooting up from the water fountain.

She rose unsteadily and looked around. At the southwest corner of the park, flames were blowing out of the windows of the NYU law school library. There was the boom of another explosion and the flames shot tens of feet in the air. Bystanders were screaming; some firefighters were shouting while others aimed white jets of foam at the building. All the nearby trees were festooned in white foam and yet as the foam fell on the flames, the fire seemed to find apertures and surge through, still alive.

Then another blast, this time from a building on the west side of the park, flames coursing through the windows and more sirens in the distance.

Caitlin tried to move from her spot, but her legs wouldn't have it. They slipped from under her, and once again she was on her back.

Shutting her eyes, too spent to keep them open, she saw shadows of black and amber play on her closed lids. The colors formed the hint of a face, like one of those afterimages of Abraham Lincoln she used to stare at in the encyclopedia.

You are not finished, a voice said to her. It was a familiar voice. The ascended Yokane?

Caitlin thought, *Screw you. I did what you asked.*

The face faded, along with all traces of light. But before it went, it said:

It is not I who asks.

And then everything was gone.

• • •

Ben had been walking blind; he knew that. He called Caitlin's phone repeatedly and got only voice mail. But with Caitlin's history it was a fair bet to head toward the action, and Washington Square Park was certainly that.

He heard the trouble before he saw it or smelled it.

Red lights were flashing everywhere, and fires crackled with long shadows in all directions. The bloops of sirens sounded as smaller emergency vehicles sped down side streets to join the fire trucks. The sky was a seething orange and smoke was blowing every which way.

Ben approached a cop at the north entrance to the park. "Please," he said, "I need to get in. I think my friend is in there."

"No one is allowed at this time," she replied.

Ben pulled out his ID. "I'm from the United Nations. I'm really worried about her."

"Sir, I cannot let you in. Injured persons are being transported to the Lenox Hill emergency room on Twelfth and Seventh."

Frustrated, Ben glanced west, where the fire trucks had clumped together.

"Are they having trouble putting out the fire?" he asked.

"It's under control," the cop said, but Ben noticed her hesitation and the surprise in her eyes. He walked away before she could think twice.

The west side of the park was obviously going to be impassable so Ben headed around the quieter east side instead. All the park entrances were blocked by police but there was one ambulance over on the east side, and EMTs were carrying someone on a gurney toward it.

Ben's feet sped up before his mind caught on. He was running by the time he realized the patient was Caitlin. He got to the vehicle just as they were lifting the gurney into the back. His stomach lurched as he saw her face, her closed eyes.

"Let me through!" he shouted at the small knot of bystanders and paramedics, pushing at them. "I know her. I have to go with her."

"Sir, you can't—"

"I'm her boyfriend," Ben snapped at the EMT, and climbed into the ambulance. "How bad is it?"

"She's unconscious," said the paramedic sitting beside her.

"*How* unconscious?"

The paramedic flashed him a look. Ben noticed that the man was sinking his thumbnail into the nail bed of Caitlin's right pinky finger. Then he let go of her hand.

"No reaction," he said as the door clunked shut behind them.

Ben felt his heart stop for a second. He picked up Caitlin's hand and held it as the ambulance peeled away from the park.

• • •

Shortly after Ben had left, Flora rose from her stool.

The stone seemed to have calmed and stabilized, and she wanted to try to reconnect with Mikel.

Ambling down the basement corridor, Flora reached into her pocket for her phone to check messages and alerts. As she climbed the stairs to the first floor her phone rang in her hand. It was Mikel calling via the radio.

"Caitlin O'Hara is in danger!" he called over static.

"What do you mean?"

"The Galderkhaani . . . I spoke with them. They want her to go back and change *everything*!"

"Dear Lord."

"Is she still there?"

Before Flora could answer, she felt a hand grip her chin and a sharp point press against her throat. In a mirror across the room, she saw that Casey Skett was holding one of their ancient knives to her neck. With his foot he closed the door of the office behind them.

"Flora?" Mikel shouted urgently over the static. "Flora!"

"Hang up," Casey whispered.

Flora ended the call.

"I'm going to sit you down now, Flora," Casey said. He put one of his knees behind one of hers and nudged until she took a step. "But even when I let you go, remember that I can still kill you before you can scream."

He nudged her again.

"What are you doing Casey—" she started.

"It's time you understood *our* point of view," Casey said, and walked her across her office.

• • •

In the basement, the stone had flickered brilliant green, just once, after Flora left. Adrienne was not asleep—not exactly. Her eyes were still open and suddenly she was swimming joyfully in the sea, entirely in touch with her senses in a way she had never experienced.

She was frolicking with penguins, hundreds of swimming penguins, but taking her time, not yet ready to return to shore. There was so much information to take in. Every part of her body seemed to be tuned, monitoring the changing swell of deep water all around her. A map was forming for her, a village she was remembering as if she were someone else. Then she was back on shore, locating masses of ice and whales swimming hundreds of feet away in the same direction as the penguins. They were all heading toward a long cliff of ice, the ocean running beneath it. She heard the call of home just as they did, and her will and her consciousness and her body were wholly one.

My god, she thought. *I can feel* everything.

• • •

Jacob O'Hara drummed on the wall. There was no answer.

"Mommy?" he said and signed, eyes still closed.

"She's not here right now, Jacob," a sweet voice told him.

The boy rubbed the sleep off and looked up to see a vaguely familiar face. His eyebrows reflected his confusion.

"Remember me?" Anita tried to sign. "From your mother's office?"

"Your signing is bad," Jacob said mildly, reaching for the box with his hearing aids.

"I am pretty terrible," she admitted. "So maybe you will show me how to do it better?"

The intercom buzzed down the hall. Anita motioned that she'd come back, then headed to the white box on the wall and peered at its screen. In the predawn light the camera showed a very thin black woman with high cheekbones, a kerchief over her hair and a blue bag in her arms. Behind her stood a younger black man wearing sunglasses.

Anita hit the "talk" button. "Yes?"

"I am a friend to Dr. O'Hara," said Madame Langlois. "She is in the coils of the great serpent. Let me come in."

EPILOGUE

There was nothing to hold on to.

Caitlin tried again and again. Her strongest memory of Jacob in their shared history was not moving her. She tried reaching for Ben. She even attempted to invoke the night they spent together, when they'd expanded so far beyond themselves that reality was eclipsed by total joy. Though the memory warmed her slightly, Ben wasn't there.

In fact, she could not feel a path away from this place. Nothingness surrounded her.

"Azha?" she called tentatively.

Nothing.

A cold death seemed to have taken over the tiles, too. She felt nothing from them, not the ones in the South Pole, not the two just to the north.

It's not possible to feel nothing, she told herself. *Not unless—*

But she wasn't dead. She couldn't be. She still had conscious thought. Then those thoughts turned to the dead of Galderkhaan—all those she'd been speaking to. They were dead. They had conscious thought.

Frightened now, Caitlin argued with herself. She was fairly sure that Rensat and Pao were gone, truly gone, so she took comfort in that. Perhaps the void left by their departure was responsible for what she was feeling—some kind of psychic aftershock, a spiritual coma. Maybe she would come out of it if she was patient.

But that wasn't happening. Nothing was. That was the operative word right now for all sensation: nothing.

Self-doubt began to fill her, along with exhaustion and the urge to give up.

"No!" she said. "I have a son and I'm getting back to him, goddamn it!"

Her voice didn't even echo. It didn't have a sound. It was only in her head. What was this?

I'm breathing, she suddenly realized. *I must be in shock*.

Deciding to assume that she wasn't dead and still had a body, Caitlin chose to remember the moment when she was most thoroughly inhabiting it, when she had been almost completely consumed by her body, all other consciousness blanked out. That wasn't a time with Ben or any other man. It was the overwhelming pain of giving birth to Jacob. She remembered the joyous agony, felt it, reached through it—

Still, there was no hook. There was no connection.

Caitlin wanted to weep but moaned instead. She tightened her hands into fists.

Wait—you did *that!*

She felt her hands, balled tight. A surge of excitement swept through her. She flexed her fingers. She couldn't have done that if she were dead or injured.

Toes—she tested her toes. She felt them, too.

Relax, she told herself. *You're alive—just let this happen now.*

She went back to thoughts, to images.

My god, she told herself, almost giddy with the thrill of it: these images were unfamiliar but they felt exactly like dreams, nothing like any of the visions she'd experienced over the last few weeks. No emotions were associated with them, either her own or anyone else's. She was simply watching a huge sheet of ice move, creeping a millimeter forward. Then, in the kind of non sequitur of a normal dream, suddenly she was watching eels twist and plunge through the ice, which of course was impossible. Fish—strange fish, but maybe not strange for South Polar waters—leaped for the sky, a sky of vivid blue, with clouds and . . . *nets*? Huge cigar-shaped *balloons*?

Well, this is a dream . . . a lucid dream . . . allowing me to editorialize on the strangeness of it.

And then she was awake, with the normal if pronounced feeling of early-in-the-morning laziness.

The sun was shining on her eyelids. Had she lain in the damn park all night? Was she in a hospital room? She breathed in, stretching out her arms, and smelled faint traces of sulfur and jasmine. Then she spread her fingertips into the sunlight for warmth, and the sensation was hers but the hand was not.

Nor was the world of strange buildings and airships that surrounded her.

ABOUT THE AUTHOR

GILLIAN ANDERSON is an award-winning film, television, and theater actress whose credits include the roles of Special Agent Dana Scully in the long-running and critically acclaimed drama series *The X-Files*, ill-fated socialite Lily Bart in *The House of Mirth*, and Lady Dedlock and Miss Havisham in the BBC productions of Charles Dickens's *Bleak House* and *Great Expectations*, respectively. She is currently playing the roles of DSI Stella Gibson in *The Fall* and Dr. Bedelia Du Maurier in *Hannibal*. She lives in the UK with her daughter and two sons.

JEFF ROVIN is the author of more than 130 books, fiction and nonfiction, under his own name, under various pseudonyms, or as a ghostwriter, including numerous *New York Times* bestsellers. He has written a dozen Op-Center novels for the late Tom Clancy. Rovin has also written for television and has had numerous celebrity interviews published in magazines under his byline. He is a member of the Author's Guild, the Science Fiction Writers of America, and the Horror Writers of America, among others.